P9-CER-290

An

INVISIBLE

Woman

NOV 2004

An

INVISIBLE

Woman

Des Plaines Public Library
1501 Ellinwood
Des Plaines, IL 60016
WITHDRAWN

Anne Strieber

A Tom Doherty Associates Book
New York

This is a work of fiction. All the characters and events portrayed in this novel are either fictitious or are used fictitiously.

AN INVISIBLE WOMAN

Copyright © 2004 by Anne Strieber

All rights reserved, including the right to reproduce this book, or portions thereof, in any form.

This book is printed on acid-free paper.

Book design by Jane Adele Regina

A Forge Book
Published by Tom Doherty Associates, LLC
175 Fifth Avenue
New York, NY 10010

www.tor.com

Des Plaines Public Library
1501 Ellinwood
Des Plaines, IL 60016

Forge® is a registered trademark of Tom Doherty Associates, LLC.

Library of Congress Cataloging-in-Publication Data

Strieber, Anne.
    An invisible woman / Anne Strieber.—1st ed.
      p. cm.
    "A Tom Doherty Associates book."
    ISBN 0-765-31093-7 (acid-free paper)
    EAN 978-0765-31093-4
    1. Widows—Fiction. 2. Socialites—Fiction. 3. Single mothers—Fiction.
    4. Homeless women—Fiction. 5. New York (N.Y.)—Fiction. 6. Murder victims'
    families—Fiction. I. Title.

    PS3619.T7525I58   2004
    813'.6—dc22

                                                                    2004047176

First Edition: November 2004

Printed in the United States of America

0 9 8 7 6 5 4 3 2 1

To my husband, Whitley,
for whom I have never been invisible

Acknowledgments

Thanks to Russell Galen, who sold it,
and Beth Meacham, who liked it.

An
INVISIBLE
Woman

CHAPTER 1

On the day her world ended, Kealy Ryerson was at war, but not with the enemy who was at this moment loading his gun. She was at war with crow's-feet, blue-spotted legs, and a rebellious waistline. She used to laugh off the effects of the years. "I'm just gonna be me, however I happen to be." And Jimmy was cool with that.

Yeah, sure. You bet.

In fact, what had happened as she floated so easily through her forties was that she slid into a bubble of invisibility. Or, rather, partial invisibility. Because she was not invisible to other women her age, far from it. They were watching every little detail of her disappearance and, she suspected, feeling the same quiet sense of relief that she did when somebody else suddenly found herself dealing with butt drop or turkey wattle: *Not me, oh God, not today.*

Men, however, are not like women. To them, women who are not flushed and trembling with youth are not there . . . at all.

At first, what a woman notices is nice. The world is becoming mysteriously less annoying. Then it hits her: I'm not annoyed all the time because construction workers and sleazeballs have gotten more polite.

But then she asks herself, Has that guy over there cuddling a hundred-pound beer gut and eyeing the femmes *really* changed? And then he whistles. The familiar piercing wail of the jungle male actually kind of relieves her . . . until she realizes that he's not whistling *at* her, he's whistling *through* her—at that darling thirty-something marching along behind her.

He's mine, she screams in her heart. *Don't you* dare *take my pig away from me!*

But the truth is that her sleazeball doesn't even know she's there. For him, she has ceased to exist.

And then some jerk steps in front of her in line at the deli, and she kicks the guy—and he's astonished. He didn't see her, he's so sorry!

Then she thinks, *My God, what about my* husband? She does an inventory of the weeks, the months. No, he's not sleeping around. But he is sleeping. A lot.

Emergency surgery! She pages through *Vanity Fair, Vogue,* all the usual suspects, for names of doctors to the stars. She finds Dr. Clayton Ambrose. He hasn't done any stars, but her GP recommended him.

Kealy had gotten a week to herself by telling Jimmy and the kids that she was going to London to the Chelsea Flower Show. Jimmy certainly didn't want to go to any flower shows, and the kids wouldn't even want to hear about it.

She'd spent her recuperation in a room at the Helmsley, ordering off the Atkins menu and watching soaps until her eyeballs fell out.

When she'd "come back" from her sealed chamber, there had been an extraordinary reward. Him: "You look wonderful!" His dear smile into her still slightly puffy eyes said, *I know and I'm on your side.* Then the kiss, and he really meant it and she was young again and all was well . . . tolled the bell.

Now, this morning, she was walking down Madison, having just left Georgette Klinger's salon where she'd had a postlift facial and makeup in preparation for tonight's Defense Bar Awards dinner at the Yale Club.

A construction guy muttered, "Lick me," as she passed, and she was proud, yes, proud. Behind her, she heard a female voice mutter angrily, but she didn't look back.

Then he started making a sound like—what? A parrot? An alarm clock?

Oh, no, my God, that's not him, that's my cell phone.

Can't be. Nobody has the number. The phone is for emergencies only.

She fought it out of her purse and opened it.

"It's me, hon."

"Jimmy?"

"Get out of town. Right now. Take a plane. Run."

"Run?"

"Do it! Now!"

The line clicked, went dead. She became as still as a mouse in a snake pit. This phone was for defense lawyer hazard numero uno—the dreaded *Cape Fear* scenario where the crazed client comes back from stir with blood in his eye. And she had just heard The Message: *It's happened. Run.*

But then what? And where? And what about the kids? And Jimmy himself, for God's sake.

Immediately, she hit callback. It rang, rang again—"You have reached James Ryerson. Please leave your message at the sound of the tone."

What the hell? The damn thing had to still be in his hand.

Drought parched her throat. Jimmy didn't talk in riddles. Jimmy was straight with you, always. Jimmy expected this to be done. N. O. W.

Yeah, just drop everything and jump in a plane. Come on, Jimmy, this is me. I'm your wife, not your child. And you're scaring me, Jimmy, my God, but you are scaring me!

Shaking hands punched in a call to Al Sager, Jim's tough in-house PI. Al had been with Jimmy since before he and Kealy had been married, doing the investigations that pulled in the key witnesses and uncovered the crucial evidence that enabled Jimmy's clients to walk out of the courtroom . . . or didn't. Al always knew where the boss was, who he was with, even what they might be discussing.

"Where's Jim?" she asked, her voice under pressure trading its uptown posh for a snarly twang.

"At lunch with the Manhattan DA," Al said. "They're at Louis's on Chambers Street."

Kealy's boiling thoughts were stilled by surprise. *With* Mc-Garrigle? Jimmy was a defense lawyer. He fought McGarrigle, he didn't eat lunch with him. Unless he was desperate.

So he was desperate. God, please, I love him so—

"You want me to reach out?" Al asked, interrupting what must have been a pretty long silence.

"No," she said. She closed her phone.

She pounded along the pavement, trying to think this thing out. Jimmy had called her with this warning in the middle of a meal with the DA.

Sweat popped out across her upper lip. Her life had seemed so safe for so long that she literally rocked as she walked, fighting dizziness and a speeding heart.

Jimmy would have explained things carefully, that was his way, unless—well, there could be only one reason that he'd been so brusque, sounded so curt. He wasn't with McGarrigle at all. He was in trouble right now. The call had been a last-ditch attempt to warn her about something that was already happening to him.

She lunged into her purse for her phone. Okay, how did you get information on the goddamn thing? She hit 555-1212. No good. 1411. No damn good! 411. Thank you, God. "A number for Louis's Restaurant in Manhattan."

They rang it automatically. One ring. Two. *Answer, oh, God.* Three. "Louis's."

She talked past her heart, which had all but stoppered her throat. "Martin, this is Mrs. Ryerson. Is my husband still there?"

"Yes, ma'am. Do you want me to call him?"

"Please."

She waited on the corner of Madison and Fiftieth, amid the bus reek and the clangor of construction.

"Mrs. Ryerson, he says to telephone him from the plane."

"The plane?"

"Yes. That's what he said."

She closed the phone. Her lips, now as dry as leaves on a cutting cold day, slid open. What about life, appointments, commitments? Above all, what about their teenagers, both away at school?

Her stomach began digesting itself.

She stepped to the curb and hailed the cabs that were streaming uptown like a school of schlocky old carp. All were full; none stopped. A bus roared past followed by another school of cabs. All full. Then an empty appeared, sweet and clean and just made for a desperate lady.

She hailed, it glided to the curb—and something crashed into her from behind. "Sorry, I didn't see you," a crisp voice snapped as a blisteringly handsome guy dressed in Paul Stuart perfection slipped into the cab.

"That's my—"

It took off. The hell of it was, she knew the guy had been telling the truth: he had literally not registered her existence.

Now here came a hack so blown that even New Yorkers were staying away. She hailed it, practically getting in front of it to stop it. She approached, drew open the door. The totaled-out crackhead peering over the seat at her was wheezing louder than the practical joke under the hood. She entered. The backseat stank of cheap air freshener and luncheon meat. The cabbie, she saw, was munching a sandwich.

Okay, Kealy, what now? Do you go to your man or do as you're told?

"Where to, lady?"

Come on, Kealy. Do it your way or do it his way.

"Lady?"

Jimmy's face blazed into her mind, the confident, bright face with the careful eyes. Beloved, dear face.

"Look, lady, I gotta *move!*"

She pictured herself out at LaGuardia buying a ticket to LA or Bangor and her heart began hammering. "Okay," she said, "okay."

"Where?"

"Just a second!"

Horns erupted behind them.

She had to go, he'd told her to go! But, what if—oh, God. "Take me to Louis's Restaurant on Chambers, please."

She twisted in the seat, struggling in her purse for some Tums or something. Her stomach had not only turned to fire, it seemed to be attempting to escape through her esophagus. "Please hurry," she added as she gobbled the antacids.

He said nothing. Didn't hear her, no doubt. Men had a tendency to hear only the essentials from invisible women, and sometimes not even those. Had she still been on male radar, they'd be flying right now.

"Let's go down the drive," she suggested, trying for a more sultry tone.

"Lady, the drive, they got construction in the Twenties. It's a nightmare."

Damn and double damn.

Now they were passing the reason that she didn't like the route down Second Avenue. Il Nido, with its big, black door. And, most especially, the spot in front of it where her previous life had shattered into a million pieces. She sighed, stared, drawn inevitably back to the hell of life with her first husband, Henry Henneman. Officer Henneman. Henny.

Henny had been so beautiful. He'd swept his Upper East Side princess deep into the exotic, burly, shivery-exciting world of cops. She'd gone for him. Totally.

Things had been great . . . for about six weeks. But then she'd noticed a distance. At first, it was more as if he wasn't really present on the inside. He was charming, attentive, but not there. She discovered that all of his talk was cop talk, and all of his interests were cop interests.

When she'd automatically bought her usual seasoners for the opera, he'd thrown his first full-bore fit. He not only hated opera, he resented its mere existence. It went over his head, and things that went over his head made Henny mad.

She had been attending the Met regularly since she was eleven. Giving it up made her feel strange and sad. This sadness was like a seed that grew and sprouted, invading her life like an eager cancer.

As her husband's white-hot ambition drove him up the promotion ladder, his distance and her sadness had grown, and fast.

In the end, her most intimate contact with him was defined by the sound of a shaver behind a closed bathroom door.

Finally, her marriage had become a great big list of ifs.

If Henny could be a person at home and not a cop all the time. *If* he could reciprocate some of the love she felt for him. *If* he could be less mechanical in bed. *If* it were less than a month between times.

A lot of ifs, but her big, strong boy in blue was too involved in his cop world to notice. Being the wife of this young god had turned out to be a ritual of loneliness and left-behind.

She'd fought both their Ozone Park lifestyle and her boredom by going to work. Her dad was a lawyer. She took her Cornell degree a step farther and become a paralegal with a Legal Aid job paying $18.35 an hour . . . and met one James Ryerson, defense lawyer to the highest of high-profile baddies.

She didn't see him often—an inexperienced para like her didn't exactly run in the same crowd as a superlawyer.

But then—well, one day after he'd been around the Legal Aid office for no real reason yet again, she'd just decided to call him. She'd suggested a drink. He'd taken her to dinner at Lutece. Dear old Renee, the headwaiter, had asked her if she'd been away. Sitting there in the Garden Room again, back in the cushioned world she'd given up for love, she had cried all over her foie gras.

Jimmy was smart, full of humor, full of drive, sparkling like some perfect male crystal. He had bespoken tailored everything and had a big S-Class that he drove with casual aggression. His was a life like the life she'd grown up in, and this desperate, lonely girl had just let him take her in his arms and carry her back up the elevator to the big rooms with the paneling and the views.

Jimmy's gentle pleas had compelled her to take Henny to a fateful dinner. She'd chosen one of the elegant haunts of her previous life, Il Nido.

She had told him there not that she had a lover, but that she wanted to call it quits. As her words sifted away into the dark of the restaurant, Henny had taken a long pull on his wine, then smiled slightly—one of those inturned, ironic smiles of his that said that he knew, had always known, even from the beginning of damn time, and he, the detective god, was not surprised—never—by the betrayal.

Then, a surprise: he'd confessed that he was ready to call it quits, too. She had a lover, okay, then he could admit it now: he had a mistress. He'd hammered one white hot rivet into her heart after another, revealing that he'd had her since before they'd been married and had never even considered giving Mindy Barner up. Sergeant Mindy Barner had driven him home nights, had eaten at Kealy's table, had been her advisor in the art of handling a New York City cop.

The pain had been greater than anything she'd ever known before, the agony she'd felt as her veal piccata slowly got cold.

"I needed a wife from upstairs," Henny had told her. He'd used her dad's political connections. They were the kind that could help a young cop one hell of a lot, and they had.

Look at him now, two decades later. He was chief of detectives and would be chief of police soon.

Despite all the years, Henny was still an open wound. In the whispering of her soul, she still loved him.

No she didn't. That was ridiculous. It had been two decades. She'd loved a kid, not the man he had become. She didn't even know Chief Henneman. He was out of her life.

Be that as it may, the cab was banging across Fourteenth Street before she could once again release the image of Il Nido's door from her mind. At least those lonely thoughts had pushed back the terror for a few moments.

Then a new fear chilled her heart. What if this was another breakup?

But no. Jimmy came sliding over to her side of the bed at least two nights a week. He still trembled when he held her, still devoured her with his eyes, whispered words of mad love in elevators, made her laugh, came home with crazy little presents, liked nothing better than spending time with his girl.

"Come *on*," she muttered as they hit a developing traffic

backup north of Canal Street. But then an ambulance—a rattling old meatwagon, in fact—appeared. It was blasting on its siren
to clear a path for itself in the morass ahead. She was punching
Louis's number in again on her cell phone when she became aware
that not only was the whole area howling with sirens, the cabbie
didn't know how to trail an ambulance, and they were losing
ground fast.

Now, wait a minute, what was going on around here, anyway?
What was that huge blue-and-white van about? She'd never seen
anything quite like the gigantic, bleating monster, honking the
loudest horn she had heard in a lifetime of Manhattan horns.

Ahead, conventional police cars were unloading cops who were
rushing out into the street waving their arms. When she saw that
they were stopping traffic, the fear came back and it hit her hard.

She got out of the cab, paid the doper, slipped and slid her way
among the steaming, honking trucks and raging taxis to a jammed
sidewalk. People were pressing curiously toward the disturbance
ahead. As she pushed past one person and then another, she
cursed under her breath, a tight little "Oh, shit."

Then she understood that the police activity was focused on
Chambers Street where Louis's was, and she began to run.

CHAPTER 2

A huge cop blocked her way. When she tried to get around him, he moved with her. His gold buttons stared at her, his eyes through her. "Officer, *please*."

No response. Didn't see her at all.

She was so close to him that she could smell his Old Spice and his thick, sour sweat.

Beyond him, she could see an army of flashing lights; she could hear the shouts of what appeared to be some sort of SWAT team pouring out of the giant van.

"I really must get by," she said. Her own voice sounded weird to her—thin and high and breathless, and she knew that she was more scared right now than she'd ever been in her life.

No reaction whatsoever. If there was a cop Mount Rushmore, he'd fit.

She called past him to a classic brass hat, a guy so covered with gold stripe that he looked like an electroplated zebra. "Hello! Officer!"

The head turned, tiny eyes peering suspiciously out from under the rim of his officer's hat.

"I'm the wife of James Walter Ryerson. He's down there. He's with DA McGarrigle."

At the sound of the DA's name, the eyes narrowed, and now the barricade stirred, too. Somewhere deep in the meat behind their faces, thoughts were stirring. Zebra came over. "You got ID?"

She pulled out her wallet, dug for her driver's license. Holding it out like a policeman would his badge, she said, "Let me through, please."

He gave her license the same dubious glance that he might something thrust into his face by a street-corner lunatic. A bit of twinkle in his eye communicated that he thought her ridiculous, and she withered inside with impotent fury. "You're a reporter, right?"

"My husband is down at Louis's Restaurant having lunch with the district attorney. Perhaps you've heard of him. He's the attorney James Walter Ryerson."

Zebra blinked, looked away. When he turned back, his eyes were scared.

"What's happening, Officer?"

His lips turned down. He might as well be smelling a damp mop as looking at a very damn nice woman. She remembered this kind of guarded, unwilling attitude very damn well. This had been Henny's way. A lot of cops are killed in their hearts by the disastrous combination of corruption and human suffering that formed the blood and bone of police work.

"Mrs. Ryerson," Zebra said. He took her arm, his hard voice going distressingly soft. He drew her in to and through the police line. She knew instantly that Jimmy was involved and the sergeant was taking her to him and therefore it was maybe very bad.

Unaccustomed smells filled the air: a high, creepy stink that she associated with guns and hunting, and a sour cream and rare meat stench that just might be blood.

She pulled away from the cop and went forward on her own, barely able to stay up on her damnable heels. As she drew closer, the hard, cold truth of the street revealed itself to yet another terrified wife.

He lay with his arms spread in the classic posture of the victim surprised, a Jesus without a cross. A film fuzzed his eyes. His expression brought to mind that terrible picture of Robert Kennedy clutching his rosary on the floor of the Ambassador Hotel in Los Angeles.

"He's hurt!" she said—or rather, shouted. But then she saw that the pen she'd given him two Christmases ago had mixed its black ink with the bright red blood of his heart, and she knew that it was more than an injury that had befallen her husband.

A woman's cry echoing against dark city windows is among

the loneliest sounds in the world. *It's us,* thought the part of her that wasn't screaming. *This time, it's us.*

Nobody came near her because they were cops, and they knew that the only thing to do with this kind of suffering was to wait it out.

There were no thoughts, no plans, nothing but the helpless gasping of somebody new to agony. Her parents had died in hospital rooms full of flowers. If you had asked her, she would have said that she had known grief, but this was like nothing she had ever known, or even known was possible.

An officer drew black plastic over Jimmy's face and that was good, because its emptiness had been horrifying to behold. You wanted to believe that this complex, wonderful man would be touched in death by anger or courage, not this blankness.

Then she saw Mike McGarrigle coming out of the restaurant surrounded by cops. "Mike! Oh, Mike, help us!"

"Kealy!" Breaking away from his guards, he came to her. He threw his arms around her.

"Kealy," he said again, backing away a little, "please know that everything my office can do, it will do. Please know that." He enclosed her waist in an arm that seemed incredibly strong, incredibly reassuring. He drew her toward his limousine.

Deep instinct made her pull back. Her husband—he needed her.

"Kealy, you can't stay here."

"I can't leave him, Mike!"

He pulled a little harder and she yanked herself away from him. "*I can't, Mike!*" She snapped her jaws shut, astonished that it had been a scream—a horrible, wailing *scream.*

There was silence. Her own cry had left her ears pounding.

Then the police surrounded Mike, urging him toward his car. He shook them away. "Kealy, darling—"

"Who did this to him, Mike?"

"There's a lot I have to tell you."

"Please, sir," a policeman said, a man full of brass and authority. "We have to get you off the street."

"Do what Jimmy told you, Kealy."

"Mike, tell me—"

"You get where you're going and call me. And get off this street."

He was bundled into his car, which was sucked up by a crowd of protective uniforms, and then was gone.

The indifferent city swirled around her, intent only on its eerie mechanical journey to nowhere, ignorant of everything but the next urgent breath. Under its hard, cutting sky, in light that was either the clearest or the most pitiless in the world, she gazed at her husband's dead body. He didn't need her here or anywhere. His needs had ended.

But hers had not, and what she needed right now was not to go running off into the fog of this thing, not knowing who she was running from or why.

A sergeant appeared, reaching out to her with his big workman's hands. "Mrs. Ryerson, we have to get you off the street now, ma'am."

An EMS paramedic came out of a newly arrived ambulance, a young man with curly hair and nicotine-stained teeth who mumbled that she could accompany the body if she wanted. She shook her head, and the crew began the loading process.

Her mind pitched and tossed like a wild horse: reach the kids, get off the street—and do it all *now!*

The tearing scratch of the body bag's zipper being closed was so awful a sound to hear that she forever after would remember the next few moments as totally silent.

"Mrs. Ryerson," a voice shouted. A young man with an open raincoat was running toward her. But then she saw a camera crew flailing wildly through the barrier behind him, their press passes dangling around their necks.

"Mrs. Ryerson!"

It hit her like a fist: no matter how it looked, these people might not be reporters at all.

Slipping between detective sedans and crime scene vans, she sought escape.

Behind her another voice yelled out, "Kealy!" Its familiarity sent a sickening bolt of energy right down her spine, sickening but also reassuring. She stifled the impulse to turn around and confirm that it was Henny.

Ahead was the Chambers Street subway station. Hearing the rumble of a train, she took a gamble, hurrying down into a world that she hadn't much visited since her days as Henny's wife, when she had to live by subways and busses and chasing sales at grocery stores.

The train squealed to a stop. She fished for her MetroCard. The doors rolled open.

Behind her, the horde came roaring down the stairs.

Would a MetroCard that hadn't been used in months still work? She thrust it into the slot.

"Mrs. Ryerson!"

The doors closed as she burst through the turnstile.

The doors clicked, jerked, then opened again. Men poured on to the platform. A hard hand came down on her shoulder. She jerked forward.

The hand slipped away and she was in the train.

It began moving out of the station, lurching and banging its way into the tunnel. Her fists twisted together. She felt like she was going to throw up all over these bored, unsuspecting people.

She had to run and keep on running, never let them get her.

A thought burned its way to the surface: the kids. What if he was after the kids, too?

She had to get her kids safely home. Then run. Run forever.

CHAPTER 3

Even as the clanging and shrieking of the accelerating train assaulted her, the living faces of the people around her remained oblivious. She looked in amazement at a mother involved with her baby's intricate stroller, then at a young man, all sweaty and wearing running clothes, who stood with his eyes closed, his ears plugged by headphones. A black family, dressed formally, sat staring gravely into empty space.

The world absorbed tragedy like a pond absorbs tossed pebbles. She remembered Jimmy's voice, that awful edge in it—the cry of a lovely, wonderful, dear and dying man.

She watched the other faces. What about that sullen guy with the bag clutched in his hands—was he eyeing her? Or the runner—wasn't he looking her way? A couple of twenty-five-year-old hunks wouldn't be interested in an invisible woman, wouldn't even see her. But they did, both of them.

The doors opened at the Fulton Street stop and she dashed out, crossing the platform and taking the stairs two at a time.

People thronged the bargain stores and hamburger joints along Fulton. There was an edgy line in front of a Chinese takeout, everybody trying to get fed during their fifteen minutes away from the counter or the kiosk. A camera store's windows announced hopefully that it had lost its lease and everything had to go, a button shop was improbably thronged.

Trying to quell the dizziness that kept threatening to pull her off her feet, she staggered into a place called Andrew's Coffee Shop. There was a long black counter and a row of booths, lit by neon. Behind the counter, the grill hissed.

She had not been in a place like this since the days of Henny, when tight money had forced her to budget her lunches.

She went up to the counter, stood under the red-lettered sign that announced TAKEOUT, and said, "A Coke, please, a big Coke."

Her lips cracked as she spoke. Instinct sent her hand plunging toward her purse for her lipstick.

When the Coke came, she took it to her face and rubbed the moist coolness of the glass against her dry, flaming cheeks, ravaging her makeup and to hell with it.

Then her nervous hand proceeded to slip. She made a grab, but the Coke went all over the counter. The counterman looked down with a theatrical shrug. "You want a new one?" he asked as he applied a rag to the mess.

"No," she said into the tired smile on his face. She saw the kindness in the laugh lines that were crinkling around his exhausted eyes, then her gaze was drawn to the simple gold band that he wore, third finger left hand. Somebody's husband, so precious.

The little place became stifling. And that man back there—wasn't that the jogger from the subway? Or, no, maybe not.

Jimmy, oh, God, how can I live like this? She almost wished that the jogger would blow her head off and get it over with. But then the actual horror of dying washed her with sweat. She didn't want to, no way. She had to run, and what if this was some scorched-earth maniac, after their kids as well? Who said he wouldn't be after them? *She had to save her kids!*

She dashed out into the barging, snarling street. A cab came, but before she could raise her hand a gray suit had blasted past her at such close range she was practically knocked out by the dense musk of his Drakkar Noir. He crossed the street in front of the cab, got into a parked car.

Had she been invisible to him, or was he planning to follow her cab?

Head down, she backed away from the curb. She turned and began walking up the street. Because her eyes were tearing so badly, she did not see the car that came around the corner behind her, a black Chevy moving with sinister grace. She did not see it stop, did not see it double-park just out of her line of sight.

As she headed back into the subway, two men got out of the car, one heavyset and wearing a dark suit, the other a Chinese guy who had on his face the excessively careful expression of a young man with too much power.

She remained unaware of their approach, did not notice them even when the Chinese guy passed her and stationed himself twenty yards ahead, improbably searching in his pockets for something.

As she walked, she tried to think. The thing to do was to get the kids home, then make the next leg a long one—Paris, Bangkok, Moscow. But what then? Did they just keep running forever, or what?

The Chinese man turned around and began moving away from the scene, staying ahead of her. His companion drew close behind her, pacing her with the expertise of a streetwise pro.

Only now, when it was far too late, did she feel the first uneasy twinge. Then she did exactly the wrong thing: she turned around, looking to see if the man behind her was really as close as he felt.

She found herself looking into a familiar face, once dear to her. Henny's cold eyes had been saddened by the years. His hair was now speckled with gray. But he was still the same beautiful man who had swept her off her feet. He'd been doing guard duty at the Black and White Ball, had Officer Henneman. He'd been on the make, trying to land a society girl.

He had been the best looking man she'd ever seen. His nervous, overly polite charm was delicious after the cynical, panty-busting sophistication of the boys in her crowd.

"Kealy," he said in the provocative, totally deceptive tone he used with all women, "slow down."

"Henny," she replied. Her voice annoyed her by breaking. Then she cried, and it made her feel so damn ridiculous in front of this man she had rejected. But when he took her in his big arms it was an incredible relief, almost as good as a daddy hug would have been.

Henny said, "As soon as I saw the bulletin, I came out for you, Kealy."

"Oh, Henny, what happened?"

"We have no idea right now and maybe you can help us. Are you up to that?"

"Henny, my children haven't been told. I have to tell my children." Seeing him, hearing that high, girlish shudder in her own voice, brought it all to the surface again, even worse than before. She found herself gasping, and thought, *It can't be like this. I'm stronger than this.*

"She's shocking," the Chinese guy said.

"Get in, babes," Henny told her, opening the door to the backseat of his city-issue Chevy. He got in the front seat.

As she settled herself in, he turned around. "I'm so sorry, Kealy. So damn sorry we had to meet up again like this."

"Mrs. Ryerson," the Chinese kid asked, "you sure you don't want the salts?"

"What salts?"

"If you're going to faint, ma'am."

She shook her head. On the cop shows, an EMS tech appeared at this point and offered Valium. Not *salts*, for God's sake. Then one of the cops would always ask, "Ya wanna see a reverend?"

"Ya wanna see a reverend?" the young detective asked.

"Just give me another second." The thing was, every time she collected herself, Jimmy's voice came back to her, that sweet, lovely voice telling her to run: his last, dear act of consideration and protection for the woman he loved. Whereupon she was lost again, rage and panic making her temples pound and her teeth grind.

"Henny," she said, "I want—" Then she stopped, choking back the bawling sobs that wanted to replace the words. Defensively, indicating that he was not to press her, she raised her hand. His own hand came along the back of the seat. Before she could even think about it, she had touched his fingers.

She realized that, despite her state, both detectives were watching her like detectives do. Of course she wasn't a prisoner and the doors weren't locked, but it felt that way, and from being on the side of the defense for so long she knew it was meant to.

"You were racing down to Louis's just before he got shot. Why was that?"

Henny's gaze might be wistful, his gestures might be tender, but she could see that for him this was also a witness interview.

Why did she feel so uneasy telling him things? Tragedy is intimate, extremely intimate, and sharing intimacy with him made her feel somehow like their marriage was still going on inside her in some way, in a place that ought to be entirely private—especially from him.

"You need to give me an answer," he said into her silence. "You understand that we're required to consider the domestic angle, Kealy."

She had not understood that, and she was shocked to realize that she would be considered a suspect. "He called me on my cell phone. He told me to leave town immediately."

"Whereupon you disobeyed him immediately." A flicker of a smile passed through his face, and she felt her cheeks flush with anger. His right eyebrow lifted, asking the next question: Why?

When she was unresponsive, he persisted. "So he calls you, tells you to run, and you go straight down to the restaurant. For starters, how did you know where he was?"

"I phoned his PI, Al Sager. Al always knows his movements." She knew that she needed to say more, but the image of Jimmy lying there in that street so totally motionless was still burning in her mind, stopping all thought.

She tossed her head, flicking the tears out of her eyes.

Henny kept right on. "Thing is, he came back to the table after stepping away to use his phone in private. The call that must have been this dire warning. So he knew that all hell was breaking loose, and yet the waiter says that they finished up normally."

"You've talked to Mike?"

"Yes."

"Then ask him."

"I'm asking you."

"He told me to run, that's all I know."

"So after their lunch, Jimmy—who has just told you to get

the hell out, your life is in danger—this same man strolls right out of Louis's as bold as you please, and pop pop, everybody thinks it's a backfire until they hear the screaming."

"He screamed?" She knew that Henny would come back here and hold her if she asked him to.

"Hon, he probably never knew what hit him. The street was full of people. They did the screaming."

"Henny, I have to go home now. I have to get in touch with my kids. They're both away at school."

"I know that." His eyes moved away for an instant.

"You do?"

He nodded, watching her carefully. The Chinese kid had become as still as a snake about to strike.

They couldn't have found out that her kids were away at school, not in the past few hectic minutes. So Henny had been keeping up with her life. But why?

He sighed, as if releasing something, some suspicion of her, perhaps . . . or seeming to.

"Lemme drive you home."

"Thank you, Henny."

The Chinese guy, who was called Detective Sergeant Wu, held out the flasher and used the horn.

On the way she put in the dreaded, essential calls to her kids. The first was the slightly easier one because she knew that she would not speak to Allison directly. She talked to Isabelle Proctor, the head at Andover Prep. There was a small, stifled cry of shock when Kealy uttered the words "shot dead." In the front seat, Henny hunched his shoulders as if it had started to rain in the car.

Andover had what Isabelle described as a "DIF routine," short for *death in the family.* Of course, it had happened before at the school. Everything had happened there before. The place had been a puppy farm for three hundred years.

Allison would be put on the five-o'clock shuttle from Boston, accompanied by a friendly teacher all the way to the apartment. Barring flight delays, she'd be home by seven-thirty.

Then she called Mark at Cornell. He was a wonderful boy with a secret that he imagined, in his boyish innocence, he was keeping from his mother. "Hi, hon, it's me."

"Hi, Mom. You just caught me. I'm late for French."

"Mark, you get on the next plane home. There's been a terrible event." She paused, started again quickly. Don't make him wait. "Dad has died."

There was a choked sound of surprise. Mark's relationship with his father was complex, full of trouble, full of love. It was the kind of relationship that was going to leave regrets that were likely to be agonizing.

"A car will come for you. It'll take you to the airport. Julie Moore will call you in the car and tell you your flight."

"Mom?"

"Honey, keep going, keep going."

"Oh, Mom, it hurts. Jesus! What happened to him? He was healthy!"

"He was shot. It was the thing we feared." She was longing to enclose her nineteen-year-old in her arms, even while in another kind of agony over what her poor girl must be enduring now in Isabelle Proctor's office. "You try to stay as pulled together as you can. The car will be there as soon as possible."

"Mom, don't hang up!"

"Honey, I need to get your travel plans going. You be strong. Remember, we Ryersons, we are very strong. When the hit comes in, the team locks arms."

"I'm locking arms with you, Mom. I'm locking arms with Ally."

"That's the way. I'm on my cell phone. You call me back if you need to."

"Mom, I love you."

He sounded so like his dad.

She kissed the phone, whispered "Marko," his childhood nickname, and hung up. Then she sat there staring at the bald back of Henny's scalp, hating whoever had done this to her family with a fire she hadn't known was in her.

She called Julie, Jimmy's secretary, and told her to set up Mark's transportation. In reply, there were only disjointed sobs.

"Are you sure you can do this, Jules? Do you want me to?"

"No—no, Kealy. Of course not, love. You just get home, I'll do it."

Canal Street passed, and they headed up the Bowery.

"What steps are you taking?" Henny asked.

"I'm getting them to come home."

"I mean, about his warning?"

"I'm not sure. I want the kids to be safe. That's the main thing."

"Do you think they're under threat?"

"I don't know!"

"Way I look at it, Kealy—a cop's viewpoint—is, whoever's out there, who's to say he's not gonna come after your kids?"

That had been obvious from the beginning, but hearing it still made her beg heaven for just one more Tums. She touched the window, drew her finger along the glass. "You think it's revenge, then? Some con who thinks Jimmy shafted him?"

"It's a starting point, for sure."

"I didn't know it was possible to be this scared."

"You got a reason, Kealy. Goddamn good reason to be scared and to run like hell."

"Where do we go, Henny? And when do we stop?"

He did not reply, and his silence was terrifying.

A woman in jeans walked three spindly greyhounds. A cab pulled past the car. Three skateboarding boys hopped onto the sidewalk, went rumbling off. Hard laughter snapped, was gone. A man standing in the doorway of a flower shop shouted up at somebody who would not open their window, shouted from amid a sea of roses.

She wondered what the killer looked like, what he was doing right now, what he ate and drank, who he loved, what had turned him into what he was. She could feel him, actually feel him in the way you feel somebody staring at you from behind your back, that feeling.

She imagined him watching from a window, a roof, the door of a convenience store, watching his target pass in the police car.

Out there in that swarming, heedless city, hidden among its many secrets, she sensed something she had never known before, the same thing that makes the deer sigh his sigh of danger, that makes the duck rise into the foggy dawn.

She sensed death, stealthy, as it might come from amid those roses, or from the cab that had just passed, or from the roofs above, or from the immense mosaic of dark windows that glared down on you in New York, always, wherever you were. Death had come into her world, and that seemed very strange, that and the thought of orphaned children.

CHAPTER 4

They pulled up in front of 1075 Fifth Avenue, her home for nineteen years, a building as familiar to her as her own body.

Henny leaped out of the car and came back to open her door. Then people were running at her, swirling around her, waving microphones, jamming tape recorders into her face and screaming, screaming for information, a howling babble of questions.

The two detectives took her arms. The three of them waded into the crowd. She realized that the detectives weren't shielding her from reporters. They were being subtle about it, but they were acting as bodyguards.

She could not have been more grateful when Frank swept the doors open and she entered the privacy and quietness of her marble lobby, softly lit by its graceful old chandelier. When the doors closed behind them, Henny's shoulders hunched in what was coming to seem a characteristic posture. It was also a new one. Swaggering Henny had become like a man being rained on.

He pointed to a door. "Where's that lead?"

"Service closet, I think."

"And the one in the back?"

"Leads to the super's apartment."

Suddenly he came toward her. He reached out to her, enclosed her left shoulder in his big hand.

Instinct made her draw back, and he released her like she had burned him. "Don't so much as go outside, Keelster, not until we're ready for you to make a move. You agree?"

Before she could respond, the elevator doors opened on Lester Young, who had been running the car since long before she and Jimmy had bought their co-op. His eyes were wet and sad. "I'm so sorry, ma'am."

The silence that followed this one remark was eloquent. On the way up Henny, standing beside her, said not a word.

Then the elevator door slid back and they were in the private foyer of her apartment, which took up the whole of the sixteenth floor.

"Jesus H.," Henny murmured. Seeing Niagara Falls or the Grand Canyon for the first time, he might have said the same, and in the same tone.

With the possible exception of Mike McGarrigle, she hadn't expected anybody to be there, but instead of Mike Jimmy's partner, Simon Osborne, and his new aide, Christa Lawrence, were waiting. Veronica stood beside them, a sentinel in a black uniform and white apron. Her face was composed but her eyes were red. She'd been with Kealy and Jimmy since the beginning. She wasn't a maid, or not only that. Kealy knew that she loved Jimmy dearly, knew it and loved her for her fussy, wonderful mothering of her employer.

She opened her arms and Vee came in, shoulders shaking, sobs stifled as best she could. The two women, dear friends, melted into each other. Kealy felt supported; she felt protective. Vee said, "They've been bringing food ever since it was on TV. They come and they're crying and bringing food, Mrs. Ryerson."

She turned, then, responding to the buzz of the back doorbell. Seeing the way she moved, shoulders stiff, head high, Kealy found a whole new level of admiration for her.

"I need information," Sim said. His gray eyes were swimming, eloquent with grief and fear. He and Jim had been together for twenty years, two tough, smart lawyers who had carved out something very unusual, a practice in criminal defense that had also made them rich. Moving past her, Sim repeated, "I need information."

She heard the elevator doors sliding behind her and turned to see Henny staring out at Sim, his face impassive. Then the doors closed and he was gone, dropping back down into the grayness that seemed to define him now.

"Wait," Sim barked, rushing forward, his hand out, intending to block the doors. He pounded the call button. "Chief!"

Kealy knew that Henny wouldn't be back.

Sim seemed to know it, too. He stopped pounding. Then he leaned against the door.

Kealy knew that he was afraid. Of course he was, frightened to death and grief stricken. She now knew the feeling well, but she also knew she needed to be alone right now. The grief had to really and truly explode out of her before the kids came back. God, it had to be before then. And she needed to think about where to go. How did you cover your tracks? What would prevent them being followed?

Turning her back on Christa and Sim, hoping they'd get the message, she went into the living room and sat down onto the couch.

Christa followed her immediately, then sat down beside her and took her hand. Sim came and stood over them, so close that Kealy felt as if he might fall on her. "We have to talk about this right away, Kealy."

"Not now, Sim, please."

"Kealy—"

"Please, Sim." She turned to the girl, who was stroking her hand. "Please." Christa drew back.

Sim sat beside Kealy, moving with the swooping grace of a crane. "It's just—I'm hoping you can help us." When she didn't reply, he went on. "Kealy, what's worrying us is if this is an angry client."

"Did Jimmy warn you, too?"

Sim blinked. "Warn?"

"He called me on my cell phone. He told me to run. Immediately. Get on a plane."

For a moment, Sim covered his face with his hands. Then he stared off into the bright afternoon light that was pouring in the picture window. "He knew it was coming, then."

"Did he warn you, too?"

"No."

"Then maybe you're not at risk."

"We work our cases together, for God's sake! Of course I'm at risk. What did Henneman tell you?"

"The cops have nothing. But Mike McGarrigle appears more informed."

She heard Sim suck breath, let it out. "McGarrigle, yes," he said, "Jimmy was with him."

"Do you know why?"

"He didn't tell me a thing. I didn't even know he'd gone to lunch."

"Maybe he told Mike what was happening. That's what I'm hoping."

Christa had begun to cry softly.

"Take it easy," Sim said absently. He regarded Kealy. "This warning changes things. I think we all need to take it very damn seriously. We need to find this man."

"You need to, Sim. I need to get the hell out of here."

His face sunk into itself. Then his eyes became hard little beads. For a moment she thought he might strike her.

"I'll need a little of your time," he said. "Tomorrow morning, an hour to go over his cases with me. Meet with Mike and Henneman."

"I don't know much about his cases."

"You might know something!"

"Don't shout at me, Sim."

"I will shout!"

"Mr. Osborne!"

"Shut up, Christa! Look, Kealy. I've got to have you there."

"What about my kids? I want them on a night flight to Rome or Athens or somewhere. With me."

He played a card. "Think about them running for the rest of their lives. That's what'll happen to them. You need to stay here and face this."

"Look, Sim, my life is definitely in danger. Jimmy warned

me. My kids—God, I hope not. But you did not get a warning, Sim. So my guess is this thing is very personal. And I'm the person in jeopardy, not you."

He took deep breaths. "I get chest pains," he murmured.

"Do you want some water, Mr. Osborne?"

"No, thank you, Christa. Set up a meeting with McGarrigle and Chief Henneman." Sim emitted a long, ragged sigh, and now Kealy knew something more: she knew what Sim actually wanted to do. He didn't really want to investigate. He didn't even want to run. What Sim wanted was to back into a dark corner somewhere, and howl with the pure terror of a trapped animal.

CHAPTER 5

At six-thirty, Kealy prevailed on Vee to go home.

"I'm not going anywhere, Mrs. Ryerson."

"You're finished for the day. And I want you to know that you'll continue to be paid, no matter what."

"What do you mean?"

"If we have to go away for a while, for our safety."

Tears formed in the corners of her eyes. She shook her head almost angrily, then threw it back, proud, defiant Vee. "Of course. I understand."

They clasped hands and Vee slipped out into the back lobby. "Vee!"

She stopped. "Yes, ma'am?"

"Use the front. I don't want you in an unmanned elevator."

She nodded, then went silently through the house and was gone by the front door.

At first, Kealy was thankful for the quiet, thankful to be alone. But only at first. By seven, waiting for Allison and Mark had finally started to give her the shaking crazies. She resisted the almost overwhelming compulsion to call them on their cell phones, but she had never in her life wanted to see two people as badly as she wanted to see them.

She couldn't believe anybody would go after them. But how could she be sure? If Jimmy had thought so, he would have warned them first and they would have said something when she called them.

She hadn't smoked since Jim had taken the last one out of her mouth the night he popped the question. She went to Vee's secret stash of cigarettes that she kept in their old cookie jar in the kitchen. A single white pack, partly crushed, came out with her hand. What in God's name were Generic Unfiltereds?

She found a big box of Diamond matches back in the knife

drawer, opened it and struck one, then applied it to the crinkling tip and drew. The taste was incredibly bitter. Then her throat seized up and she felt a wave of unease, like just before you get really carsick. She all but spat out the butt. Vee damn well wanted her ciggies to work.

The lock clicked on the front door. Momma Bear tossed the cigarette into the sink and ran.

And there was Allison, standing in the foyer with red eyes, fists clenched, her dear face breaking to pieces like a lovely little mirror. She flew so fast into Kealy's arms that the two of them almost went over backward.

A Niagara of tears, helpless, howling sobs that slowly subsided. The poor kid must have almost cried herself out on the way home. A little girl's voice wailed into her momma's shoulder, "My daddy, my daddy . . ."

She'd been his angel, his star. She had loved him with the utter devotion of a good daughter.

"I want Daddy, Momma. Oh, Momma, I can't *stand it!*"

"We have to, we're strong, we have to stand it, baby!"

Inside her, deep down where the primitive part slides its way along the bottom of the soul, Kealy Ryerson tasted true hate. Hate for the man who had done this, for whoever had broken Ally's precious young heart.

Suddenly Kealy realized that there was somebody else there. Blinking away her tears, she saw Mr. Steinmetz, Ally's English teacher. He was a narrow man with a kind, weathered face.

"Thanks, Mr. Steinmetz," Kealy said.

Allison broke away and gave him a brief hug.

"She's been a brave girl," he said.

"Mr. Steinmetz is the best, Mom."

"I'm so sorry, Mrs Ryerson, and I bring the condolences of the whole school."

"Thanks so much."

There was one of those moments when nobody quite knows what to do. "Umm, let us give you something to eat. You must be starving."

"I'd better be getting back."

"The neighbors have been leaving food all afternoon. We've got a feast in the kitchen."

"I've got the nine-thirty shuttle to catch."

"He has Lit at eight," Ally said. "Tell everybody I love them."

The sadness in her voice when she said that almost made Kealy lose it again. But she fought back the tears, fought hard, quelled them. Ally needed her to be strong.

Mr. Steinmetz stepped into the foyer. The elevator came and he was gone.

"Mom?"

"Yes, darling?"

"Is it okay to be hungry?"

"It's natural when you're feeling grief. That's why everybody brings food."

Kealy and Allison went into the kitchen. Allison ate three-bean salad, deli potato salad, and a cassoulet that Kealy knew instantly had been made by her friend Bitsy's cook, Marie Prado. Under each dish, Vee had left a note in her round, neat hand of the name of the donor.

"Where's Vee, anyway?"

"I sent her home."

"Why? I want Vee."

"Oh, all the reporters and cops swarming around downstairs—it's best that she not be subjected to that."

The truth was, it might be dangerous to be Kealy Ryerson's maid just now. She was going to call Vee, tell her not to show up for a while. That was going to be another hard call.

She and Allison sat together on stools at the white counter, eating directly from the dishes. Afterward, Allison went to her room. Kealy followed. She did not want her daughter to be alone.

It was a fluffy, soft lair, with a canopied bed, a pink velvet chair, and matching ottoman. The two of them had so enjoyed furnishing this room. It was girlie and comfy and felt so safe. Deceptive now, of course.

Allison threw herself down on the bed.

"Mom, would you tell me a dancer story?"

These were stories from Kealy's days as a dance student at Juilliard, back before Henny, when she'd had dreams of balletic stardom. Kealy did not have it in her to tell a dancer story now. "I wish I could, baby."

"Mommy, he can't be dead."

"Oh, baby, that's just how I feel."

"I keep hearing him. I *hear* him!"

Kealy sat down beside her daughter, stroked her hair. Her dad used to say, "that girl is coated with boy glue," and tease her about all the "slack-jawed youths," as he called them, who used to hang around the apartment. "Ally, clean up your room, it's covered with drool," he'd say after the boys skulked home.

At nine Mark came bursting in. This boy whose bottom she had powdered was now rippling with strength, easily powerful enough to embrace the two grieving females who sank into his arms. Kealy felt the strength that remained of Fortress Family, the walls that had not been shattered, the towers of love and respect that still stood tall. *Do you see us, Jim?* she asked her heart. *Do you still exist, are you with us?*

When her son spoke, his voice was surprisingly hard. "Do they know who did it?" He was like his mother: in him, also, grief expressed itself in the form of anger.

"The cops are clueless."

"I don't understand that, Mom. I mean, it happened in broad daylight on a busy street. There must have been a hundred witnesses."

Jimmy's warning had never been far from Kealy's thoughts. Soon, she had to tell the kids. They would not want to run, she didn't think. The warning would be what convinced them.

"I want to walk," Mark announced. "I think I want to walk all night."

"No!"

"Mom?"

"I—I mean, obviously not. It's not safe on the streets at night."

"Around here? Come on, Mom."

"No!"

"Mark, Mom says no!"

No sense in keeping it back. The time was now. "There's something you both have to know. Right before . . ." She trailed off, fighting to understand just how to say it. Nothing to do but plunge ahead. "Okay, I guess I just have to say this."

"What, Mommy?" Allison's eyes registered distress.

"It's okay, honey."

"No, it's not."

"No, you're right. It sure as hell is not. Before it happened— just a few minutes—Daddy phoned me on my cell phone. I had just left Klinger's—Jesus, it seems like it happened fifty years ago and five seconds ago both at the same time—"

"What did he say?" Mark asked.

"He told me to leave town, to go at once. The next thing I knew, he was dead on Chambers Street."

The color drained out of Allison's face. She wailed, "I thought it was Kelly Neil. I thought it was a *joke!*"

"Allison, what are you saying?"

"On my answering machine at the dorm, before I knew that anything had happened, there was a message that sounded like Daddy, but I just assumed—oh, *Mommy!*"

In that terrible moment, Kealy Ryerson learned what it meant to go cold with fear. *He had warned the kids.*

"What," Mark asked his sister, "was on your tape?"

"He said to leave immediately. Call Al Sager and tell him where I went. I thought it was that jerk, Kelly, and I *erased* it, the last thing my daddy ever said to me!"

Kealy looked at Mark. "You?"

He shook his head. "I missed a call from him. He didn't leave a message."

Kealy's mind was racing. He'd called them, therefore they were in danger, too. She had not thought this, had not expected it. But it was true, irrevocably and finally.

She had to get them out of here.

"We better do what he said." She glanced at her watch. "The late flights to Europe'll be taking off in two hours."

"I'll call for reservations," Mark said.

"Of course."

"Mommy, we're just leaving in the middle of the night? What about school?"

"First or coach?"

"Honey, we have to."

"But when do we come back?"

"When it's safe."

"What if it's never safe? Then what happens to us?"

There followed a silence, as each of them faced the intensity of the danger and the totality of their helplessness.

"Jesus!"

Mark bolted into the family room, dove for the TV remote.

"What's going on?"

"The News at Nine, Mom!"

"Oh, Mark—"

"We need to see this."

Todd Gibson on Channel Five was reporting on the story. There was a clip Kealy didn't want to watch, of her racing across the sidewalk with her arms up like she was warding off gnats.

"Mom?"

"Yes, son?"

He laid his arm over her shoulder. "I love you, Mom."

"Me, too." Allison put her arm around Kealy's waist.

"We'll get through this, kids. We'll win this thing."

Then another face appeared: Henny, being interviewed on the scene by reporter Gay Freund. "Chief Henneman, are we even close to an identification?"

"That's our house," Allison said. "That's right downstairs!"

Kealy was confused. It looked like the interview had been taped a couple of hours ago. That would have been just after Henny had left her off. How had they ever gotten a man as tight-lipped as Henny to do this?

"Mr. Ryerson was attorney for Salvatore Bonacori. We're treating this as a mob hit."

"No way," Mark whispered.

Kealy was stunned speechless. She knew Mr. Bonacori. "I introduced them," she said faintly. "He wasn't—Dad wasn't in the *Mafia!*"

Henny continued, "Mr. Ryerson and his firm are under investigation for racketeering violations and money laundering, among other things."

"Can you say why the hit took place? Is this the beginning of a mob war?"

"That's all part of the ongoing investigation. Thank you, Gay."

They cut back to the studio. Todd said to his coanchor Kyra Dawes: "Mobsters going down on the streets of New York. Some things never change."

"Mom?"

"Shh!"

"Yeah, Todd. It's great to see 'em go, but you hate for it to be out in public like this. Good folks could've been hurt."

Weatherman Burt Pantera appeared. Mark cut off the TV. He turned a pale, shocked face to his mother. "Mom?"

"I introduced your father to Sal Bonacori."

"You? You know a mob boss?"

"He's on the board of the Opera Guild."

"What's going on," Allison wailed.

Kealy had not the faintest idea what to say. Mark went to the wall phone in the kitchen. "Give me Henny's number."

"Henny?"

"You were married to him, you're bound to have his number."

"Calm down, Mark. Keep your head. You barely know Henny."

"Yeah, I barely know him, but I need to know him a lot better."

"He's just doing his job."

"Mom, given that Dad was not a mob lawyer and Henny is

your probably extremely jealous former husband, I doubt very
much that he's just doing his job. What he's doing is one fuck of
a job on you!"

"Mark!"

"Mother, please give me that number. This is some kind of
sick, jealous bullshit he's putting out, and I want it stopped."

Kealy fumbled for the card Henny had given her, read the
number off. "You be civil, Mark."

At that instant, the phone rang. Mark grabbed it. A moment
later, he handed it to his mother. "Medical examiner's office," he
said.

"Your remains are going to be released at seven," a voice said.
"You need to have a hearse waiting."

"A hearse at seven A.M.?" She hadn't thought that far into the
future, which struck her now as remarkably stupid. There had to
be arrangements, a funeral, all that. The world would expect him
to be buried from St. Thomas on Fifth, where his family had been
respected parishioners for seventy years.

"You need a funeral home with twenty-four-hour receiving,
ma'am. In a case like this."

"I'll use Cooke on Madison," she said. They must offer twenty-
four-hour service; they were the mortuary of choice for the whole
silk-stocking district.

After Kealy hung up, Mark made his call. "Chief Henneman,
my dad isn't a Mafia thug, so stop planting sick stories like that,
because it's—"

He listened.

"Well then, put him on, Sergeant! . . . Chief Henneman, this
is Mark Ryerson. You told the media that my father was some
kind of a mob lawyer, and I—"

As he listened, his face grew redder and redder.

"My father was not a criminal, and any investigative team that
thinks that is a bunch of morons!" Mark slammed the phone into
its wall-mounted base so hard that the whole instrument jumped
from its moorings in a cloud of plaster dust and flying screws. It

clattered to the floor, its wire-tangled insides separating from the housing.

"They're setting him up because he's a defense lawyer and they hate our guts! Dad was upholding his oath. That's what he was doing, being a good lawyer. The law works because it enables fair representation of bad people. Dad lived the law."

"Jesus, you guys, *look!*" Allison was pointing at the broken base of the phone. Attached to the innards by one strand of black wire and another of red, was what appeared to be a small microphone.

CHAPTER 6

Mark tore the microphone off its wires and crushed it. "Assume it's not the only one."

Kealy said, "First thing, don't panic."

"Excuse me, Mom, but why not when it's clearly panic time? This is—who put this here? What do they know? Whoever they are, they're all over us."

"We've got to get those reservations," Kealy practically screamed. She went into the living room, picked up the phone, dialed information. "British Airways, please."

Mark came in. He put his finger on the receiver button. "Mark?"

"You can't make a plane reservation on that."

"Mark, we've got to go. Immediately!"

"You're broadcasting. You understand that."

"No, I—"

"Mother, we got rid of one bug. Probably every telephone is bugged. Every room. Probably this—us, talking right now—somebody's listening."

She put the phone down. "I see."

"You mean they're listening to us right now?"

"Ally," Mark replied, his voice gentle, "I think we have to assume that."

"Mom, are we in the Mafia? Are the police investigating us?"

"I don't know."

"I think we can assume these are police listening devices," Mark said. "I think that Henneman was telling the truth. Dad was under investigation."

"I don't want people listening to me in my house!"

"Ally, there's not much we can do right now," Kealy said. "We'll get it straightened out in the morning."

Allison slapped her hands to her ears and screamed. Kealy went to her, tried to hold her, but she tore herself away and kept on screaming. With Kealy fluttering around her like a nervous moth, the screaming developed into a full-scale panic attack. Her face turned red, her eyes wallowed.

"Baby, just try to stop. Just try!"

Allison's head shook, she howled.

Mark shouted, "Stop! Hey!"

She did not stop.

Mark slapped his sister, quick and sharp—but with a clumsy gentleness, also, that said how unaccustomed he was to striking people.

Ally gasped, too astonished to keep screaming. Then she backed away from her brother.

"You hit me!"

"Sis—oh, Jesus!" He tried to hug her.

Allison burst into tears and ran off toward her room.

"Mom?"

"Cool it, honey. You did right."

"I did? I—"

"Listen, we have to work this out. We have to think."

Mark went to the cupboard and pulled down a bottle of scotch that hadn't yet reached the bar in Jimmy's den. He opened it and poured himself some.

"Want?" he said, raising his eyebrows to Kealy.

"You're not twenty-one yet, young man."

He knocked back the scotch like a pro. "No, I'm not."

"We need to call Mike McGarrigle. Daddy was with him when it happened, and he must know something that can help us."

"We can't use the damn *phone!*"

"Don't be short with me, son."

"Okay! Sorry. You should never have sent that scum to Dad."

"I introduced him to a member of a very distinguished board."

"But you knew—I mean—the name? Who he was?"

"I didn't think. He said he needed a lawyer."

"Dad was bound by his oath to accept a client who claimed innocence. You realize that? You realize that you *made* Dad represent a mafioso!"

"He could have said no!"

"Not Dad. Dad was a stickler. With no conflict that would allow him to recuse himself, and no professional issue involved, he was bound by his conscience to say yes, and that's what he did. Mafia lawyer! Your former husband is a real piece of work, Mom."

"Well, I guess I know that."

"What we need to do is to completely search the house and see if we can find any more of these things. Then we need to cut on the alarm, and try to see if we can figure out a next move."

Kealy had a wonderful, sweet, obvious idea. "We can call Al Sager on one of our cell phones. Al is going to know even more than Mike. Al is going to get this whole thing solved."

"Mother, forget the phones for now, okay? And bear in mind, whatever we say in here, right now, is being listened to."

Allison reappeared, red of face but much more collected. She went straight for the scotch.

"Ally!"

"Mother?" Her smile was not nice. She drank straight from the bottle. "Prep school style," she said.

"You don't drink at school!"

"If I did . . ." She took another pull.

"Oh, God," Kealy said. "I just can't believe this of your father."

"Because it isn't true."

"Mark, I don't think we—I mean, can we be sure? Are we?"

"It isn't true, and I'm going to prove that! This is a cheap cop setup orchestrated by a jealous scumbag who hates Daddy for the reason that he stole you from him. Surely you can see that, Mother."

Kealy was appalled. Henny was not that kind of a man. He was tough and dedicated and honest—for a cop.

Allison wheezed. "Sorry I blew it." She looked from one to the other of them. "Given that we're gonna get killed, we might as well go down fighting. I want to stay right here in New York and clear my daddy's name."

"I agree, Mom. I think we need to face this thing down."

"Somebody is out there who wants to kill us and there is no way we're staying here."

"The first thing we need to do is get rid of these damn bugs. Before I take apart all the phones, let's check the switch box."

"Where's the switch box? In the basement?"

"In Dad's study."

The study hit Kealy like a slap far worse than the one Mark had given Ally. She could hardly bear to glance at his desk, with those infamously cryptic notes of his scattered across it. Every month or so, she'd come in and gather them all up and make him go through them, throwing out the ones he could no longer decipher, which was usually every single one of them. Never again, never another laugh, never another hug. Never another night together.

Mark went to Jimmy's closet where he kept his backup files and trial videos. "I think it's in here."

As he pulled the door open, the light came on. He became silent. Very still.

Kealy moved toward him. The first thing she saw was that the file cabinets were standing open and empty. Something had been poured over the videos that left a stink of melted plastic.

"Acetone," Mark said as he picked one up. "They're totaled."

"This was not done by the police."

"No, obviously not."

It was like rape. That's how it made Kealy feel. She wanted to bathe, to scour herself clean. *He* had been here. "I think it's time to make those plane reservations."

"You do that now and whoever in this family he wants to kill is dead."

"Then I'll go over to Bitsy's and do it."

"Mother, I don't think you understand. What's been done to these records puts a whole different light on things. I'm changing my mind about the bugging devices. They were probably put in here by whoever trashed these files, and the police don't trash files. Dad was being stalked by a professional who was in here, who did all of this, and who then killed him *even though* Dad knew he was out there. That's how good this guy is. Or group. Could be a group? Mafia hit men. Professionals, all the way. And now they are stalking us. Wherever we go, they will find us, people who can bug apartments and trash files and kill right out in the middle of the street and get away with it."

"I'm your mother and I'm ordering you to run."

"You, who brought Sal Bonacori into the picture?"

"I introduced Dad to an opera patron who was obviously rich and said he needed a lawyer. Why not? It's part of the reason I do all my boards and balls and charities—to help your father."

"Mom, there's something I have to ask you. I want you to tell us the truth, me and Ally. To your knowledge, did Dad ever commit any kind of a crime?"

She thought. They'd been so intimate. He'd often discussed cases with her, but never anything that suggested mob involvement. He was deeply upstanding, deeply honorable. "No way."

"Mom, we're better off here in a place we know, where we have friends."

Maybe Henny, the police, some judge perhaps, could force them to go with her. "If I have to, I'll get a court order and make you come."

"Mom, listen to me. Face this: we can't escape the kind of skilled professionals who are involved here. Say we go to London or Bangkok. You talk about helpless! At least here we've got some resources and we know the damn streets."

"He's right, Mom. And I want to show them my daddy wasn't a mafioso! He was a great lawyer, Mom. We can't just leave with his reputation in the mud."

"For God's sake, have you both gone insane?"

"Mother, if we run, sooner or later we are going to be caught. If we stay here and do everything we can to aid this investigation, then maybe we have a chance to live—and to tell the world that Dad was *not in the damn Mafia!*"

"He's dead and he can't help himself, so we have to, Mom."

She didn't know how to escape from anybody. They were right about that. Professionals would find them easily, no matter how far away they went. She did not say this to the kids, but if this was a professional operation, then the reason that Jimmy had warned them was different from what she had assumed, and it was sinister. Professionals wouldn't kill them for spite. Professionals would kill them because they knew something—probably without realizing it—that it was very damn dangerous for them to know.

"Sim's having a meeting in the morning with Henny and Mike," she said. Her stomach quivered.

"Good. We'll be there."

"This made noise," Allison said, gesturing toward the closet. Her voice was flat. Kealy knew the tone: it was grief beyond grief. She was past all tears, all hysterics.

"Yeah," Mark agreed. "Lots of noise."

"So, when did it happen?"

"Vee was here all day," Kealy said faintly. But Veronica's loyalty was beyond question.

Mark was kneeling into the mess. He lifted a notebook by its ripped cover, dangling it open to the twisted metal binder rings that had held the pages. "Empty," he said. He pushed the shredded remains of the others with his toe. "They're all empty."

Allison opened the phone box. "What would I be looking for in here?"

"It looks clean," Mark said. "I guess."

"God, I just remembered something," Kealy said. "There were carpet cleaners in this room day before yesterday."

"So put down the carpet cleaners on the suspect list," Allison said.

"And take Vee off."

"Don't take anybody off," Mark said.

"Vee has been with us for years. She loves us."

"Mother, nobody loves us right now. Nobody except you and me and Ally."

As they left Jimmy's study, Kealy closed the door firmly. She would not return to that room unless she absolutely had to.

Mark went to the fridge and got a beer, opened it, and tossed the cap in the trash can. He took a long pull. "You know what I want?"

"What, hon?"

"A Glock 17." He pointed his finger toward the dark window. "And a big, beautiful thug to shoot it at."

CHAPTER 7

Kealy's sleepless night ended in a shrouded, rainy dawn. At three, she'd gone on the Internet to find out what the rules were about carrying a gun in New York City. She'd found out that they were simple: you couldn't.

Again and again, she'd patrolled the house, checking the doors, the windows, the kids. Mark's room was full of cigarette smoke and Ally had the scotch with her. But at least they were both sleeping.

Her shower stall had felt so much like a trap that she'd barely been able to finish bathing. Carrying out her routine behind the frosted glass had practically driven her mad. Afterward, she'd slugged Maalox and taken a Prilosec.

During the night, she'd also realized that Al was the key. Al would be their salvation, even more than Mike. If Jimmy had bodies buried, Al knew where they were. But there weren't any. Jimmy was no criminal. It just was not possible.

Her question was, why would Henny believe it? Or, maybe he didn't. Maybe it was jealousy. Henny had always been a hard man to read, and judging from yesterday, that had in no way changed.

After making herself up, she closed the door to her room and telephoned the funeral home. Speaking carefully, she gave them detailed instructions. The funeral would be Friday, it would be from St. Thomas. There would be a closed coffin of the finest mahogany. She told them all the arrangements she wanted, including a High Mass at the church, and to expect about five hundred mourners. He was to be buried in the Ryerson plot at St. Stephens' Park, next to his father and mother, and his grandparents and their parents, on back to the unreadable stones on the edge of the plot. Ryerson is a Dutch name. They had been here since the beginning, this family. New York had been built on the strong and distinguished backs of people like the Van Damms and the Schuylers and the Ryersons.

A Mafia lawyer, indeed.

She found Mark making coffee, drank some with him. The moment was wordless, a sad dance between mother and son. Ally came out looking as if the shock of it all had entered her expression permanently. Her eyes were moist, but they were also sad and mad, not scared, which Kealy decided was a step in the right direction.

"Is everybody ready to do this?" she asked.

No responses.

"I called the car for a quarter to."

"If it's not Ned, I'm not going," Ally said.

Ned was their regular driver. "If it's not Ned," Mark said, "nobody's going."

"Can they put time bombs in cars?" Ally asked.

"They can put any kind of bomb anywhere," Mark replied.

When they reached the lobby, the press, which was still camping on the sidewalk, started in at them like famished hounds.

Fifth was packed with traffic and slick with rain, the sky above it choked with fast, fat clouds, the air gray. Amid blaring horns, a city bus dueled with a cab for space; a gang of uniformed boys ran up the sidewalk on their way to one of the nearby schools; an old man in a long, expensive raincoat stormed through the reporters blocking his way.

"This isn't good," Mark said.

Head down, Kealy plunged toward the door.

Frank stopped her. "Don't go out, wait for the car," he said. "You got a shark attack out there."

"Yes."

"You could go through the basement."

She shook her head. She'd forgotten to schedule the limo for the side entrance, and now it was too late.

Allison's hand came into hers. Soft little hand, as cold as a dead sparrow.

Right on schedule, the car appeared, a black sedan nosing

along like a big old grouper outside the wall of double-parked press cars.

"Now do it," Frank told them. As they started walking, she looked from face to face among the press, wondering which ones were really reporters and which had other briefs. As soon as they started moving, the crowd erupted, surging toward them.

"They're like animals, Mom," Allison cried. The reporters, cold from the night and wet from the morning, went after the kids.

"Hey, Mark, what's it like to be a Mafia kid? You get any perks? You get your drugs wholesale?"

Poor Mark, hate flashed in his eyes as the flashbulbs popped. What a contemptible way to exploit a young man's grief. Kealy looked for the face that had blurted that evil stuff, but it was hidden in the hoods and umbrellas that were deployed against the mean little rain that sifted down.

As Allison pressed forward, the crowd suddenly closed around her. The next thing Kealy knew, she could not see her daughter. Grabbing Mark's arm, she shoved ahead. Reporters, moving fast, blocked her way.

She heard a voice snap at Allison: "You know Meadow Soprano?"

A microphone plunged into Kealy's face. "Is this a mob war? Are you up for a hit, too? Are you under investigation?"

"Leave us alone," she said, pushing the man aside so hard that he cursed and almost fell. Instinct caused her to lunge after him, trying to help. Mark broke away from her and then he was also gone in the crowd. Kealy could see the black roof of the limo, but were the kids in it?

"Give me a break," she cried. Microphones struck at her like snakes.

"Is there a grand jury involved? Was your husband a capo?"

Finally, the limo door was just ahead, and Allison was making room for her, scooting into the middle seat. Kealy dove into the car, locking the door the instant the chauffeur closed it. "Fuck 'em," she said.

"Mo*ther*," Allison responded.

"Dad wasn't a crook," Mark said. He looked straight into his mother's eyes. "Was he?"

"I can only say what I said before."

"Okay."

Jim's office was in the magnificent old Smolen Building on Forty-sixth and Fifth. Built in 1921, its lobby was a soaring masterpiece of pink and white marble. The elevators were brass cages, their ceilings painted with trompe l'oeil skies through which golden airships soared. Mark looked up in silence as they ascended. The kids had loved those paintings when they were young. How many questions Marko had asked about the antique aircraft that flew in memory there.

There was a huge black wreath on the oak doors of the office, so big that Kealy found it oppressive. She had not understood before just how intimate real grief is, or how much privacy it needs.

The reception desk was empty. From the offices beyond, there was total silence.

"Mom?"

"I don't know where they are, Allison."

Then Henny came out of the big oak doors that led into the office suite. He seemed to glide with a buzzard's somber majesty. When he saw the kids, he blinked as if he had been struck a mild blow.

"Kealy, there's bad news," Henny said. His unpleasant assistant, Detective Wu, had appeared behind him. "We got a call a couple of minutes ago—sit down—" He motioned woodenly toward a love seat. "Hi, kids," he added in what sounded like an almost prayerful undertone.

"Hi," Allison replied.

"This is a rough one," he continued. "Al Sager got killed."

Allison made a ragged noise. Mark was taut, motionless.

"They handcuffed him to a radiator. Then they burned out his apartment." He sounded embarrassed, as he might sound confessing his professional failures to some supervisory board. He gestured back toward the offices. "There are also files missing from this office. Hundreds of them." He regarded her with that deceptive gentleness of his. "We're hoping that you have some useful records at home."

Mark was the first to pull himself together. "Our apartment was entered. The files Dad had here were destroyed or stolen. And we found a bugging device."

Henny sighed. "When you start needing a drink before ten in the morning," he commented to Wu, "it's time to retire." Then he addressed Sim, who had appeared in the doorway that led back to the offices. "You got a bar? Maybe somebody to pour me a little Stoli?"

"I sent the staff home," Sim replied. "It seemed best."

"Cleaners," Wu said, "is what we're looking at. Professionals. A thing is known, and they are cleaning up all knowledge of it. Paper and people."

A sensation of suffocation made Kealy suck a long breath. She could almost smell the smoke of Al's death. "He was one of the best," she said, "so tough, but such a sweet man."

Sim's voice was thin, as if this latest horror had dissolved his strength like acid dissolves metal. "The police are culling what files we still have, that we can release to them. The ones we can't release—we're hiring a private detective agency." There would be major issues of confidentiality in a defense law office, of course.

Wu, who had lit a small cigar, seemed to have become preoccupied by a picture that Kealy had chosen in happier days, a pale Morris Louis whose serene order belonged to another version of the world. "Cleaners," Wu repeated. He turned to Kealy. "And the manner of the death—you should consider that a warning."

"Oh, yeah, like we need a warning, for God's sake," Mark said. "The poor guy. Jesus!"

In all three of their minds, there was the same thought: it could have been us.

"Look, as far as I know, Jimmy had no problems with his mob clients. They were just ordinary defendants, as far as he was concerned," Sim said.

"There are always concerns," Mark responded, which was not the answer she had been expecting to hear.

"On Channel Five," Allison announced, "you said he was a criminal, Mr. Henneman. Why did you do that?"

"There's been an internal investigation," Sim responded. He handed Kealy a report in a black folder.

"Lemme see it," Mark demanded. Kealy leaned over one of his shoulders, Allison the other, and they looked into the heart of darkness.

"JWR met SB 14:26, walked 43rd St. to 7th Ave. Disc. Patroni," read one handwritten entry. Another said, "SB-JWR phone cntct 10:44. Patroni issue." The hand seemed to race along the pages. "JWR-SB at Cent. Club. Lunch. Patroni."

Mark looked from Sim to Henny and back. "Is this about the guy they found dead on that construction site? Billy Patroni?"

Henny nodded. "Patroni beat a rap, murder one, walked out of the courtroom a free man. Three hours later, his own people off him and dump him. We don't know why and we don't know who did the hit. But it's probably an internal Bonacori thing. Thugs rubbing thugs, it's not priority stuff, to tell you the truth."

Kealy thought, *If they believe that Jimmy was not only in the mob but one of their lawyers, then our protection isn't priority stuff, either.*

"My father knew about this? He was involved?"

"These notes were made by Al Sager and handed over to me. He was probably killed for them last night. Fortunately, the murderers were too late." Sim dropped a hand on Mark's shoulder. "Good men go wrong, Son. It happened to your dad, I'm sorry to say. Somehow or another, he backed himself into a corner he couldn't get out of."

Kealy pulled the report out of her son's hands, thrust it back at Sim. "I want to find out about this from the DA. If Jimmy's dirty, he'll know about it."

Sim jumped in. "What probably happened here was that Bonacori took your dad out because some disagreement caused a loss of trust. When the underlings defy the boss—well, this is what the Mafia is famous for."

"Bonacori actually did the killing?" Mark asked.

"Not personally. But he'd have given the order." Sim smiled, an expression sour with pity. "My only regret is that we didn't call the police in sooner. He would have gone to jail, but at least he'd still be alive."

"What about you, Sim? Are you in danger?"

"I'm being very careful, obviously."

"We agree that we might be looking at a Bonacori hit," Henny said. "With cleanup done on Jimmy's PI."

On the surface, he seemed almost beaten, the way he was delivering himself, his tired eyes regarding her with hollow indifference, or perhaps dislike, she wasn't sure.

"So what you're saying is that my husband was a crook and got offed in the normal course of Mafia business. Am I right?"

"No way," Mark said.

Henny and Wu both turned toward him, moving like two ungainly tanks aiming their turrets.

"That's what everything points to," Wu said.

Kealy went to the receptionist's desk and picked up the phone. She called Mike.

"District Attorney's Office."

"This is Kealy Ryerson."

She was put through immediately. "Kealy?"

"Mike! Tell me, is it true about my husband?"

"Kealy, that's not the question. The question is, where are you?"

"In our office. I'm with Sim and Henneman and Wu, and they're telling me that Jimmy was taken out by Sal Bonacori. A Mafia hit."

"The kids are there, too?"

"We're all here. What difference does that make?"

"Listen to me. I want you to put down this telephone and get out of there instantly. Take your kids and do exactly what Jimmy told you to do. Christ, you should've done it last night!"

"Mike, I want to know if my husband—"

"You get where you're going. Then call me."

"Was he under investigation?"

She waited. But all that came back was a dial tone. She looked at the phone, then at the men who were watching her, at Sim with his concerned, disappointed face, at the impassive, self-aware Wu, and at Henny's used-up eyes.

For one of those awful, perpetual moments that come at times of extreme stress, the only sound was the careful whisper of their breath.

"What did he say?" Sim asked.

"He said—" She thought frantically. How did she answer? She'd just been told that one or more of these men was the enemy. She could give them nothing further. "He said how sorry he was. How much he respected Jimmy."

"See, Dad isn't a crook," Mark said doggedly. "Bonacori killed him because of something he knew. If a lawyer gets evidence of a crime about to be committed, he has to report it. Confidentiality doesn't count, then. That's the why of this hit."

"Kealy, you need to focus on telling us what you know," Henny said.

"What *I* know?" She fought the dryness in her throat, the trembling in her voice. She forced herself to continue. "That's just the problem. I don't know anything."

Henny laid his hand on hers. "Kealy, if you can, you need to tell us why Jim thought you were in danger. Unless we know that, we can't help you."

She was in the worst of all possible situations: she had come into unexpectedly dangerous currents, and had no idea how to save herself. Never before in her life, not even in one of the few nightmares she had experienced, had she felt like this. She opened her mouth, sucked for breath.

The antique clock against the far wall, one of her own collection, began sounding the ten-o'clock hour. She heard in its voice a chorus as if of the solemn dead warning her to leave, leave, leave.

"Kids," she said, trying and failing to keep the quaver out of her voice, "we have to go now. We have to go."

CHAPTER 8

As she rose to her feet, Sim came with her. "You need to finish this, Kealy."

"We don't know anything and all of Jimmy's files we had are stolen. Even his trial videos are ruined."

"There might be something that seems trivial to you," he said gently. "But maybe it contains the whole key. That's what we think. That's got to be the why of these warnings."

Mark turned on Henny. "Get Bonacori! Then we're fine."

"We need evidence."

Sim added, "We need you to think back, Kealy. Try."

Inside, she was screaming. She had to get out of here with her kids and she had to do it now.

"Daddy told you everything, Mom," Allison said. "Maybe if you go through it all—"

Henny made a small sound, a sort of sigh. Sim took Kealy's elbow, began ushering her back to her seat. She shook him off.

"Come on, kids," she said. She headed for the door.

"We're not finished," Sim snapped. "Not nearly!"

"Come on," she repeated, and to their credit her kids did as they were asked.

Sim came out with them.

She hammered the elevator button.

"Kealy, it's dangerous out there," he said. He grabbed Mark's shoulder. "Help her, calm her down."

"Mother—"

"We'll call you," Kealy said.

As the doors closed, Kealy heard Wu's faint curse: "Goddamnit!"

Allison turned on her. "What are we doing?"

She faced her kids. "We have a problem. Mike wasn't there, you noticed that?"

They waited.

"He told me to do what Jimmy said. He made it clear that we were in danger from somebody in that office."

Allison went pale.

"The second this door opens, we have to move, and fast."

"Where do we we go?" Allison asked.

The elevator stopped at the busy lobby. The limo was right at the door. "Don't go near it!" Kealy looked around. "We have to find another exit."

"Are we running?" Allison asked.

"If we are, this is a major mistake, Mother."

Kealy saw that another elevator was dropping, bypassing all floors. It must be them, using an emergency key.

Before the kids could continue, Kealy was crossing the lobby. There was nothing more to say, no time to stop and explain.

A glance back showed her that the comandeered elevator was passing the fourth floor. "Come on!"

"May I please know what's going on?"

"Trust me, son. We've got to get a cab."

"The limo—"

"Stay away from the damn limo!"

They went toward glass doors. Behind them, the elevator was opening. She could see Henny coming out, looking left and right.

If there was no cab outside, they were going to be caught. Now she ran, prancing along on her heels, cursing herself for putting them on without a second thought. They came out on to Forty-seventh Street, which was swarming with people—shoppers, diamond-district merchants, tourists looking in windows choked with jewels. Not a cab in sight.

"Mother, please!" Mark shouted. His father's son, he did not like surprises, he did not like being out of control. She grabbed his wrist and tugged.

Still no cabs—no, there was one, a guy getting out. "Taxi!"

"Where are we going?" Mark asked.

"Anywhere," she barked. "Help me, run for that cab!"

She felt him dig in instead. "Mother! Stop this!"

"Allison, get the cab!"

Two women coming out of the Gotham Book Mart got it.

"Jesus God!" She went out into the street, found herself staring into the grille of an oncoming crosstown bus, heard its horn blaring, then was up on the sidewalk in front of the brick building where she and Jimmy had so very long ago shopped for his favorite Broadway show albums at the old Music Masters store. Still no empty cabs. "Come on," she yelled at the kids.

They began crossing the street, but not quickly.

The next moment, there was a scream, so high and terrible that it rose above the roar of traffic. Kealy saw that three strange men had come barreling around the corner from Madison Avenue. They were a few feet from Allison, who was shrieking but not moving, apparently frozen with fear.

"Allison! Run! Run!"

As Kealy watched helplessly, Mark went back to his sister. He took her arm, drew her forward. Kealy thought that one of the men had a steel-blue snout poking out of his fist, a gun. She could easily believe they would kill a child.

"Help us! Somebody!"

The traffic thundered on, indifferently swirling toward its million separate destinations. A huge truck appeared, totally blocking Kealy's view. She screamed then, her voice an inarticulate wail built around the names of her children.

And then there was movement in the traffic—the enormous truck was rolling past. And the kids—the kids were *under* the truck! Shrieking, Kealy dashed toward it, yelling at the driver to stop, stop—but he heard nothing, his windows were closed, he was too high up, he was too unconcerned with anything except the traffic ahead.

Then there was *pop* then another *pop* and she bellowed, "My kids, my kids!"

But there they were, rising from the traffic with improbable dignity, their eyes glassy with terror, their faces pale.

"Come on," she said, and darted into the Gotham Book Mart. It had a basement, an upstairs, lots of nooks and crannies. She knew it well; they'd bought a substantial part of their collection of twentieth-century first editions here.

Mark broke ahead of her. "Come on," he said. "Mother, come *on!*"

Kealy hardly heard her son. She was looking back, fighting heaves of fear. Through a gap above some books, she could see Henny standing in the doorway. On his face was what she thought must be the most dangerous smile she had ever seen.

If she tried to run like this through the streets of the city, she would die. Her children would die.

He had caught up to her just as she was making her way through to the back of the bookstore and out the other side. When he realized what was happening, he'd barked at Wu, "Get us around the block fast, Detective. Get plainclothes on it, get uniforms on it."

As he maneuvered the car, Wu issued the orders into their phone.

Henny remembered. Their marriage had been such a disappointment for him. She'd been splendid, her body glorious in its harmonies, but so cool, so unreachable. She'd forced him to retreat into his work . . . and into the arms of a girl.

They went screaming up Sixth Avenue, whipped onto Forty-eighth Street. "Not too fast, we'll bop a civilian."

"There they are." A flash of her hair, gold in the sun, a flash of her rich silk suit. A memory: kissing the swooping curve of her neck.

Forty-eighth Street was jammed, cabs and vans at war with a huge eighteen-wheeler that probably shouldn't have been there at all. "Christ," Wu muttered.

"Stop the car."

"You got it."

Henny dodged between two cars and came up onto the sidewalk, looked toward Fifth. Where the hell had they gotten to? He went back the way he had been coming, thinking that they might have taken a cab or even that their limousine had caught up with them.

Why had she run like that, right the hell out of the meeting? Didn't she understand the kind of alarms such a thing would set off? What had Mike said to the woman, anyway? Either too much or too little, that was obvious.

It had not been pleasant to see her as scared as she was in that office, her red, teary eyes shifting constantly from face to face, almost beseeching. The kids, too, broken, the boy looking as if he'd been given a death sentence, the girl's expression flashing with the desperate defiance that any detective could tell you concealed fear.

Christ, maybe they went into the Sixth Avenue subway. But even they wouldn't be that stupid. The subway would be a death trap for them. Nobody got away using the subway.

Now out of contact with Wu, he flipped open his cell phone. "Alert transit," he said. "They're underground."

"I alerted transit."

"Give them detailed IDs. Tell them they're on the Sixth Avenue line. I'm coming back to you now."

He started toward the car, which he could just see mired deep in traffic.

This family's situation was extremely dangerous—to a lot of people besides them, and in a lot of different ways.

"We're in trouble, Mr. Wu."

"I know it, Chief."

hey had gone down past two long racks of books, then
through a door where they encountered offices. An elderly
man in a blue jacket had looked up from his work with a
ledger. "Excuse me?"

"Sorry," Kealy had said as he rose from his chair.

He'd come toward her, his face twisting into a grin. "You took
a wrong turn here, folks."

Ahead they'd found a dark brown door, partly opened. Then
they were outside in an alley full of boxes and Dumpsters and debris. For a moment, it had seemed as if they were trapped, but
then Mark had found a door into another store. A moment later,
they'd come on to the sales floor of Harvey Electronics on Forty-
eighth Street. "Hello there," a salesman had said from behind a
counter full of DVD equipment.

Just as they were going out onto the street, Mark had seen the
three men again. They'd ducked into the subway. There was no
alternative.

Kealy hurried along behind them, letting them lead her into
the underground world. She could ride the Lex comfortably
enough, but beyond that the thing was a maze, and at the moment
the idea of a maze was terrifying.

She fumbled in her purse for her MetroCard. "You need one
of these," she explained as she moved toward the token booth to
get two more.

"Mother!"

They had MetroCards.

"Shit," Allison said.

"What's the trouble?"

"There's no train!"

Mark trotted down the platform to the far stairs, Allison close behind him. Kealy felt her hair tickling the back of her neck as she ran.

Then the kids disappeared. "Mark? Ally!"

"Mother," Allison said, signaling for silence.

Kealy realized that they had stepped back under a stairway at the far end of the platform. She joined them. Fighting to catch her breath, she told them what Mike had said on the phone.

"God damn it," Mark said with quiet intensity.

There were two men, one in a tan jacket, the other wearing a sweater. They were moving methodically down the far platform, across the tracks from them.

Where was the train?

The man in the jacket jumped down to the tracks. Before she realized what she was doing, Kealy screamed. She cut it off, but too late. His face turned their way, rested on the stairway.

"Oh, God, he knows."

"Of course he knows."

The man reached the center divider between the uptown and downtown tracks. He started to step over, but the rails were singing and he hesitated. His partner was running along the platform, leaping up the stairs five at a time, disappearing overhead as the train came banging into the station.

They got on, but the doors didn't close. Outside, she could see a quickly moving figure, see it coming down the stairs. She was transfixed again by the shape of dark metal in a fist.

A bell rang and the doors slid closed. They rolled out of the station.

"Did he get on?" Allison asked.

"I don't know," Mark said.

"I don't believe he did," Kealy said.

"If he had," Allison said, "we'd know it."

"The danger is that they'll intercept us at some stop," Mark said. "We have to keep changing trains." He went to the nearest map, a badly scarred one on the wall beside the door opposite them.

"We need to end up on an A," Allison said.

"Why an A?" Kealy asked.

"Give me your cell phone, Mother," Allison said.

"It won't work down here," Mark said as he returned from the map. "Anyway, we want to stay off the air right now."

"We've got to get to Kennedy," Kealy said. Jimmy had warned her, Mike had warned her, now they were being chased. It was time to at least try to do this.

"If the police are involved, we shouldn't show up at an airport."

"We need West Fourth Street for the A," Allison said.

"Where are we going on an A train?"

"Momma, you remember that girl who got on probation in the NyQuil incident?"

"All too well. The one with the peculiar name."

"Lushawn is a family name, Mother. Like Kealy, I might add. We're going to her house."

"We're going to Kennedy."

"Mother, it won't work."

"And this will?"

"Lushawn can help us."

"Where does she live? In SoHo? In the Village?"

"There's a distant land out there called Brooklyn. And her house happens to be close to Kennedy."

The change at West Fourth Street was uneventful, but at the last minute Mark decided to take another line, the R.

The train bounced and screeched. It was awful in here. No wonder people called the subway "the Beast." Allison, who had picked up a discarded copy of the *Post* suddenly gasped. Dropping the paper, she gripped Kealy's arm.

Mark got it, silently showed his mother. There was a photograph of Al Sager's blackened body on page three. RYERSON BLOODBATH: HIT NUMBER TWO—HE'S FRIED.

"Bonacori's the key," Mark said.

They rode on, coming to a stop where Allison took them across the platform, down some stairs, and onto another train. Pausing at a pay phone, she made a quick call.

Kealy was rather surprised that Allison had a friend who lived out in Brooklyn. But the Wainwrights and the Carlottos both lived in Brooklyn Heights, and there was even a rather good tennis club there, the Casino Club or the Castle Club or something. Along with the good families in the Heights, there were iffy people, too—a writer who had gone running after his wife with a cleaver, for example. So it wasn't surprising that a child who could get drunk on NyQuil would come from the Heights. The notorious Saint Ann's School was there, a ramshackle skyscraper full of geniuses and the offspring of celebrities.

"How many stops?" Kealy asked as they pulled out of a station.

"Sixteen," Allison said.

How could there be sixteen stops between here and Brooklyn Heights? Kealy began to count. They passed Astor Place, then Bleecker Street, soon after Brooklyn Bridge–City Hall. Shortly, they were in the East River tunnel.

"You were wrong," she said, getting up, "that was five stops. The Heights isn't as far as you tend to think." They were in the Borough Hall station, the doors standing open. Neither kid moved.

"It's six more stops with a change, Mother. We're going to Church Avenue."

Six stops? But that was—where *was* that? Then the doors closed and they pulled out.

Kealy needed a shower and a change of clothes, some food. She needed Vee to make her a nice sandwich, and then she'd spend the afternoon in her reading nook. The nook would be flooded with spring sunshine . . . if the sun ever came out again.

In a booming cavern of a station, they changed to yet another train. It was a long time coming, and they stood as far away from the turnstiles as they could, hiding themselves between the rows of steel pillars that lined the platform. Some black children came along the platform and regarded them with grave, careful eyes. "This isn't particularly safe," Kealy said under her breath.

"Safer than Fifth Avenue, Mother," Allison replied, "for us."

A transit policeman appeared on the station, coming slowly down the platform. "Should we be afraid of the police?" Kealy asked.

"We should be afraid of Henny Henneman."

"Who can make use of any police resources he wants to."

"Exactly."

The train appeared, came into the station and stood a moment, its electric motors humming. They stepped in and Kealy felt a rush of relief. It had been like being naked in public out there on that platform.

As the train rattled along, the passengers grew fewer and fewer, until finally there were only five other people left in the car. Kealy and the kids were between them wearing easily five thousand dollars' worth of clothes, most of which was invested in this sadly disheveled Chanel suit of hers. But Mark and Allison were also in proper mourning; she had seen to that back a thousand years ago when they'd been getting dressed. The people elsewhere in the car were all young, were all black, and were wearing the sort of *très formidable* athletic shoes that Kealy associated with muggers.

More time passed. When there were three stops left to go to the end of the line, they suddenly burst out into the light. The train had become an elevated. Kealy could see colorful, teeming streets out the windows, looking like the sort of pictures Jacob Riis took of the Lower East Side at the turn of the century, with the difference that the people crowding these streets were black rather than Jewish.

Then the doors rolled open once again, and three more black teenagers with Kangol ratcatchers on their bald heads came strolling in, looking remarkably dangerous.

She realized that her own kids were leaving the train. But this was a black ghetto. They couldn't leave the train here, they'd be killed.

"Mother, come on!"

"Ally, this isn't . . . our neighborhood."

Allison grabbed Kealy's wrist and dragged her through the door just as it closed. Kealy saw before her what might as well be an alien planet, and a hostile one.

CHAPTER 10

The subway went rattling away into yet-deeper depths of Brooklyn, followed by a whirling mass of empty cups and anonymous pieces of paper, among which Kealy recognized a Doritos bag and the shattered remains of an appallingly large box of Stayfree Maxi Pads.

"Wait," Allison said. She and Mark were surreptitiously watching a man who had gotten out on the far end of the platform. A mugger? Kealy thought not. He was too aged. Actually, he looked rather dignified. He went slowly down the steps, a man protecting a bad hip.

"Where are we?"

"Just a sec." Allison went to the edge of the platform and looked down into the street. "He's getting on a bus," she said "Come on, Ma."

She followed them dumbly, having no idea if there was any sense or direction to this escapade. One thing was certainly wrong, though: in a neighborhood this black, they could not possibly disappear.

"Where *are* we going?"

"Mother, to Lushawn Davis's house. I told you."

"But she goes to Andover, she can't possibly—"

"Live out here?"

"No matter where she lives, this is a slum. We can't stay here, it's not safe for us."

"Maybe not all that safe," Mark agreed, "but you've got to admit that it's also not a place where those guys who were after us are likely to find us."

As they passed a newsstand, Kealy observed that even the gum was kept under lock and key. Farther along the block there were bars on every window. Then it got worse: every other storefront was shuttered and looked as if it had been sealed up behind thick armor plates taken from some battleship.

Even so, some of them had been peeled back, no doubt with crowbars. Their black interiors exuded cold, muddy vapors. Inside one of them, she could glimpse dots of light: crack pipes being smoked, she would assume.

She noticed one pair of hungry eyes after another look her up and down, pausing each time to gaze at the gold clasp on her Gucci purse.

"I don't understand why we're doing this," she said, but neither kid answered. Now they were in a block of what fifty years ago had probably been homes for poor workers. The houses were narrow and mean, their blank windows suggesting stark interiors. Many were burned out, many ruined. Anybody who still called the others home might as well be homeless.

They crossed an unseen boundary into a more populated area. Here fruit stands sold plantains and breadfruit, coconuts and durians. A black girl was coming toward them. "Yo, baby, you is still breathin'?" she asked.

"Wassup," Allison replied. To her mother's amazement, she sounded exactly like her young black friend. They slapped hands. "Here my bro."

"Hey," Mark said, and *they* slapped hands.

The girl then looked at Kealy.

"An' here be my momma," Allison said.

Kealy cleared her throat. Feeling like an utter fool, she said, "Yo," and raised her hand for the obligatory slap.

"I'm Lushawn Davis, Mrs. Ryerson." The girl extended her hand to shake. "Very pleased to meet you."

Kealy's own hand sailed down into a shake. "I'm *so* pleased to meet you, Lushawn. I've heard so much about you."

"Best we get you upstairs," Lushawn said. She laughed, tossed her head. She was a lovely girl, tall with a proud face and a firm gaze. "This is an edge neighborhood, Mrs. Ryerson. You really couldn't be more inappropriate for these streets."

They entered a three-story building faced with weathered aluminum siding. Inside, it was even older. There were strong smells of cooking and cigarettes, the wailing of an infant and what sounded like Caribbean music, and voices droning from at least four televisions. A drunken staircase led up into the shadows, and into the shadows was where they went.

Kealy was deathly scared and feeling extraordinarily lonely. She had not known that her children could emulate the mannerisms and speech of these people, and the fact that they could do it so comfortably meant that they were living even more of their lives than she'd thought entirely out of her view.

The more alone she felt, the more she dwelt in the little room in her heart that was being carefully and lovingly furnished with memories of Jimmy.

"My Lord, you look *exhausted*," a huge black woman said from the top of the stairs. "Baby, you come on—you kids *help* your mother! Come on, honey, let's get your feet up!"

Kealy sank down onto Mrs. Davis's couch. She wanted to believe that she was safe here, that this woman would care for her, that she would slowly recover her strength and find her safety here. But she knew the truth: despite the warmth she was feeling from Lushawn and her mother, this sad little place offered her and her children only an illusion of refuge.

"There, we're gonna make you better," Mrs. Davis said. "You drink this." She offered Kealy a chipped, brown-stained mug full of hot black coffee.

"Have you any cream?"

"Cremora okay?"

Then the house shook, the house thundered, a blasting, annihilating avalanche of sound. Flashing across the top of the single dirty window that offered the room's only access to the outside world, Kealy glimpsed the fat body of a jumbo jet no more than five hundred feet overhead.

"You get used to it," Lushawn explained. "When the wind's from the east, we get Kennedy traffic."

Kealy could not possibly get used to sounds like that. Her

ears would be destroyed, her ears were not perfect, hadn't been since a very different version of herself had enjoyed getting them almost blasted out of her head at rock concerts. But that had been the sixties, a very long time ago indeed.

"Mother, you need to call Mike now."

"Do you think this is what he meant? To get ourselves into this sort of a situation?"

Allison glared at her.

"I mean, he expected us to be abroad, was my impression."

"Flatbush is farther away from Fifth Avenue than London ever could be, Mrs. Ryerson."

"Please forgive me, Lushawn, I meant no offense."

"Call him, Mother."

She dug into her purse for her book, reflecting as she did so that they had arrived very quickly at the bottom. She picked up the phone, which stood on a small table beside the couch.

"Use yours," Mark said.

"I thought we weren't supposed to use our cell phones."

"Ours both have GSM. Yours doesn't. If you use the land line, somebody could get the number. Your cell phone can't tell them anything they don't already know."

She dialed her phone. She knew all about GSM. Jimmy had explained the satellite tracking system to her. With GSM phones, the kids could be tracked in case, God forbid, they were ever kidnapped. They'd taken out their batteries in the subway.

"District Attorney's Office."

"This is Mrs. Ryerson."

"Mr. McGarrigle—haven't you heard?"

"When do you expect him?"

The voice stayed silent.

"Hello?"

"Mrs. Ryerson—there was another—he's been shot, ma'am. Shot in his own living room."

With a small, tight cry, Kealy slammed down the phone. She turned and her kids' eyes widened. They could see the terror.

"We'll take care of you," Mrs. Davis said. She was now in the kitchen, hammering something that she had enclosed in a gray dish towel. "This is just what you need."

Kealy backed away from them. She fought to speak, swallowed against the dryness in her throat. "Mike," she managed to whisper. "Killed."

"Mommy?"

"Mike's been killed! The DA!"

"What DA?" Roselle Davis asked.

Allison said, "He was the last person we were sure of."

Mark added, "He knew what was happening. He was going to help us."

"Jesus," Roselle said. She came over to the couch and put her hand on Kealy's forehead. "You're running hot, lady." The bag of crushed ice that replaced the hand was deliciously cold. Kealy closed her eyes. First Jimmy, then Al, now the district attorney himself. You'd think a man in his position would be untouchable.

Whatever this was, it was clearly huge, maybe even bigger than a single Mafia don like Sal Bonacori. But what could be bigger than that, what awful thing?

She pressed the ice against her forehead, listened to the humming of the air conditioner. With her free hand, she sought for Mark. He took the hand, and his grip was strong. But what did that mean now, the fact that her boy was strong and healthy and good. Bullets don't stop for the good.

CHAPTER 11

There was thudding outside, and Mrs. Davis seemed to stiffen a bit when she heard it. It got louder and louder, until it reached the door. There it paused. Then there was a click, then a muffled scraping sound.

Kealy looked toward the door. "What's happening," she asked in a voice gone soft with fear.

The door opened and a man came in. Kealy looked frantically from Lushawn to her mother.

"You're late, Ollie," Roselle said.

"Had a time."

He had tools with him, which he carefully put down beside the door. "This is another shit job they got me in," he said. He advanced into the room, but stopped stone still the moment he saw the Ryersons.

"They're friends of mine," Lushawn said quickly.

He looked straight at Kealy. She surveyed his wide face, and worried that it was so unreadable. "You don't belong here, lady."

"Good afternoon," Kealy said. Rising, she extended her hand. "I'm Mrs. James Ryerson. Kealy."

"You need to be getting moving."

"Ollie, they need to be staying."

"Now that isn't wise, Sister. They're gonna get hurt, they hang around here." He nodded toward Kealy. "She is. Those kids look pretty fast."

"This a Christian home, Brother." She moved in front of Kealy. "They stay."

"There's somethin' wrong you're not telling me. This isn't any social call." He gazed at Kealy. "If you looking for a donation for that school of Lushawn's, you've come to the wrong place."

Kealy didn't know how to explain herself. "We're not fund-raisers," she said.

"Then just what are you?"

"In a manner of speaking, fugitives."

"Shit, Sister! You gotta get these people outta here!"

"Ollie!"

"You don't know what kinda trouble these people are gonna bring into your Christian home, Sister!" He glared at Kealy. "You on the run from the cops?"

"I don't know."

" 'Cause I'm on parole, you will recall, Roselle Davis. If I get caught harboring fugutives—well, *shit!*"

"I know that! I know that every second of my life. And I also know that this woman and these two children are in need. We've got to let 'em stay, Brother."

"Can you tell us we're gonna be safe, lady? If you stay?"

Kealy could not answer him.

Lushawn said, "May I speak?"

"You better," her mother responded, " 'cause we've got to make them go if your uncle says so."

"Ally stood up for me before the disciplinary committee when I was about to get kicked out. She told the truth, and that's why Patty Miller-Carlucci admitted that I hadn't been the one who got drunk on that NyQuil. Ally is why I still have my scholarship."

Ollie sat down in an old armchair. "This sure isn't any place for the likes of you folks, is all I have to say."

"Nowhere else is either, it would seem. We've run out of places."

Ollie leaned forward, and his face radiated a sympathy so plain that it rather shocked Kealy. "You run out of places, so you end up with us. That tells me you're in danger. Am I right?"

"Yes, you are."

"You think it's all right to bring danger into this home?"

"Well, I—"

"Because it's just a black home?"

"Of course not!"

"Then I want you to tell me just exactly what brought you

here. Because I've got to make a decision, and I want to know what I'm deciding about."

A teenage boy appeared from a bedroom. He was wiry and huge, and Kealy liked him immediately, his bright eyes, the enthusiastic way he sped into the room. "You're too rich to be running from the cops! I bet you're on the run from the Mafia, aren't'cha? That's why they're here, they know the greaseballs don't come in no nigger ghetto." He produced a huge pistol from underneath his jacket. "I'm offering myself as protection. Two hundred dollars a day."

"You get that piece back in that drawer, Jo-Jo Davis, or I'm gonna whip your tail for about the tenth time this week. Shit, you're a piece of work, bo!"

"We hear the word 'guinea' round these parts, lady, we go for our guns. Like Comrade Lenin said." He blew into the barrel, twirled the gun on one of his long, thin fingers, and tucked it back into his belt.

"My brother is a communist at the moment," Lushawn explained acidly.

"I also haven't gotten kicked out of school for chugging NyQuil."

Allison's young friend closed her eyes. "I did *not* get kicked out, I did *not* chug NyQuil, and I am going back to school after break." She shook her head. "It's so hard."

"You ever heard of Murrow? School named after Edward R. Murrow? Well, I'm the smartest damn nigger they've ever seen, and that school is full of smart niggers."

"This is an entire household of smart people," Mrs. Davis said. "But smart Jo-Jo isn't doing what smart Uncle says he's gotta do."

"And that isn't wise, because I'm going after your tail right here in front of this white girl, and she's gonna laugh her ass off, am I right, white girl?"

"This is Ally Ryerson, Uncle Ollie," Lushawn said. "And this is her brother, Mark, and her mom, Mrs. James Ryerson."

"Well, I'm pleased to meet you, and I'm still waitin' to hear why your presence in this house ain't gonna mean fuck-all for us, if you'll excuse my *indelicate* language."

Jo-Jo disappeared into the kitchen. When he returned, the gun was nowhere to be seen. "Nigger need a piece, but mine has to stay in the house. This the ghetto—you know, Mrs. James Ryerson, you read about it in a book. Where us children of slavery rob each other, shoot each other, and drug ourselves senseless. Where the murder rate is dropping only because the cops don't fill out forms on no dead niggers. But the niggers are just as dead."

Ollie turned on him. "As for you, you keep your mouth outta the gutter with that 'nigger' stuff. That 'hood talk don't move me."

"Yessir. I spose ta talk lak yew, lak a Carolina cracker." He grinned wide and licked his lips, a caricature of an old-fashioned black minstrel.

His uncle glared at him.

"Just give them a little time," Roselle said.

"You know why they're here, Sister?"

Kealy said, "My husband was murdered yesterday. We were warned that we were in danger, too, but we don't know why."

Now Ollie gave her a really careful look. "Damn. Your husband—he's that lawyer, ain't he?"

"Yes."

"Oh, my. That is sad." He looked toward the kids. "I'm sorry for you-all." Now he turned his attention to Roselle. "I know damn well we're making the mistake of the century."

Roselle smiled at Kealy. "That's a yes."

"It'll just be for a few hours," Kealy said. "Just a few hours." She really wanted an aspirin very badly.

"We need the police on our side," Allison said. "We have to find a way to trust them."

"What we need is Sal Bonacori in a coffin," Mark added. "That'd clear this whole thing right up."

Jo-Jo smiled. "Wait a minute. Just a minute. You said Bonacori? The Mafia boss?"

"He's apparently involved."

"Oh, Lord," Ollie said.

"I was right! They *do* have a Mafia problem." Jo-Jo stood to attention. "Five hundred bucks, I give you a Mafia corpse."

Ollie reached out, cuffed the escaping kid. "Like some thirteen-year-old black kid yet to need a blade is gonna do a Mafia boss. You're a born fool. I don't know what you daddy was thinking, the day he popped you in the oven." He turned to Kealy. "Now listen here, lady. What I want you to tell me is, why do you only need the one afternoon? From what your kids say, half the wiseguys in New York are chasing you. So just why do you think you're gonna be okay in a few hours?"

"We can take a night flight to Europe."

"You got passports?"

That was a problem. She said, "We'll need a little more time." She went to the phone. It was a risk, but she needed those passports. She dialed Vee's number.

"Vee, don't ask any questions. I need you to go to the apartment and get our passports."

"Mrs. Ryerson! Where are you? Are you okay?"

"We're fine. But both Al Sager and Mike McGarrigle have been killed."

"I know, I saw the TV—and listen, there are people watching my place. And yours. I went back this afternoon, saw a carload of 'em."

"They're watching you as well?"

"I think they're undercover cops. My whole neighborhood's steaming about it. They aren't even black, Mrs. Ryerson. It's so obvious."

Was it safe for Vee to do this? How in the world could she deliver the passports if she was being watched? She'd be followed right here to this apartment.

Then Kealy saw how it could be done. It was simple; good ideas always were. "Vee, tomorrow morning, you go back to the apartment. Get the passports. Then you go to Jimmy's funeral. Give them to us there."

"I'll have them with me."

In the back of her mind, Kealy had been suffering over the
funeral. It couldn't wait, and she was very uneasy about going,
and she certainly didn't want Ally and Mark to risk it. She told
herself that it was a good plan, that the funeral would be
crowded, that it was the perfect place to get the passports.

"I love you, Vee," she said. After she hung up, she turned to
Ollie Davis, who did not look like a very happy man at all. There
was nothing to do, though, but just plunge ahead.

"Mr. Davis, we need more than an afternoon, it seems. We
need tonight and part of tomorrow." She did not add that her full
plan was to intercept Vee entering the church, then go straight to
Kennedy and get on the next flight to any other country. The risk
of doing this was great, but it was obviously not greater than staying here.

Before he could respond, everybody in the room heard the
word "Ryerson" coming from the television, which was always
left on, providing background chatter that was mostly ignored.

On the screen beside Tim Harvey, the Channel Eleven news
anchor, was the portrait Avedon had shot of her, the one that
Jimmy had kept in his office. ". . . family of Mafia lawyer James
Walter Ryerson has been missing since this morning."

"Shit, a *Mafia* lawyer, yet."

Mark leaped to his feet. "He's not a Mafia lawyer!"

"Police sources have stated that they are in grave danger and
are running in fear of their lives. A five-thousand-dollar reward
has been offered by friends of the missing family for information
regarding their whereabouts."

Jimmy's photos of Allison and Mark joined their mother's on
the screen.

Then Henny appeared. "If you're in hiding because you're
afraid, you need to come into contact with the police. Mrs. Ryerson, the safest thing for all of you to do is come in."

Kealy thought perhaps they should do just that.

"Man, they sure don't like you people," Jo-Jo said.

Kealy was confused. "What do you mean?"

"They just converted everyone in the city into a bounty hunter," Mark said, his voice leached of tone.

It had seemed so decent of them, but it was really cunning, wasn't it?

Ollie said, "You've got a nice number on you."

"What does that mean?" Kealy asked.

"The chief of detectives is asking you to come in. That doesn't happen every day."

"That detective could be part of our problem."

"You're white," Jo-Jo said, "and you don't trust your own police. That I don't get."

"I have good reasons."

Ollie said, "Look, you go back home now. You can't hang around out here. You might as well be walking around with a sign, 'Get Your Five Grand Here.'"

"We can't go home if we don't know who to trust!"

"What I'm saying is, you've got friends ready to put up five thousand dollars. You go to them for help. A bunch of poor people can't do a thing."

"It's a trick," Mark said.

"You have to go back to your own people. You can't do anything else, not with eight million bounty hunters lookin' to bring you in like big game."

"If we go in, Henneman is going to kill us." There, she'd said it. That was her fear. Her knowledge. It explained the coldness he'd displayed toward her in the car, the distance. He'd wanted to kill her then, but he wanted her to get her children in the net, first—which she had so very obligingly done.

"You're one paranoid bitch."

A bitch. The thing she most despised being called. The thing Henny had called her in court, right out in public, in the most painful, most humiliating experience of her life. She wanted to control herself but she couldn't, the rage just started to come.

The kids knew these signs, the sudden pallor, the clenching of the fists. "Mommy?"

"You keep out of this."

"Mother, no!"

"You damned arrogant bully! I am *not* a bitch, Mr. Davis, and don't you dare call me one. I'm a person in a whole lot of trouble that you can't even begin to understand—"

"Thas right, nigger don't know nothin'. Nigger too 'undereducated' to understand."

"And don't you call yourself that! Can you imagine how offensive that sounds?"

"Sorry. African-American. African-American too dumb to understand."

Another voice was raised, bigger than either of theirs. "Brother, you shut your trap. And Kealy, you, too. Why can't you two get along like adults? The way you're screamin', a deaf bear couldn't hibernate."

Thank God for Roselle Davis.

"She a racist bitch and she don't even know it! She drivin' me crazy, Sister, she the most arrogant damn bitch I ever met!"

Even as he spat the bitter words, their eyes met. Almost instantly, they flickered away—anywhere else.

"Time out!" It was Allison. "This is crazy. You don't even know each other."

Lushawn said, "Yeah, Uncle Ollie, these are good people, these are my friends."

Ollie blinked. Then he said, his voice very quiet, "What the hell are you gonna do? What the *hell?*"

"Ollie, I apologize. However I offended you."

"And I won't turn you in for the five grand, but I want to. And not to get that damn money when it's there for the getting— that just plain pisses me off!"

Mark said, "I could sure as hell stand a beer."

"We got beer," Ollie said. "Bud, Bud Light. Help yourself."

Mark went into the kitchen, followed closely by Jo-Jo.

Roselle said, "Half this street probably knows we've got white people in here. I mean, you folks showing up, that was noticed for sure."

"We need to get our tickets," Kealy said, again picking up the phone. "I've got it all planned." Into the phone: "A number for British Airways reservations, please." They went to many obscure places, BA did.

Ollie rose up, put out his hand and took the phone. His movements were firm but gentle. "You're gonna use a credit card, aren't you?"

"Of course."

"Can't do that. They'll track you down in ten minutes flat."

"Then how do we get tickets?"

"You wanna do this right, you gotta use cash."

"Cash means going to an ATM. We'll be recognized."

Ollie continued. "Bounty hunting's a profession in a neighborhood like this. There's four or five good bounties live on just this one block. I mean, there are all kinds of people around here worth money, and all kinds of people trying to earn that money. So you're in the wrong place for sure."

"We need cash," Kealy said, "if we're going to be able to pay for three tickets."

"I'll go out and get it for you," Lushawn said.

"No, we ain't gettin' involved! We can't dare do that, girl!"

"Ollie, they're my friends!"

"He's right," Allison said. "We can get money at the airport."

Jo-Jo burst in. "He gone down the fire escape!"

Mrs. Davis leaped from her chair and sped past her son into the kitchen, Kealy right behind her. She could see the dark brown back of Mark's jacket turning amid the black steps and girders. "Mark! *Mark!*"

She watched him drop into the debris-choked alley, then start loping toward the street.

Ollie was all over Jo-Jo, grabbing him by his shirt, lifting him off the floor. "Where is it?" he asked.

"I left it right there," the boy said, jerking his head toward the table. But there was no gun on the table. The gun was gone.

There was no warrant, just the piece of paper with which
Henny had deceived the doorman. Considering the exhaus-
tive forensic search that had already been conducted here, he
didn't really know why he'd come back.

Even so, he stood in the living room of her beautiful home
and had a lot of very complicated feelings. When he'd brought
her here after the murder, he had not been able to bear the sense
of inadequacy and loss that it brought him.

Often, when he happened to be passing 1075 Fifth, he'd wondered about her in her beautiful life. He'd heard from some assi-
tant DA that she and Jimmy jogged around the Central Park
Reservoir, and he'd found himself jogging there, too.

There was such a view, so many lights even at this late hour.
The view in his most recent apartment consisted of a chimney
climbing a wall. He had always wanted to live the Manhattan
lifestyle, but money was tight. He had supported Marie and his
boy Charlie, made a decent life for them in Cop Land, that strip
of Long Island towns that hug the Queens border like sympathetic
whores propping up a tired old john.

It was a hike across this living room, a hike into the kitchen.
Once again, he examined the broken phone. Silver-gray dust still
covered it, but the only prints they'd found had belonged to the
family.

They had combed this place thoroughly, had found a spike microphone in the living room wall, but it had not been set right and
wasn't operational. There were two more in the master bedroom,
both working. The rest of the phones were clear, but they had
been opened anyway.

They'd come up with nothing, and he was coming up with
nothing now. He moved into the dining room. How much was a
table like that worth? Ten grand, twenty?

"Kealy," he said. He thought of that fast, sharp voice of
hers—how could a voice like that be so damned sexy? It was because of what went with it: the cast of the eye, that little smile of
hers that said so much about her womanhood.

He treated me like a common prostitute, she had testified at the divorce trial. *I was just one of many.* It could not have been more true, and he could not have been more—"Stupid," he said aloud.

He'd known damn well that it would hurt to come here. He'd known that it would hurt a lot. So maybe that's why he'd done it, to enable her to punish him even in her absence, and by her absence. Because he was to blame for her suffering and her danger, he was entirely to blame.

They hadn't picked up a single thing on this family of three helpless, street-dumb civilians since they walked into the Sixth Avenue subway. Despite a manhunt that had put every patrolman in the city on alert and fanned bulletins across the United States, and with the help of Interpol, through Europe as well, there had been not one legitimate sighting.

How did people who had no more street knowledge than a gaggle of five-years-olds evade them like this? The commissioner and the mayor were on his ass. "Every day that passes, it gets more likely that they're gonna turn up dead," the commissioner had said with his usual scintillating insight.

Well, yes.

"Kealy," he said. *"Kealy!"* Then he went striding back into the best room of all, the room where you could still smell the love. She had decorated it in green, no doubt to make it restful. But no healthy man could rest in that big bed, not with Kealy's alabaster curves sliding between the sheets.

He sat down on the edge. She must have given Ryerson one hell of a lot of love in this thing. Under the satin coverlet, silk sheets. How would it feel to be naked with Kealy in silk sheets? He rolled over, inhaled the faintly perfumed scent of the coverlet.

Then he cried into it, cried as he had cried a hundred times since the divorce.

He shut it off. No time now. He had to be tough as hell. The die was cast for Kealy Ryerson. He rose up, went into the study. This was where forensics had concentrated its effort, and there was dust everywhere, especially in the little closet, which still stood open, its gutted interior visible as a shadowy shambles.

There was nothing. The place wasn't inspiring him at all. There'd been no damn point in coming here. It was just opening old wounds. "Kealy!"

Only the humming echo of his own voice replied. That and the faint rumble of the sleeping city outside, a siren raised, a dog howling in the park, the voices of lovers drifting up from the late-night sidewalk far below.

He was one very lonely policeman. He had a very damn hard job to do.

Ryerson's funeral was tomorrow. The family would show up. They were certain to, if he knew his Kealy. She had been loyal to that creep from the first moment she bedded him. Henny still remembered when the light of love had begun to leave her eyes. That was when Ryerson started in on her, it must have been.

Dead. Good. What a bastard.

Tomorrow at the funeral, Henry Henneman would do what he had to do to the woman who once he had loved.

CHAPTER 12

H e's gone after Bonacori," Allison shouted.

Lushawn went thundering off down the stairs. Kealy grabbed her purse and followed.

Al's and Mike's murders had made her boy feel cornered—accurately—and he was lashing out like a trapped lion. Well, he *was* a lion, just like his father. A brave, tragic lion.

In a taxi she'd beat him to Bonacori's house. She'd tell the Mafia chieftain everything, throw herself on his mercy. She knew where he lived. He threw spectacular fund-raisers there for the Opera Guild.

Allison caught up with her. "Mother, you can't go there!"

"I sure can."

"But—you—he'll kill you!"

"It's me or your brother. I think my choice is clear."

"Does Mark even know where he lives?"

"If he didn't know or couldn't find out, he wouldn't have run like this."

"What about me? What happens to me?"

"Mark's our immediate priority."

"I could lose both of you!"

Kealy looked into the face of a passing woman, then lowered her eyes. Had the woman noticed them shouting at each other, perhaps then recognized them from the TV? She gave no indication.

She'd been dreaming lately about being naked in a crowd. Well, this was the real thing. You don't know anybody. Everybody knows you. And to think she'd been worried about being invisible. At the moment, she was the most visible woman in New York. Eat your hearts out, ladies.

The beautiful Lushawn had turned out to be one hell of a fast woman on her feet. Those long, lithe legs had pumped along behind Mark for what had seemed like hours, forever getting closer. Mark was just about to quit. But then he found himself beside the open door of a bus. He jumped in just as it took off. Lushawn appeared beside the windows, running to keep up, but she had dropped back. He'd last seen her bent at the waist, gasping and heaving.

He didn't know where the bus was going, and he sat well to the back, trying to make himself inconspicuous, primarily concerned with keeping the huge .45 concealed under his clothes and avoiding letting people see his face. Anybody would understand his wanting to carry a weapon in this terrible area, but the police would be forced to stop him if they saw the thing—and that must not happen. After, it wouldn't matter, not when his sister and his mom were safe. With what was wrong with him—the secret that he and Dad had been living with since last October—to him it meant that his own life mattered less. That hurt like hell, but it was the truth. Dad had always said, *We roll with the blows, Marko, but we do it together, and that's going to make it better. That's what it's about, being father and son.* He was so great and Mark's heart was breaking in a thousand ways. *Dad, I'm gonna save your ladies, then I'm coming home.* His throat constricted, the tears flowed, the bus ground along the bustling streets of a Caribbean neighborhood. The life outside, people in bright clothes, shops with their goods spilling out onto the street, presented an astonishing contrast to the broken neighborhood a few blocks back. Mark watched with a kind of envy, from the dark of the dying. He thought, *I didn't get to live hardly at all, Dad, but that's okay. Maybe I'll get to try again.*

He'd told Dad about being gay because he told Dad everything. When he knew for certain that he was HIV positive, he'd called Dad and said, "I need you. I have a problem."

Dad had been at the airport within the hour. They'd met at the Ritz-Carlton. Dad had never asked how he'd become positive. All he'd said was that he'd done some research and made an appointment for Mark with Dr. Seamus O'Hara at the Mayo Clinic, who was the best AIDS man in the country.

Right now, Mark's viral load was undetectable, thanks to Seamus. But Seamus had said to him, "We never know what to expect. If we're lucky, we'll get a cure before your disease begins to defeat us."

Then Dad had been shot. Mom's words had gone off like an atomic blast of grief in his brain, a literal flash, blinding, soul-crushing. He'd been brave for her on the phone, then he had curled up on the floor of his dorm room and screamed and screamed into a pillow, so loud that kids had come to the door. Timothy Greene, lovely Timmy, had consoled him, had helped him get himself together enough to at least go home.

Dad. Mark had taken this as his mission: to become a terrorist against crime, to save his mom and his sister and destroy the life of Dad's killer even if it meant giving up his own.

The thing was, how could he possibly pull this off? Bonacori must have bodyguards, for one thing. Also, Mark had never shot a pistol. More importantly, he'd never shot a man, and it might be hard to actually do that, no matter how much he hated the guy.

Dad had made sure Mark had met Bonacori. He always wanted him to be informed, to understand, because he thought of his son as a future partner. "He's the last of the great Mafia bosses. You will see true evil, and you will witness me testing the strength of my oath, because I loathe him but I have no way to recuse myself."

This was why Mark knew that his dad wasn't a criminal. No man would say a thing like that to his own son and not mean it, no man with a soul. And his dad had one of the great souls, he damn well did.

Oh, Dad, Dad. He repeated it like a mantra. Oh, Dad my beloved, father of my mind and my heart, I will avenge you, I will shoot him in the leg, and then in the balls—yes, I will be brutal and hard and I will make him struggle and suffer on the dirty ground. Dad, then I will join you, I will go into the light and be with you for ten thousand years, my father.

The bus stopped at Joralemon and Court. Downtown Brooklyn. He saw cabs. "Hello, Mr. Bonacori," he whispered as he stepped to the curb to hail one. "Hello, there."

There were no damn taxis and Allison and Lushawn were sticking to her and refusing to leave.

"Mother, don't you understand that you can't do this? Why don't you get it? If you end up on Bonacori's doorstep—"

"Please God send me a cab!"

Twenty-sixth Street and Eighty-eighth Avenue," Mark said to the back of the driver's head.

The driver sang out, "Villa Vivolo?"

"You got it." It was where they'd eaten, he and dad and Sal Bonacori, in a private room with pale wallpaper. There had been a painting of the sea; they'd had lasagna with three cheeses. He didn't recall Bonacori's address, but the house was a couple of doors down and he thought that he'd recognize it.

Bensonhurst, with its alternating bleak cityscapes and quiet, tree-lined streets, had a curiously European appearance. It was where Little Italy had gone as Manhattan's Chinatown expanded. There were cafes open to the sidewalks, people strolling, a living, immensely detailed world that seemed impossibly unaware of the rage and hate that rode in this cab.

The interior of the bus was jammed with young people whose accents identified them with the Caribbean. Kealy sat with the girls, wishing that they would listen to sense, knowing that they would not leave her.

Block by block, the bus crept closer to the center of Brooklyn.

Men in battle felt as Mark felt, but he knew nothing about battle. He stood in front of the restaurant, looking down the quiet street. And then he saw it, he was sure that this was the house: tall, silent, every shade drawn. It looked like a house of evil, and he knew that was exactly correct. "Dad," he whispered, the gun dragging heavily under his jacket, its barrel pressing his thigh. He moved toward the house, went up the steps, rang the bell. There was a hollow chime, then soft movement very close to the other side of the door.

CHAPTER 13

S tanding on the sidewalk, they looked up at the tall house. Its tall first-story windows gave it an air of Gothic watchfulness.

"What do we do now?" Lushawn asked.

Kealy had absolutely not the faintest idea. Knock on the door? Break in? Maybe there were cellar stairs, maybe she could sneak in. But not the girls. "I want you girls to go in that restaurant and wait. Stay away from me."

Allison marched to the top of the steps and rang the bell. "This is what to do next," she said.

Before Kealy could take another breath, the door came sweeping open, and she found herself staring into the dark cave of the front hall, her daughter in front of her. Before Allison stood a boy of perhaps twelve, with dark hair and a line of sweat gleaming along his child's soft lip. Inexplicably, he had a roll of duct tape in his hand—that and a toy ninja knife.

They were silently let in. Then the boy turned and walked into the gloomy central hallway of the elegant old mansion.

"He told us you'd be coming soon," he said over his shoulder. Then he added, "I'm sorry I busted him up a little before my dad recognized him. But he'll be fine. Just sore."

Kealy had expected to find Mark dead, but instead here was this strange, rough child with his big eyes apologizing to her. Then a figure emerged, a squat man in an Egyptian-cotton club shirt, blue pants, and white patent leather shoes. Sal in casual dress looked like a golf caddy on his way to a wedding. The head of one of the great New York crime families, a man her husband had called evil, gave her the sweetest smile.

Age had brought a certain distinction to his face, the Hapsburg pout characteristic of certain northern Italian aristocrats.

Maybe somewhere in the family's hard past there was a failed duke, a burned castle, a flight into the night.

"Get the kid, Paulie."

The boy disappeared, his feet thundering on stairs somewhere in the back of the house. Bonacori regarded Kealy with the same liquid eyes that he had bequeathed to his son. "My Paulie was on him like a tiger. He came in here with a piece. So stupid."

"He thinks you're responsible for Jimmy's death."

He sucked air through his teeth, shook his head. "Your husband was gonna keep me outta jail. I go to jail, my Paulie ends up in foster care, and Papa in the kitchen—well, they got a bed waiting for him in Droolerville."

The old man who must be Sal's father—wearing a neat blue suit under a gleaming leather butcher's apron—appeared with young Paulie. Between them was a pitiful stick-figure of a young man, his mouth covered with duct tape, his clothes disheveled.

All three women rushed to him, Lushawn arriving first. With a cry, she embraced him. Then her eyes flared at Paulie Bonacori. "You hurt him, you prick!" Gently, she removed the duct tape. He licked his lips, took a gasping breath.

"I knocked him out is all," Paulie said. "I took his gun so he wouldn't kill my dad." He looked ashamed, then, glancing away from those accusing eyes. "I did him a little." He reached out his hand, took his father's. "My dad hadda pull me off."

"He's real protective," Sal said, and there was pride in his voice. "He's, like, a brown belt."

"I'm a black belt, Dad."

"Since when?"

"Since Sensei gave me my test."

Seeing the silent something that passed at that moment between father and son, Kealy knew at once that Sal Bonacori was a very loyal man. There could be no question now, if there ever had been: men like that are dangerous. She knew. Her husband had been like that, loyal to an extreme. It made him a wonderful person to have on your side, but God help his enemies. And God help Sal's.

She and Lushawn and Allison took poor beaten-up Mark to the couch and sat him down. "Momma," he gasped, "I got us killed, Momma!" He threw his arms around her. "I'm so sorry!"

"Honey, be quiet." She appealed with her eyes to Bonacori. She had no reason to trust him, but what else could she do? She was here, her kids were here. "Sal," she said, "if there's something you want from us, you can have it. Anything we have."

"You look a mess, Kealy. I can hardly recognize you."

She knew that her suit was ruined, her face wretched, her hair like something teased in hell. "It's me," she said. She laughed a little.

"Who killed Jimmy?"

She could hardly believe the question, and she could *not* believe that he would have any reason to ask it if he knew the answer. Even Mark reacted to it, sitting up slightly.

"We're in the dark. But they threatened us, Sal. All of us. We thought—"

"You thought it was me." He looked at Mark. "You came here to avenge your father. That is an act of courage. But you got the wrong guy."

"That can't be true."

"It is true," Paulie said. "I know everything my dad does, and he didn't lay a finger on your old man!"

Sal regarded Mark. "You got a lot to learn about this world, kid."

"We all do," Allison said. "Because if you aren't responsible, then we're even more in the dark than we thought."

"If that's possible," Kealy added.

"Okay, so this is what I can tell you. First, my family—people like me, you understand, I'm not sayin' anything one way or the other about organized crime, here, you get my drift—but my family, my personal people who are mostly my blood, we got rules."

"You're not involved in organized crime. That's what you're saying."

"I'm saying there are these ethical things." He pronounced the word as he might the name of an exotic fruit. "Ethical things," he repeated. "First off, no killing of women and children. Wives and kids, this is out. Plus, no cops unless in hot pursuit with their guns drawn. I mean, there are rules in this thing we have, you got that?" He thrust his chin out at Mark. "You got that, son? 'Cause that's why when you brought a piece in here—"

Mark groaned.

"The rules are why you're alive, Mark. Why I foreswore from blowing your head off." Mark's pistol appeared in Sal's hand. "You always do things right, Kealy. I mean, with style. But this is a really miserable weapon. This is gonna kill the shooter, too, 'cause what it's mainly gonna do is blow the fuck up. Excuse me."

"I'd like that," Lushawn said. "It's my uncle's."

"No, no. Consider it confiscated." Again, he sucked air through his teeth. "You got a big-time problem, Kealy. Big-time." He regarded her. "You have suspicions?"

"What do you know about Henny Henneman?" Kealy asked.

"Good cop. Not a friend of ours."

Mark requested aspirin. Kealy's heart ached for her boy.

"Get him a Vicodin, Paulie," Sal said to his son.

The kid went off.

Mark continued, his voice hoarse. "My father told me that you were an example of true human evil. That's what my father thought of you."

"You ever consider the ministry, kid? You got the disposition of a preacher."

Paulie Bonacori brought a Vicodin and a glass of water, and helped Mark take it with a gentleness that was at odds with his proved ferocity.

"Hits like these are very unusual," Bonacori said. "They're not normal. I mean, guys I heard of here and there would never do hits like these. A big lawyer. You talk about drawing attention. Then a PI, another big attention getter. Then the DA! I don't think in all the years I been following organized crime—I'm writing a history book about it, I'm a professor of crime, you could say—I never heard of nobody hitting nobody that far up the ladder."

A silence fell as each person in the room came face-to-face with the depth of the problem.

Allison said at last, "Mr. Bonacori, we don't know what to do."

As if noticing Lushawn for the first time, Sal looked her up and down. "You got a reason for bein' here?"

"She's my roomie," Allison said, "from school. We're staying at her—"

Kealy did not want that revealed. "It's a long story, Sal. The question I'm trying to get answered is if you know who might be our problem."

"Whoever the big guy is, he's so powerful that he feels he can off a DA without fear of getting caught. You know how much juice the commissioner of police is gonna put on that case? You can't even imagine. As much as it takes, even if it takes every detective and every plainclothesman on the force. Ten thousand men, it don't matter to him."

"So who might he be, and how're we gonna deal with him?"

Sal went over to Mark. "How's your gut, kid?"

"Hurts."

"Paulie, you got a hell of a fist on you, boy!" He could not conceal his pride in the tightly wound little monster. "You're gonna have a coupla bruises." His eyes gleamed. "Your boy had me under the gun." He nodded toward Paulie. "He took care of his dad."

Paulie burst and bristled at the same time, pride and defensive belligerence making him flush and almost strut. Kealy thought that he had a lot of strengths, this child, but it wasn't at all obvious that he was being taught proper standards of behavior.

But he also wasn't her problem, and she had plenty of those. She thought that she would try to extract knowledge and even help from Bonacori. Why not, if he wasn't against her?

And yet, how did she *really* know? People could be duplicitous, people could lie. This man could be expected to be an expert liar.

She had to face it: this was no more safe a place for her and her kids than the rest of the city. And maybe, if they were lying, it was far less safe. Maybe it was the lair of the wolf.

CHAPTER 14

Papa Bonacori, the grandfather of the clan, had been preparing a dinner that, when it was set out on the wide table, was glorious. Silver platters gleamed beneath the light of the enormous chandelier. Kealy remembered this lovely dining room with its magnificent Louis Quatorze table and chairs, rosewood intricately carved with rose flowers, its fine Persian carpet glowing richly with hunting scenes and the magnificent reproduction wallpaper. It was an elegant, superbly decorated room. But the food. Kealy could hardly believe the food that was being laid before them now.

"Mr. Bonacori," she said, "this is—well—"

Grandfather Bonacori smiled, his eyes crinkling. "It's a few minutes, it's nothing."

Sal said, "Italians, somebody is born, we eat. Somebody dies, we eat. A deal is struck, we eat." He spread his hands. "Please sit down to my table."

Papa Bonacori said, "Eat, eat."

"You gotta be careful, Papa's gonna make you a dish you can't refuse," Paulie said.

Sal regarded Kealy. "So what's your plan? You got to have a plan."

"My plan is to get out of the country."

"You'll get hit either in the airport before you leave, or when you land. You need a better plan."

"What else can we do?"

"You gotta find out who's after you. Then you gotta get them first."

"Oh, well, the law—"

"It didn't help Mikey-boy, it ain't gonna help you." He glanced at Mark. "You had the right idea, kid. Just the wrong guy." He smiled, nodded toward the food. "Now you see the way we eat every day, am I right? Not like the Opera Guild, all that light-weight stuff they like. This is real. A real Italian dinner, a serious meal."

At each place was a salad tossed with pale slices of porcini mushrooms, celery, snowy flakes of *parmigiano-reggiano* cheese and woodsy, delicate slices of perfectly white truffle. And that was just the beginning. Kealy dug into her salad. "Do you have any ideas that might help us?"

"I got suspicions. It ain't *la cosa nostra*. I mean, my business is fucked. I'm fucked, we all are. The wiseguy is a dead guy. All you gotta do is get indicted and you're heading for jail. It used to be, it was hard for the Feds to get convictions. See, the way the organiz-ation works—so I hear—is the farther up the ladder you go, the less evidence there is of your involvement. Now, the bigger the boss, the harder he falls, evidence or no evidence." He directed his glittering black eyes toward Mark. "You know what the conviction rate's been on the bosses?"

"High," Mark said.

"Jimmy the Chin. No real evidence there, but down he goes. Gotti the same—I mean, there was *no* probable cause. And his son, they ate him alive, too."

On the word "ate," he reached to the middle of the table for a large silver bowl that was decorated with plump little angels and garlands of silver ivy. The bowl was filled with tagliatelle and a steaming meat sauce Bolognese.

His father, standing in the doorway, nodded and smiled. "Eat," he said.

"What else can we do?" Bonacori roared with laughter as he next went to a side table where there stood four bottles of wine. *"Gemma,"* he announced, "made by my cousin. This is 1982, a very good year."

Kealy wasn't interested in wine, not even superb wine, not now. She wanted as much information from him as she could man-age to get. "Are you saying that whoever's putting the bosses away is somehow responsible for all this?"

He regarded her, smiled thinly. "Exactly. Young suits are

moving in on us. Somehow, you're in their way, so you and your kids are expected to join darlin' Jimmy where the roses grow."

"What young suits?"

"Big-time ones. They got the clout to kill a DA and think they can get away with it. Not to mention a major lawyer."

"So we're right to run?"

He stopped pouring wine. "Stop with this run! You don't run! You find out what the fuck's goin' on, I'm tellin' you. You can do it, you got Jimmy's records. It's all laid out in there somewhere or he wouldn't be dead."

"The records he had at home were stolen."

"He has a safe in his office."

Bonacori knew a lot about Jimmy's arrangements. Kealy wondered how much truth there was in appearances. As far as she could remember, the only thing in the safe was two hundred thousand dollars' worth of bearer bonds, which she did not intend to mention. "I can't possibly go to the office. We can't even go out in the street."

"I need help, too, lady. I got an indictment coming down and now my lawyer's a goddamn corpse."

"What about us?" Mark asked. "We might get shot in ten minutes. We need your help more than you need ours."

Paulie Bonacori wagged a finger at him. "You shut up! You said enough, you done enough!"

"No. No, I don't think I have." He addressed the father. "Because you're not really offering us help. You're actually asking us to help you, and we can't do that without risking our own lives."

"Look, you gotta get information. It might be useful to me, yes. I'm about to get burned for a crime I haven't committed yet. That's good, isn't it? The Feds are saying I got a million bum phone cards I'm gonna sell on the street. The operative word here is 'gonna.' I'm gonna go down for a crime that I haven't committed yet!"

Allison responded—her voice, Kealy thought, surprisingly adult. She was growing up by the minute, poor kid. "You have your problems, Mr. Bonacori. Serious problems. But we're in a much worse situation. We can't get information for you."

"I told you, I'm lookin' at time for a crime I didn't *fucking* commit! That's my problem! That's what I care about!"

Mark said, "I care about the lives of my mother and my sister."

"Getting whatever's in that safe is gonna help everybody. You need information as much as I do."

"I don't think there's any information there, Sal. Just personal materials."

"Look, Kealy, you don't know what's in there. But my guess is, your husband was killed for it. Maybe it's even got the answer to my ace question."

"And what's your ace question?" Allison asked.

"My dad's ace question is who stole the ten million dollars' worth of phone cards the FBI's charged him for using in a scam."

"Phone cards?" Kealy did not know what phone cards were.

"Little cards with an account number on them. You call an 800 number and you get so much long-distance time, depending on the value on the card. Only these cards are special. One of 'em might say it has an hour on it for $4.95. Only it ain't got no hour. It's got, maybe, ten minutes. You buy it right from your corner grocery, and you get ripped off."

"That's vicious," Mark said.

"Yeah, it is vicious. Thing is, I paid a certain price for these cards. Good price. I had no reason to think they weren't legitimate. Then somebody is selling them—I mean, selling *my* cards, right outta my warehouse—and the next thing I hear, public complaints are coming in. And guess who's left holding the bag? Mr. so-called Mafia boss who didn't even sell the damn cards and sure as hell didn't get any money for them is left holding the fucking bag."

Whoever this was, they'd succeeded in not only robbing a legendary criminal but actually framing him for a crime he had so far only planned to commit.

"That's why I'd love to see what's in Jimmy's safe. My guess is that he found out who's inside my business selling my cards out from under me. That's sure as hell what that PI of his was workin' on. I think this is why our Jimmy went off to the DA. He fingered the thief and my case was gonna get dismissed."

"This can't be about phone cards," Mark said. "People don't kill district attorneys over phone cards."

"Well, let's look at it another way. It's ten million dollars. And I think people *do* kill district attorneys for ten million dollars, especially if there's an added benefit that the murder ends a threat of jail time. What you gotta do is get in that safe. Odds are, whatever Al Sager came up with is in there."

"They'd've cracked the safe by now."

"It might not be so easy to do that in an office with heavy-duty security. I sure as hell wouldn't try to go in there, not with the best pete guy in the business, 'cause your husband's got a lotta technology between the door and the pete, you know what I mean."

"Will you tell us how to escape, Sal? We have no idea how to run, how to change our identities, anything."

"Can't you fuckin' *hear?* You run, you die!"

"You are talking to a mother and two children!"

At that moment, Papa Boncori came in carrying more dishes. The boy got up and took the two bowls of vegetables from him, one containing Swiss chard gratineed with Parmesan cheese and the other diced potatoes pan-roasted to a luscious golden color. As these dishes were put on the table, Papa returned with a loin of pork steaming with meaty flavors and roasted to nut-brown perfection.

"We're not going to attempt something we can't possibly manage. Especially not to save a man like you."

"Your kid's a prig," Sal said. "That surprises me."

"Yours is an up-and-coming criminal. That surprises me."

Bonacori chuckled. "You gonna be a wiseguy, Paulie?"

"Wiseguys is stupid."

Sal raised his eyebrows at Kealy. "See? Not such a bad answer."

"I'm gonna be a boss."

"You're nothing but a bunch of common criminals," Mark announced. "Even the child!"

The magnificent loin was placed before Sal, who didn't even acknowledge it. He was glaring at Mark. His face was purple, his spit flecked white. "You've been on your fuckin' high horse ever since you came in here with that asshole special in your fat little hand and tried to plug me!" His fist came down so hard that his glass snapped right off its stem and wine swept like dark blood across the sparkling white tablecloth. He turned on Kealy. "And you're a damn fool if you think you can get out of the hole you're in by goin' to Moscow or China or somewhere! You're dead people, you understand? 'Cause this is bigger than the Mafia and a whole lot meaner. This is big law and big business working together to create bigger crime than we've ever seen before. Compared to these shits with clean fingernails, we're a bunch of gentlemen. Women and children, they don't mean fuck to these guys! Somehow or another, you're in their way. So you're toast, end of fuckin' story."

Allison burst out, "Who are they? God help us, who are they?"

Kealy went to her, Mark went to her, Lushawn went to her. The Bonacoris watched, Sal still purple, his son crackling with belligerent energy, the old man smiling and nodding like he was in a receiving line at a ball.

"Ally—"

"He's right. We're dead because we can't investigate and we can't escape! We don't know how to do any of it, we're stupid and helpless! And oh, Jesus, they killed Daddy!"

Kealy held her kids.

Lushawn said, "We're gonna find a way. Because there is one. You aren't dead yet."

"You do your own investigation," Kealy told Bonacori. "Running is our only alternative."

"Shit, this wine is goin' through the crack in the table!" He pushed his chair back. "Fuckin' wine stain on my pants!" He sopped at it with his napkin. "Fuck!"

"Listen, Sal, I want you to calm down. My kids are crying, Lushawn looks like she's seen a ghost, and look at your boy— look at him!"

Paulie's truculence was gone. He had his head in his hands. "Now, what you have to do is get your organization, and—"

With a snarling growl he raised the big silver platter with the loin of pork on it and slammed it down on the table. "Can't you goddamn well hear, you stupid cunt! I ain't *got* no fuckin' organization. Nothing's left! You think I'd be wasting my time trying to make a deal with some Fifth Avenue bitch if I did?"

"Come on, kids," Kealy said. "We're leaving."

"Thank you, God," Lushawn muttered.

"Oh, you're leaving? You're *leaving?* Here the boss of bosses throws you and your gaggle of tramps a party and so *you're leaving!* I guess us Bensonhurst greaseballs ain't got quite enough style for your nigger here, right? Fine. You leave here and you go out on that street, you are fucking dead and you know it!"

She moved quickly away, the kids with her. This thing with this man had to end right now or somebody was going to commit murder. She was practically running by the time she reached the front door.

Then he barged up behind her and grabbed her by the shoulder. He spun her around—but his face was now mild. "You got to help me," he said.

"I've got to help my kids."

The door was opened and the kids were dragging her out. As it slammed, there came a huge thud against it from the inside—and then silence.

The night was yellow from the sodium vapor street lighting, which glowed in the fog that was rolling in from the harbor. The cars parked along the street were dark and still. But some of them had tinted windows, and maybe there was the brief glow of a cigarette end from behind one of them.

"Move it, guys," Lushawn said. "We gotta get outta here right now."

As they went down the steps to the street, an unexpected sound rose from deep in the house behind them, a high, lonely wailing.

It broke Kealy's heart. "It's that poor little boy," she said. "He puts on a tough front, but that poor little boy is terrified."

"He's hell with his fists," Mark muttered. "A damned expert."

As they hurried toward the subway stop, the screams of child-ish terror were repeated again and again, echoing in the silence of the night, only slowly fading.

"Now, where do we go?" Allison asked. "Can we go to a hotel?"

"Come back to our place. You can use my bedroom."

"Lushawn, your uncle won't like that."

"My uncle's gonna be pissed as hell, and he'll probably throw you right out. But he's generally not around at night, so you've got a place until morning. I think."

From deep beneath the street, there came the harsh, rum-bling roar of an incoming train. They ran, because subways were scarce out here at this hour.

"Maybe we oughtta just ride it all night," Mark said as the doors closed behind them.

"You come home with me. It'll be all right."

Kealy did not give voice to her thoughts, but she wondered if anything would be all right for them, anything at all, ever again.

CHAPTER 15

The goddamn Feds had contact!" Henny was screaming into the phone. He didn't give a damn what time it was; this was vitally important and the commissioner had better damn well wake up for it.

"We get any payout?"

"That's why I'm on the horn at two A.M. Not only did they have this contact at ten, they did not give chase, they did not bulletin anybody, they merely noted it and let it pass into the Bonacori surveillance log. If it hadn't been for Wu, who reads all that shit, we never would have even known about it."

"So what's in the log?"

"Listen. 'Witnesses Ryerson, K., A., M., were observed leaving the Bonacori premises at twenty-ought-six hours in the company of a young Negro woman. They proceeded north toward New Utrecht Avenue.' "

Howie waited. Henny let him.

"That's it?"

"That's all they wrote, Brother!"

"God damn those guys. You put 'em on surveillance and they surveil. Didn't anybody think to get outta the goddamn car and tail these people?"

"I asked myself the same question, Howie. But you're dealing here with a lot of rules. These guys haven't got specific orders to tail nonsuspect witnesses, so they just sit there and let 'em go."

"We gotta get them puppies back in the box soon, buddy, or they're gonna be deaders."

"There's two things about this that are good. First, we know for certain that they're still alive. Second, we know that they're getting support."

"By 'support,' I suppose you mean the black girl. I wonder

who that could be? Maybe related to the maid. Veronica Cooke is black."

"I got her neighborhood plastered with cops. No joy there."

There came a long sigh from the other end. "I prefer the Mafia," the commissioner said at last. "Working wiseguys is better. I mean, you know where you stand, don't you?"

"Yeah, but the wiseguys are a sideshow in this. Bonacori's just a cover."

"Yeah, but for what? For who?"

"It sure as hell isn't about those lousy phone cards, that I can tell you."

"No, whatever it is, it's a whole hell of a lot worse than cheating the public out of a few mil."

"Hundred thou. Most of the cards were returned to sender. The scam didn't even work very well.' "

"It's a cover. But in what way? Why does selling Bonacori's phone cards out from under him help them?"

"It helps them to hide something."

They were silent together then, two old friends, two men who respected each other. They were sharing their anger but also the sense of helplessness that came with it. The very best efforts of a chief of detectives with a sterling record, backed by a police department that was actually in reasonably good shape, had not been enough to save the Ryersons from their own fear. If only she would pick up a phone and call him, or better, call Howie. She knew Howie. She must be in total paranoid meltdown, though. The thought crossed his mind that she might actually know something. Maybe doing her was more than insurance. Maybe it was essential. He tasted his own bile.

"Henny?"

"I was just thinking, we're probably gonna lose these lives, buddy."

"I know it. A goddamn silk-stocking bloodbath. On my watch."

"Look, I gotta go. I got a long night ahead."

"One thing."

"Yeah?"

"Why Bonacori's? Why the hell did they know to go there?"

"I wish I knew, Commissioner."

"You need to find out."

Why did he have that habit of stating the obvious? That was the one thing about Howie that was damn annoying. He told him good-bye, then sat staring at the dashboard. He listened to the radio pop a 4411 on Ditmars Boulevard, then cut the damn thing off.

What had happened to him was that all the scar tissue that had covered the wound that Kealy had left was now open again and bleeding. Pouring blood. The damn thing of it was, she still had that something about her that made him want to care. He remembered back to their marriage, in that incredibly fancy church, with all those expensive people. He had experienced a fear so awful that it had almost driven him right out of the place, running like a whipped cur. He was marrying her for her money, that's what they all thought, he could see it in their too-cheerful smiles. Lying smiles. They'd made him feel cheap and dirty at his own wedding, just with those damn smiles. The way he looked at it, the marriage had never recovered from the wedding.

Shit, he'd gone back to Queens and started fucking everything that had two legs and an orifice. Marie O'Higgins. Pearl Stein and her sister, Johnnie. He became a screwing machine that couldn't turn itself off. All *she* ever found out about was Mindy Barner. But that had been enough for her. Yeah, if only she knew.

He put a foot up against the dash. Don't let the past eat you alive, Detective. Get rid of it and do your damn job. He was outside Veronica Cooke's building, staring at the door with hungry impatience. "Come on," he said. "Come on." But nothing happened, nothing at all. "Oh, Charlie," he said, "you're old man's on a hell of a case."

Charlie had been the love of his life. In junior high, his son had become a track star. Statewide. He'd even considered calling Kealy to brag, just to let her know that he was somebody, that his kid was maybe not at Andover, but he was still special. "How's it been? I'm good, I got a boy. Runs track. He's some kinda star—school stuff, y'know."

Never happened.

And then came that strange day, warm in the dead of winter, when he had heard the voice of a Vermont State Police captain telling him that his son had expired.

Henny had never been able to determine if Charlie had made some kind of horrible mistake or overdosed intentionally. He hadn't even known that his son had a drug problem. It turned out that Marie had been scared to tell him. Marie had been handling it all by herself and not doing anything right. She'd been in denial. "I thought it was a phase he'd grow out of."

The fact of his death had eaten into what remained of their marriage like acid into soft skin. Within a couple of years, there had been nothing left but bitterness on her part and just plain old-fashioned hate on his. If only she had told him. If only he'd gotten the chance to try to help his boy, to sweep clean the sky with father love. But no, she hadn't *trusted* him, the goddamn fool.

People came and went in the street, all black, all as suspicious as hell of the pigmobiles that had suddenly appeared in their midst. These people were not going to be fooled by the goddamn gray Crown Vics that were supposed to pass as undercover cars. Who but a cop would be in a gray Crown Vic?

He watched as a plainclothesman got out of his car and went into the Dunkin' Donuts at the end of the block. He'd have liked to signal the guy, gotten him to deliver a couple of crullers and a big cup of java. But that would be a little obvious, wouldn't it? This was supposed to be a stakeout. Clandestine. What a joke.

He got out of the goddamn car and went down to the goddamn Dunkin' Donuts. "Two crullers and a large coffee, white," he told the kid behind the counter. Then, in a lower tone of voice, "Make that two jelly donuts and two crullers." Okay, so he'd have to get the goddamn suit taken out again. Who cared, anyway? What's left for a twice-divorced old fart like him, anyway? He was the goddamn invisible man, as far as the ladies were concerned.

Marie had sold the house and they'd split the profit. He'd

bought three terrific suits and moved into a bachelor pad in Chelsea. He was on the town again, oh yeah, fifty pounds overweight and falling behind fast in the hair race. His pad was a sty that looked out over an alley. He'd tried to make it better by exposing some brick and installing track lighting, but it hadn't worked. Women took one look at his dungeon and they were outta there.

"What the fuck," he said to himself, stuffing his face full of jelly donut. He sucked in coffee. He hadn't been laid since dinosaurs roamed the earth.

The street had now been empty for ten minutes. There wasn't any goddamn action here at all. This was a dead end.

So who was the black girl? And why had they gone to Bonacori's? The danger of doing that should have appeared really, really extreme to them. Unless, of course, they knew.

He tore at the donut like it was a strip of blood-rare meat. How could it be that the Ryersons were so damned elusive? They must go out in the streets, they must be living lives. By now, every cop in the city had pictures of them memorized. They couldn't get out of this, they were going to be tagged eventually.

"Kealy, please come in," he said. He had to get imaginative about this. Dragnets weren't going to do it, and trying to second guess her movements was remarkably useless. "Kealy, God damn it, come in!"

Only silence answered him.

CHAPTER 16

Kealy had Lushawn's bed, a ramshackle, narrow affair that offered nothing like the comfort she was used to. But it was better than the couch that Lushawn was very kindly sleeping on.

Allison in Jo-Jo's bed and Mark on the floor slept heavily. That they could sleep like babies at a time like this made them seem so very innocent to their mother, and so terribly vulnerable.

Again and again, Kealy reviewed her life with Jimmy, trying to sort through it for a clue. But there were no clues. It wasn't hard to understand that they might have wanted to kill Jimmy. But why had he warned her and Allie? How could they possibly be a threat to anybody?

She sweated and clutched the sheets and tossed. Fighting this thing was like fighting a fishhook caught in your finger—everything you did to withdraw it only set it more deeply. Only this thing was set in your gut, in your soul.

What time was it? She got her watch, looked at it in the pale light that came up from the street below. Four-forty. Dear God, there was no place to go, nobody to turn to. And what about tomorrow morning—how could they possibly connect with Vee now? They'd be spotted even before they got to the funeral.

And what about the funeral? She knew that it would be beautifully planned, executed with appropriate decorum. But how would she and the kids ever deal with that situation? Their friends must be worried sick, and everybody would be waiting for them to show up there.

Somehow, they'd have to intercept Vee, get the passports, and duck into a cab immediately. It was going to be a very near thing, and if the police and the killers were one and the same, then it was going to be hopeless.

The only thing they might—and this was a very big might—

have on their side was surprise. Their adversaries *might* not expect them to turn up in such an obvious place.

Maybe she should try to enlist her friends after all. Call Bitsy, maybe Bitsy would help. Of course she would, and damn the consequences. But then what about her safety, and Sam's and the kids? She had to resist the temptation to involve friends.

What about Howard Bass, though? He was the police commissioner, and she'd known Howie for twenty years. Or, at least, been an acquaintance.

She was unsure—not of him, but of the people around him. He'd mentioned Henny a few times, and favorably enough. Were they close?

Maybe there was some policing authority that she could call other than the New York City Police Department. What about the FBI, for example?

The thing was, you just did not *know*. And you had not only to know, but to be certain. With young people's lives possibly at stake, nobody could gamble. A call from her might go directly to an agent who was working with the NYPD, and therefore to Henny. If big business and big law were taking over the rackets like Sal seemed to think, there was just no way to tell who was working with whom.

What was so awful was the swiftness and brutality of everything. Jimmy calls her, then ten minutes later he's dead. A few hours later, Al goes, then Mike. And now this cunning, evil business of this reward on her head, seemingly to help her. Fear made people hesitate to turn in criminals, but who wouldn't turn in somebody who needed help, especially if being a Good Samaritan involved getting a reward, too?

She flipped onto her side, rolling up into the fetal position. She'd hated being invisible before—now she longed for it and more. It would be so nice to just disappear.

A night wind had come up and was rattling the windows. She watched the shadows from the street below dancing along the ceiling. Without the faintest idea that it was coming, she fell into the black, sudden sleep that overtakes the exhausted.

It was the sun shining on her face that made her realize that her night in hell had finally ended. CNN was chattering from the TV in the living room as the tang of bacon wafted in from the kitchen.

They'd let her oversleep; it was nearly nine. She sat up, reached for her suit jacket, which was all she had to put on over her dirty slip and bra. She didn't have the basics, not even a toothbrush. She struggled into the bathroom, scuffling along on bare feet.

When she looked at herself in the bathroom mirror, it was not her familiar, fair face. This was hardly Kealy Ryerson at all. She knew how to fight this, but not without tools. She had no foundation. In fact, she had no makeup, just the powder in her purse. Her hair looked as if she'd borrowed a wig from Medusa.

"Hi," a voice said behind her.

"Allison, good—" As she turned around, she was astonished to find a completely transformed daughter standing there.

"—morning."

"It's like I dress at school." It was a harsh, punky look, made all the more ugly by a gold nose ring, of all the vulgar things. But when she smiled, the old Allison came shining right through.

Mark appeared behind her. He wore a black leather jacket, had close-cropped hair and a baseball cap turned backward. "Hi, Mom."

"Surely, Mark, you don't dress like that normally. You're so conservative."

"The clothes are Jo-Jo's." He twirled. "That's why they're too long and too tight."

She lifted the cap off his head. His hair was so badly cut that it was actually disfiguring. "Where did you get this done, Mark?"

"Ally and Lushawn gave me a new look."

"But it isn't just cut . . . it's—is that henna in it?"

The effect of the close-cropped, dyed hair was to make him appear not like another person, but like an angular and quite sinister version of himself.

The changes helped, but she could still recognize both kids easily. In a crowd, though—well, maybe it would be a little harder.

"You kids stay right here while I change," she said. "Don't leave this house."

"Mother, we won't. But we can."

Maybe. And maybe even make a quick pass in front of St. Thomas's, just enough to get the passports.

She took the rest of her suit with her into the bathroom, which had a tub with feet that had been painted metallic silver in an attempt at decorative improvement. The shower was enclosed by a ring of curtains, yellow and spotted with mildew. She showered under what proved to be a thin and lukewarm stream, washing her hair with the giant bottle of Flex Balsam she found balanced on the tub's edge.

She thought that she should feel more deeply about the plight of the people living in this apartment and all the others like it. All she could really feel, though, was an urge—almost lustful, it was so intense—to escape back into her own world. She longed for her many comforts. She also would have liked to turn the little voice back on that told you that the less-well-off didn't really have it *this* bad.

But the raw truth of a place like this had shattered that illusion forever. If she ever got back home, the memory of these brave, good people in their wretched hole was going to make her forever a different person.

When she came out of the shower, she found herself looking into the mirror in amazement. No disguise would be required to conceal Kealy Ryerson because Kealy Ryerson *was* a disguise. The stripping water confirmed the truth: she could not even recognize the hollow-eyed woman staring back at her. Kealy Ryerson was her own makeup, and the last of her youth had gone down the drain. The kids had disguised themselves. She had disappeared into a reality that was itself a disguise.

Finding no dryer, she toweled her hair and glumly put to use the one instrument she could find that might be of help—a hair pick. As best she could, she worked her hair back into shape. Forcing herself to deal with her greasy clothes, she dressed. The clothes felt awful against her clean skin, slick and soiled. The underarms were ripe. The suit, with its torn hem and accordion-like wrinkles, looked as if it had come out of a Salvation Army bin.

Entering the living room was like appearing before an audience naked. They were all there except, thankfully, Ollie. Roselle, who did a night shift with a cleaning service, had come home at six.

"Mommy," Allison laughed, "you look like you just got handed down a sentence."

The battle against invisibility had been lost in a day.

"You eat, Kealy," Roselle said around a cigarette. "A woman needs her food."

There was a plate of fried eggs on the table, a stack of toast and a stick of butter, and a couple of slices of rather cold bacon.

As Kealy ate, Roselle came over and sat down. "You get awful tired cleaning," she said. "Those offices are filthy places, you'd be amazed. Man, you are one hungry lady. Girl, get her more eggs." She sighed heavily.

After her last swallow of Roselle's fierce coffee, Kealy turned to her kids. "I think we have to forget the funeral. We've gotta take the risk of getting Vee to meet us somewhere else."

"I don't even think we should leave. I think Mr. Bonacori is right. But I'd hate not to be at Daddy's funeral."

"Mom," Mark said, "we both want to go to our father's funeral. It's still the best plan, anyway. We take the subway, arrive from three different directions. The first one who sees Vee gets the passports and we're gone."

Allison said, "We called Davis Flowers from a pay phone. We ordered a dozen lilies to be on his coffin. With a big card, 'From Kealy, Mark, and Allison: God Is Your Home.'"

"Oh, kids, that is so beautiful. Where's the quote from?"

"Me," Allison said.

Kealy did not cry easily. She cried now, though, in her contained way, flipping the tears from the edges of her eyes with the tip of a finger.

"Roselle, what do you think? Should we try this?"

"It's so crazy it might work, would be my thought."

Kealy didn't think they had much of a chance. Also, though,

they didn't have a choice. If they were quick, maybe at least the kids would get away. "So let's do it." She got up to leave.

"You gotta have a coat, woman! It's blowin' out there today."

Roselle produced a weathered black wool coat that was cut to twice Kealy's waist but barely covered her knees. Nevertheless, Kealy put it on. She'd repair the damage to her persona in London. She might look like a bag lady's bag lady now, but Kealy Ryerson would rise again.

It was a relief to leave the smoky, crowded little apartment, but it did not feel comfortable to go out into the bustling street. Suddenly there were faces everywhere, people looking at you, every single one of them noticing your white skin in a black neighborhood.

A gust of wind caught Kealy from behind and she pulled up the collars of the cigarette-cured old coat. "I wish I had a scarf," she said. It would not only give her more covering, it would hide her lunatic hair.

"Brickman's is near here," Ally said.

"Brickman's? The place that advertises on the radio?"

"None other," Mark said. "Come on, we can complete your makeover."

Brickman's was, of course, awful, with low-rent de la Renta knockoffs in the windows, draped inexpertly on atrocious plastic mannequins. The store itself reeked of popcorn, but it seemed to consist almost entirely of bins piled high with absurdly gaudy scarves that could not possibly have been created by the designers identified on their labels. Allison seemed to know the place well and soon appeared with a simple black woolen square. With it tied under her chin, Kealy looked like a babushka.

She could have started crying again, but she refused to. She followed her kids out onto the sidewalk in a kind of daze. A couple passed them, heading into the place. They were her age, a tall, fine-featured man and a woman in a long cloth coat.

The strangest thing happened. She'd been fading, of course, but also fighting. But this was beyond fading. These people had not looked through her or past her, it was more than that. For this couple, she was beyond invisible. She literally did not exist.

Then some men passed, three of them, and she could see that they didn't see her, either. The kind of invisibility she'd worried about before was bush league. *This* was the real thing. "This is appalling," she said.

"What is," Allison asked. She was eating popcorn from a bag, munching happily away.

"You kids are disguised, but I've ceased to exist."

"Then we can stay for the whole funeral, Mom."

Now, there was a bad idea. "Don't even consider it."

"But, Mommy, no one will know it's us."

"Allison, after last night, you can't possibly be this naïve. And anyway, wouldn't the point of attending be so that people would know we aren't abandoning him? We couldn't exactly reveal who we are."

"We can be there." Mark's comment was stark, simple, and full of love for his lost father. These kids were loyal and good. They were brave. They wanted to honor their father, if only by a concealed presence. Kealy could not help but respect her children for the excellence of their spirits. She also ached to be near him at the last important moment of his life. But it took more to fool a professional than a baggy coat and a scarf. "We have to keep to the plan."

At that instant a uniformed policeman walked right into her and practically knocked her senseless.

"Watch it, Sister," he yelled, storming at her. "You drunk, or what?" Then his angry eyes met hers. For a moment, she thought she saw a flicker of recognition. But then a glaze appeared, total indifference.

"Of course I'm not drunk," she snapped, getting to her feet with Mark's help.

The cop brushed past, heading into a small cafe where a number of other officers could be seen eating donuts and drinking coffee.

"See, nobody notices us, Mother."

"So we can stay for the whole service."

"Daddy won't know we're there."

Mark looked at her. "I think he will."

"Me, too, Mom."

"It's out. I'm sorry."

"Mother, we didn't want to have to do this—Allison, are we still together on it?"

Allison nodded.

"We're going to attend no matter what. We're going without you."

"You're both minors and I'm your parent and I forbid it."

"We love you very much, but we can do this safely, and we're going to. We have to."

She looked from one beloved kid to the other. In the end, it was true that she couldn't stop them. If they went, she would follow them; she could not bear for them to go alone.

"As long as we don't arrive in a group. And afterward—and you must promise me this—we go straight to the airport. No debate. We do not try anything heroic, and we do not make ourselves known to friends. If any one of us is recognized by anybody, we leave immediately. The instant we get into the church, the first one of us who sees Vee gets the passports."

"No, we'll all converge on her. We have to designate somebody." Allison was getting smart about this fast.

"Who does it?" Mark asked.

"She does," Allison replied immediately. "No one will notice her."

"Thank you."

"I'm just being practical, Mommy. But you have totally disappeared. Even I wouldn't recognize you. It's fantastic, to tell you the truth."

"We also want it to be a test," Mark added. "If we make it, we consider staying undercover a little longer, doing some investigation."

"Mark, that is insane."

"So is running! As Bonacori so eloquently explained."

"Bonacori has a point about Dad's safe. If we could get in there—think about that."

She didn't believe that there would be anything useful in solving the case. The contents of the safe had always been personal. "Probably all that's in it is our bearer bonds. No, we stay away from the office."

"What's our alternative?" Mark asked. "Run forever? That's not such a great option. If Bonacori's right, we'll be like a fox trying to climb a tree to escape the hounds. Just a question of time."

That she could not deny.

CHAPTER 17

Kealy sat staring at the floor of the subway, trying to believe that she really was so faceless and unnoticeable that not even people like Bitsy and Julie would recognize her. And Henny.

She and Allison had their hands entwined. Mark, on the other side, was shoulder-tight beside her. Her love for them was so intense right now that it seemed as if it had actually filled her physical body, inhabiting her very blood. *That's the thing*, she told herself, *that will get us through, this love that sustains us, this family love.*

She had never in her life felt this proud—this really proud—to be what she was, just a woman, plain and simple, who had borne kids and was trying to be a shepherd to them as they started out in the world.

But their shepherd could not control them anymore. They would be easier for the professionals to spot than she was. She had entered the fate of all her sisters everywhere. She had become the genuine version of the invisible woman.

With a sigh, she folded her arms around her purse. The woman across the aisle had already done it. In fact, all the invisible women in the train were riding that way. Protect what you have. Nobody will help you keep it, nobody will help you get it back.

When they finally reached Sixty-eighth Street and Lexington Avenue, there was chaos on the platform. They were assaulted by hordes of young people who were leaving their classes at Hunter College, jostling eagerly to get on the train for their rides uptown to Harlem or out to Queens.

On the way, they'd discussed their routes to St. Thomas's. Nobody would acknowledge the other two, and nobody would enter the church. As soon as Vee appeared, Kealy would get the passports. At that point, Kealy hoped, the kids would be willing to leave.

The indignity involved in attending her husband's funeral this way was unspeakable. But, as ten A.M. and the beginning of the service drew near, she was so very relieved to be here. No matter the danger, she belonged as close to him as she could be. She was part of Jimmy and he was part of her, and death does not cut such cords.

When she went up into the bright and windy morning, she returned to the neighborhood where she had been raised, where she had raised her kids. She knew every shop, every bump in the sidewalk, every house and every brick. But her neighborhood did not know her. To the place where she had lived her life, she was just another tired old woman in a cheap coat, abandoned by the world.

They had given her a route, but in her misery, she forgot it. Go west on Sixty-ninth, had they said, or was it down to Sixty-eighth? Blinded by a copious flow of tears, she walked without thinking, without seeing, without caring. She knew that this was dangerous, this was all wrong, but she couldn't stop herself. The devastating totality of her loss was sweeping her like wild waves, enveloping her in the tangle of a grief she'd thought she had mastered.

Suddenly she was in front of Umberto on Madison. She was known there, was Mrs. Ryerson. She'd gone in often for a wrap or a dress, or some accessory. They were lovely people, and they had lovely things. "Move along," a voice said, not a kindly one. She looked around, wondering who had spoken—then saw that they had a guard. She had never noticed a guard, but she supposed that he must have been there right along.

"Excuse me?"

"You heard me." He jerked his head.

Her heart started racing, blood rushed to her face. She couldn't help it; his arrogance made her furious. Plus, she was on a public sidewalk. He had no right to order her off, and his furtiveness revealed that he knew this. But she went. She knew why people who looked like she did wouldn't be welcome in front of shops like this. Women like she was—used to be—would be affronted to see some old bag gawking at *their* store. She wouldn't have liked seeing the old lady in the scarf there. Too depressing. She wouldn't have thought much about it, but she would not have stopped in.

Could she have really been that shallow—and all without even realizing it? Don't answer the question, woman. Try stopping the self-involved inner dialog for a while. Think about Jimmy, think about your kids, think about their survival.

She went on down the street until she saw the crowd in front of St. Thomas's. There was a lot of press, and about fifty members of the public stood behind some police sawhorses. Some of them were undoubtedly funeral monsters, that peculiar breed of female who appears at the funerals of men they don't know and sit huddled in the back weeping. You always wondered: were they long-abandoned mistresses or childhood girlfriends, or just women who needed a reason to cry?

Cars were pulling up, and she was appalled to see Sal Bonacori get out of a black Mercedes limousine and enter amid a great popping of flashbulbs. She looked for Mark's newly red hair. This unwanted but not really unexpected mourner would make him furious, and she did not want another outburst, not here.

Where were the plainclothesmen, or whoever it was who was watching for her and the kids? She didn't see anybody obvious. But then, they wouldn't be, would they? That was the whole point.

She passed the little Greek-run bistro where she'd grabbed many a tuna salad on the fly or stopped for a Coke after a board meeting at the museum. It was a funny little place that catered largely to the servants and nannies who populated the area, and the clerks who worked in the stores. So it was fun to drop in there with Bitsy or Julie or somebody, fun and easy and pleasant to make believe you were part of the ordinary world— and know inside, of course, that you were just having a little fun.

Dear heavens, there was Bitsy coming around the corner. Undoubtedly she'd stopped at the Polo Lounge at the Westbury for a snort before the funeral. When they went to funerals together, they always stopped for a snort, one if for the older generation, two if for a peer. From Bitsy's fixed stare, she knew that more than two had been needed for the husband of a dear and missing friend.

Oh, look at her! Look at her marvelous new dress, that splendid deep blue, perfect for mourning. It must be quite new; Kealy had never seen it before. And goodness, Bits was so lovely. Kealy could hardly stop looking at her, consuming her with her eyes. Bitsy had always bemoaned her pleasantly uninteresting looks. But seen from this perspective, she was resplendent, her skin flushed with the appearance of health, her necklace glittering so beautifully—appropriately subtle for a funeral, of course, but oh so wonderful to see.

All of a sudden, Bitsy was much too close—just steps away, coming right toward her. Bitsy could not fail to recognize a friend of a lifetime. They'd been toddlers together. Kealy couldn't turn away, though, not without drawing more attention to herself. And then their eyes met. Kealy started to say something, moved toward her to keep it as private as possible—but Bitsy took a decisive step back. A kid-gloved hand came up and covered the necklace. Her other hand reached into her purse, where Kealy knew she kept a small, silver-clad Mace spray.

Kealy stood like a wooden woman as Bitsy brushed past, a softly sweet scent of Fracas wafting away behind her.

It was damned fortunate that Bitsy hadn't recognized her, but it hurt like hell. She moved toward the church to mingle with the foregathering public. She saw Ally nearby, standing proud, tears pouring down her cheeks. She did not see Mark anywhere, and she wished that she didn't suspect that he'd gone inside. *They* would certainly be in there.

Where in hell was Vee? What if she was already in the church?

Then Sim got out of one of the firm's limos, along with his wife, Lanette, and Christa Lawrence. A dark blue Bronco pulled up behind them, and two men in equally dark blue suits exited, following them up the steps. Bodyguards.

The Reverend Gilkerson greeted the Osbornes, taking Sim's hand in both of his. There was a brief conversation, and when

Paul Gilkerson shook his head and Sim gazed off down Fifth Avenue, she knew exactly what—and who—it was about.

Then she saw that the two men were gazing directly her way. They wore dark glasses. She felt her fists clenching, her jaws clenching. But the men made no move. Their eyes were on the crowd in general, not any specific member of it.

Where the hell was Mark? He couldn't have gone in there, it was too crazy. Unless, of course, he had seen Vee and followed her in. But surely she'd be expecting to see them outside the church. The need for that would be obvious to her. She was supposed to be the one to find Vee and get the passports.

Minette James and Glenda Tripp arrived together with their husbands. Minette glanced toward the crowd, and Kealy was struck by how her cruelly narrowed eyes seemed to say *look at me, eat your hearts out.* Look at her toss her head, look at her strut. She knew well that the women in the crowd were longing to be in her marvelous black silk suit and her lovely, subtle jewels, to ride in her beautiful car and be on the arm of her wealthy husband. She knew all that, and she showed them that she knew it with an expression that was both triumphant and hideously revealing. The fact that this was about the death of a man was lost. Minette was here to be seen. Little did she know that her elegance stripped her naked.

Others came, people whom she didn't know, people she recognized vaguely, people whom she numbered among her oldest and dearest friends. There was Joan Halff from her Brearly days, and Georgie Pauley, who had been her first love. He was a grey-templed gentleman presently escorting tiny See-See Weatherall around town—dating, you could say. She was on his arm, See-See whose dashing father, Ames, had sailed for the America's Cup and been the heartthrob of all her friends.

As well dressed as they were, her friends had come here naked and they didn't even know it. The crowd knew it, though, she could tell by the hiss of breath, the quiet snap of tongues. They were here to bear witness, to disapprove, to lust, yes, but also to loathe.

Here came old Jimbo Freer, who had not been her first love, but had been the first person—well, that corpulent gentleman with the sagging eyes had deflowered her in her own game room, under the pool table. She'd been a senior and he'd been down from Harvard. He was handsome then, hard-muscled from crew and lacrosse, with a head of marvelous brown hair that made him look like he'd been bred from David Niven out of Ali McGraw. It had been a frantic few seconds, seeming in retrospect more like a sort of shared seizure. But she had been deflowered, most certainly, by that fat old man with just rubble left where the brown hair had been.

Then the great doors were shut, and the crowd began to disperse, all but the funeral monsters, who lingered nervously wondering if this was to be a "closed" or an "open."

From inside, she heard the organ begin, "Sheep May Safely Graze," from the Bach Cantata. She found herself rooted to the spot by her anguished hunger to be near Jimmy, to play her proper part in the proceedings, to feel her mourning and be comforted in it, to give Jimmy the last of her love on this earth.

Now she was worried. Where was Vee? If they didn't get those passports—but that didn't bear thinking about.

Her mind said, *Stay right where you are,* but her heart was telling—demanding, urging—her to go straight up those stairs and in.

And that was insane—insanely dangerous. But she not only had to, to find Vee and Mark, she also wanted to, for deep reasons of love and saying good-bye. So she went up the stone steps, and she put her hand on the brass handle of the big oak door. Now she was totally exposed, all alone up here, visible for a block up and down Fifth Avenue. The funeral monsters watched her like ravenous dogs waiting to see if the pack leader survived a foray into some restaurant alley.

She opened the door, and if the sextant didn't recognize her, then she was sure he would tell her to leave. Then the sextant was there, old Jim Harmon with his fat face and his big, strong hands.

He smiled gently and put his finger to his lips. She waited to see the wash of surprise that would cross his face as he realized who she was, but it never came.

Incredibly, he did not recognize her any more than Bitsy had. "Stay back here, darlin'," he whispered, showing the first kindness she had experienced since she'd become what she had so feared.

Despite his warning, she went deeper into the dim church with its smoky odor of candles and fainter one of flowers. She had to be close; this was her last time. Then she caught sight of his dark mahogany coffin, on it the spray of a dozen lilies that Allison and Mark had ordered.

Behind her, the other funeral monsters began venturing in, and she could hear the clicking of their tongues and their sighs at the opulence of the altar and the magnificence of the coffin that she herself hated the sight of.

There were really a great many bouquets. As a matter of fact, she had never seen this many flowers at a funeral. She found them soothing her hurt just a little bit, their color challenging the clouds of misery that surrounded her.

She still didn't see Mark. God, what if they'd gotten him? What if Mark—her heart started again. It had been doing this so much lately that she was becoming concerned that the fear was literally going to kill her.

She sat down beside two funeral monsters, about ten aisles behind the real mourners. At last she began to relax a little. Should she, though? Because among those mourners was none other than Henny Henneman. He was about six rows in front of her, sitting against the end of a pew, leaving a little cushion of space between himself and Al Packard. Did Al remember Henny? No, no way. Poor Henny had been socially awkward, when he wasn't off in Queens with his prostitutes and mistresses. Then he wasn't at all awkward, from what she could gather.

Had Allison seen her come in? Would she come now, too, and increase the risk that much more?

Vee was there, not far from Sim. How gray she was. Kealy had not realized how old she'd been getting. How to approach her, though?

She sat through the Mass, sat and stood and knelt, then heard Bishop Tucker deliver his eulogy. He spoke so well of him, his voice ringing with such conviction, that she almost wanted to tell the women beside her, "That's my husband who gave his life for the law, that's *my* man he's talking about." Tears flooded her face. Thank God the other funeral monsters were sobbing, too.

Then Willie Edwards and Sim and David Welles were bearing the pall, helped by the three members of the old Century Club poker gang. As the coffin passed out of the church, the choir sang "Nearer My God to Thee," and thank heavens a couple of the other funeral monsters wept openly, because Kealy could not contain her grief in mere sobs.

Through her tears, she looked up, and there was Henny bearing down on her. She must have gasped, because the two other monsters stirred. He came closer, looking straight at her, and closer yet, his eyes now flicking toward the other two, now back to her.

Then he had passed. She didn't know whether to laugh or to cry. Take off the makeup and put on an old coat and a scarf, and a woman her age simply disappeared from the face of the earth.

Then the funeral was over, and she realized that she'd made a mistake. Maybe Bitsy hadn't recognized her, and maybe Henny had failed as well. But the rest of the mourners were going to file out now, and every one of them was going to see her.

And one of them, surely, was bound to realize who she was. And that would be the end.

CHAPTER 18

Henny had stopped sleeping days ago. Late nights were the worst. Late nights, he'd pop Ambien and manage to sort of nap. The twilight sleep seemed to help a little more than it hurt. It was getting complicated with Kealy. He was thinking about her, about the old days. He'd been hung up, no doubt about it. Never should have married a girl from upstairs. But, oh God, she'd been so beautiful and she had that—what was it—that special inner spirit of hers, a combination of laughter and determination, that made him just really enjoy her. And then there was the matter of connections.

They had been physically apart for twenty years, but his heart was still married to those perfect first weeks, which remained the best time of his life, never to be recaptured, never forgotten.

And yet, despite the sweaty nights and the corroded, helpless days, he found himself drawing on depths of professionalism that he hadn't even known he possessed. He'd always thought of himself as something of a failure as a policeman, to tell the truth. But even as this terrible situation devoured him inside—or perhaps because it was devouring him—it seemed to be focusing his mind as it had never been focused before. He would do what had to be done.

The operation he had organized involved twelve plainclothes officers working out of an undercover communications van stationed two blocks up Fifth Avenue from the church. There were surveillance cameras inside and covering all entrances and exits.

He had not brought his men here to find the Ryersons. They were here for the same reason they went to Mafia funerals, to gather evidence of names and faces, see who turned out and who didn't. Ultimately Henny would use this information to draw new lines on charts in a small windowless room deep in Planning and Operations, a room with only two keys—his and the commissioner's.

He understood why Kealy had taken her kids and run, and why they did not come in. They were unable to tell whom to trust. Maybe Kealy even suspected him; it was possible. Even probable, given their unfortunate history together.

The great problem was that Mike had not had a chance to communicate with her or anybody else. He was too damn deliberate, that Mike McGarrigle. He should've briefed his staff within an hour of the meeting with Ryerson. But he'd wanted to get his ducks lined up, no doubt. Probably also to be sure Kealy was safe before he told anybody anything.

The congregation filled about half the pews. He sat near the back, next to a guy named Jake something who had laughed at him during the Kealy days, laughed at him, he thought, because he'd made the mistake of lighting a cigar with the band still on. Well, look at you, Jake, you corpulent heap of goo, and look at me, still tight enough to take most anybody.

More mourners were coming in, but not all that many. He'd arranged for the press to lay it on pretty damn thick about Jimmy being involved with poor old broken-toothed Sal Bonacori, so the crowd was a good bit thinner than it would have been.

Veronica Cooke was there, though, looking old and bowed as she came up the aisle. She'd been back to the apartment a number of times, which she was a damn fool for doing. But she was a loyal friend, that one. He had considered coming into contact with her, but he dared not place her at such risk. It wasn't his job to waste innocent lives. He looked at the back of her head. Did she know where her boss was? If not, then who was that black girl who'd been with them at Sal's place? He'd had Vee followed—guarded, really. But she hadn't made a single move that suggested she might know Kealy's whereabouts. He hadn't had her phone bugged because of all the legal complications. She wasn't a suspect and there was no way to get a wiretap warrant unless there was suspicion of a crime, and Vee hadn't done a thing.

Sal he *had* interviewed. Bonacori wasn't even able to remember seeing her, so he claimed. Kealy who? Came to my house? When? Oh, *that*—that was months ago, with her husband.

It had been a waste, just as he'd thought it would be.

Hell, maybe they'd actually succeeded in making their run. If so, he'd probably see the story of their murders in Cairo or Stuttgart or somewhere in the papers.

The thing that made him wake up in the night sweating was the fear that they would go to some of their powerful friends, thinking that this was safe when it was probably the most dangerous thing they could do.

If they were still here, living in some damned hotel or something—well, they just plain weren't going to make it very long.

His problem was that his intuition was bothering him. Normally, he dismissed things like that. They had no place in police work—intuition, hunches. That was movie stuff, just pure crap. But sometimes his damned intuition wouldn't leave him alone, and now was one of those times. His intution said she was here at this funeral. For whatever insane reason.

Here was Kealy's friend Bitsy. Bitsy had been maid of honor at their wedding, so delectable in her pale silk gown, with her dark Irish hair and milky skin.

She was not lovely now. In fact, she looked really shaken. As well she should be, with her best friend's husband murdered and her best friend on the run. Henny hadn't approached her, but he'd talked to her on the telephone. He was being extremely careful in his approaches to her circle of friends. Some of them were innocent bystanders. Some were as far from that as it was possible to be.

The Italian Mafia killed for two reasons: power and betrayal. They took out guys who hurt them, and every so often one of the bosses went down—Albert Anastasia, Paul Castellano. Young lions tending to kill off the old ones. Very understandable.

The Russian Mafia did a lot more killing, but there was still that element of predictability to it: they fought to victory and to death.

The folks who were after Kealy were beyond any Mafia. They were beyond drugs. They were the worst people on earth, and among the most powerful.

The choir started, singing some vaguely familiar Protestant hymn. Pretty enough, he supposed. Give him the Catholic stuff, though, the old ones, the Latin ones from his boyhood. Now, those hymns made you think maybe God was actually somewhere in the vicinity.

That coffin actually looked as if it belonged in a museum. How much had that thing cost? Whatever, how must it feel to spend so much money on a box that was going straight into the ground? Even Kealy had to have thought a little bit about that one.

They began to take the coffin out of the church. He wouldn't follow the funeral, not personally, but he would have two carloads of plainclothes in the entourage. Camera crews were already deployed in the cemetery. As the procession passed, he made a note to find out what florist had provided those lilies with that card from the family.

The last confirmed contact had been the Bonacori affair. It would be a great relief if the florist had recognized one of their voices and gotten the call—say—earlier today.

Suddenly his earphone, which had been silent throughout, came to life. Having practically forgotten that it was there, he almost jumped across the church. "We have a possible. Girl fits the description."

He moved quickly out, passing an aisle with three elderly ladies in it, the kind who haunted every funeral he'd ever attended in this city. Rosaries, gray hair, black scarfs: you'd think that praying for the dead was some kind of a damn hobby for some people.

"This appears to be the daughter."

Maybe this was the end of it. Maybe they had been found. By the time he reached the door of the church, he had started to run.

CHAPTER 19

"Don't look at me. Just listen."

Kealy froze.

"I'm sorry for you, Mrs. Ryerson. I want you to know that."

That sounded like the beginning of a betrayal. "Vee?"

Vee's hand slid down and squeezed her elbow. "They're watching me."

"The police?"

"Could be."

"What do they look like?"

"Sleazy white guys."

"You have the passports?"

An envelope slid into Kealy's pocket. "God bless you," Vee whispered.

Vee was taking a terrific risk just doing this, and Kealy knew she had to send her away quickly. But there was one thing she needed to know. "How did you recognize me?"

"I knew it was you, Mrs. Ryerson. You look like you do on the mornings after."

Of course—Vee had seen her like this before, the only person in the world besides Jimmy who had. So maybe it was okay.

Still, she wasn't prepared to spend any more time here than absolutely necessary, and she was getting frantic because she had not been able to spot Mark. She went to her feet.

"You call me, Mrs. Ryerson, if you need me. And remember, you got lots of friends in this town."

"I worry about the danger."

She could feel Vee nodding her head. "Those white men in my neighborhood, even the dogs're watching them."

Kealy hoped that was sufficient protection for Vee, but it didn't sound like nearly enough. "You be very, very careful." It was quite clear: if Kealy had been recognized and Vee seen with her, no telling what would happen to the poor woman.

"Vee, I have to go. I love you, Vee."

"Will I ever see you again?"

"I don't know. I—maybe."

"These've been terrible days."

"Keep well away from the apartment, Vee. Never go back there again."

She clutched Kealy's arm, then let go.

Kealy went out the side door into the tiny garden in front of the pastor's house, through the familiar iron gate and quickly down Fifth toward Sixty-eighth.

The plan had been to meet back at the subway, but when she reached the platform, she found no sign of Allison and Mark. She waited, leaning against a steel column, wishing she could disappear into the wall.

Time passed. A train came and went. She forced back the awful feeling that was building within her. If she had lost her kids—oh, God.

Another train came thundering in, riding on its roar. The doors rolled open. She stood there, hesitating, looking up and down the platform, hating the fear, sick with it.

Just as the doors were closing, somebody shoved her in. At one time she would have screamed, but she did not scream. She was beyond screaming.

"Ally was followed," Mark said as he threw himself into a seat.

"The guy's still in the station," Allison said breathlessly.

"Not in the train?" Mark asked darkly.

She shook her head. "I hope not." The train was pulling out. "You were followed?"

"Leather jacket, blue shirt, tan golf cap. Looks like a tourist."

"Maybe he was a tourist."

She shook her head. "He passed me on Sixty-eighth, then got a call on his cell phone. He turned around and came down into the station right behind me. Oh, Mommy!"

"We'll be all right, baby."

They were sitting at the far end of the half-full car. Mark leaned his head against the window behind him. "That's what we all believe, isn't it? That in the end, it'll be okay. This is America where the good guys win, right? Well, they don't always."

"How do we deal with this?" Kealy asked them.

"How do we deal with it?" Mark sat rigid in his seat. "We keep changing lines."

"Let's just get to the airport," Allison said. "I want this to *end*."

Kealy thought: my love, it never will end. Bonacori had been right. Running wouldn't help, not for long. Her only hope was that it would gain time, and maybe that time would fix this.

Mark said, "We have to be strong now. Now is when it counts."

They rode downtown, then changed at Forty-second Street and went out to Queens. Nobody seemed to be after them, but what did that mean? They didn't know how to tell, not for sure. So they did all the things to shake tails that they'd seen done in the movies.

Whenever there was an opportunity to cross the platform to another train at the last minute, they took advantage of it. They rode at random, getting out and taking taxis or walking to different stops. For an hour, they sat in a coffee shop in Forest Hills, just to watch the street. Then they took the Long Island Railroad to Jamaica and transferred back to the subway. There followed more random riding and changing.

Working out the routes together, consulting the wall maps on the trains, they crisscrossed the system, moving sometimes closer to, sometimes farther from Kennedy. "Look," Mark said, pointing out the window. They were on an elevated track, and there was Yankee Stadium. All fell quiet, all were remembering. Jimmy was a Yankee fan and the son of a Yankee fan. They'd spent many an hour in the firm's skybox, watching the ballet and thrill of baseball.

"Season starts in a few weeks," Kealy said. "I intend to keep our seats."

"Mommy, I felt his presence at the funeral. Did you feel him?"

"The funeral was essential to me. No matter how dangerous it was to be there, I'm glad I went. I thank God I went."

"I'm gonna be a lawyer," Mark said. "I'm gonna do defense."

It was the first time in nearly a year that she had heard him speak of the future.

They rode for another eventless hour. People came and went. Nobody so much as glanced at the nondescript old woman and the two punk kids. "We're clean," Mark said at last.

"You're certain?" his sister asked.

"No."

"It's two-thirty. We can get an afternoon flight to Toronto, then go from there to Paris on the night plane."

"How about Cuba? Let's go to Cuba on the night plane."

Kealy didn't see that as being at all practical. "Not Cuba, Allison. It just adds an unnecessary complication."

They got out of the subway somewhere in what might have been Jackson Heights. The neighborhood was really bustling, and that was probably good. She didn't want to look at herself in the glass of a storefront they were passing, but she couldn't help it.

Mark saw her and laughed. "You're still beautiful, Mom."

How many other invisible women clung to that lie?

"Uh-oh," Mark said.

A police car was slowing down. "Don't look at it," Kealy said softly.

"I already did," Allison replied.

The squad car kept on, moving down the retail strip and turning off into a residential area. A moment later, Mark was out in the street hailing a passing cab. Given how he looked, it almost didn't stop for him.

They went down Northern Boulevard, glimpsing a sunny marina out one window and Shea Stadium out the other as they careened through the streets and onto the Van Wyck Expressway. The roads, so often clogged, were relatively clear at this time of day. They made excellent time, arriving at Kennedy at three.

On the way, each of them retreated into their own thoughts. "Do we have a plan?" Allison asked as they approached.

"British Air," Kealy told the driver.

"Not Air Canada?" Mark asked.

"Let's just do it," Kealy responded. She'd been thinking about the Canada leg and had decided that it was too close to feel safe. Better to go to London, then really disappear.

"Sounds good," Mark responded.

Nobody wanted to talk much, not in the hearing of the driver. So Kealy kept her feelings to herself as the cab moved among the huge terminals.

As they got out of the cab, Kealy said to them both, "Welcome to the rest of our lives."

CHAPTER 20

The BA terminal was familiar territory, and they all felt a little more confident once they were inside. They'd been through here many times. Without speaking, they went straight to the glass-enclosed travel center.

"Hold it," Mark said. "We buy the tickets with cash."

Travel was usually handled by Jimmy's in-house travel agent. "How much would we need?"

"I dunno," Allison said. "Maybe a couple of thousand."

Kealy went into the travel center. "How much for a ticket to London? Leaving on the eight-thirty?"

"Round trip?"

"One way."

"Seven hundred and thirty dollars economy."

She turned and marched out of the enclosure. "There's gotta be an ATM around here somewhere." She went over to a Chase Teller and thrust her US Trust card in. "I need three grand."

"Can you get that much?"

"I have no idea." She punched in her special passcode, which supposedly gave her access to as much cash as the machine could offer. "If we can't get it all from here, we'll go to another machine."

"We can combine all our cards," Mark said. "We'll be fine."

The ATM waited. It waited some more. Then it sent out a receipt. "Funds Not Available."

There was plenty of money in her account, she was quite certain of that. Certainly three thousand dollars.

She tried again, got the same result. She made a balance inquiry. "I've got eight thousand dollars in my cash account and it won't give me any money!"

"Try a hundred dollars. Maybe the machine's got a limit."

"It's not supposed to care. This is a special card."

But the result was the same. It wouldn't even give her a hundred bucks fast cash.

Mark and Allison tried their cards, both with the same result. Kealy fought down the damn acid that was rising in her stomach. If this didn't end soon, she was going to dissolve.

"Okay, we gotta buy 'em with American Express."

As they went back to the travel center, Mark touched Kealy's shoulder. "Over there," he said quietly.

Two men were standing nearby, looking their way.

"Don't anybody look at them," Allison said.

"Are they watching us?" Kealy asked.

"Sort of. But maybe they're just undercovers watching the crowd."

They went back into the travel center. The men couldn't see them here, their view being blocked by the wall behind the travel consultants' desks.

Not ten seconds later the men appeared again, this time just outside the doors. One of them had a narrow face and thin, straight hair. He was older. The other was young and had the cold, competent look of a man trained in violence. His right hand was stuffed deep in his pocket.

"Jesus," Allison said. She was trying to watch them out of the corner of her eye. She said in a soft voice, "We've got to get out of here."

With that, she dashed straight out of the travel center and into the main part of the terminal.

Kealy followed her, Mark close behind. "We have to get the tickets!"

"Get 'em somewhere else, Mother." She plunged through the double doors and out onto the sidewalk. "Delta," she said. "It's right over there."

Mark said, "You didn't know! You blew it running like that!"

"Mark, I knew. And look—" She pointed. They were coming out the door. She turned to run farther, but Mark grabbed her shoulders. "We have to get these tickets. We have to!"

A jam-packed Kennedy Transfer bus was passing, and they

managed to get aboard. Standing in piles of luggage, swaying amid a sweaty, squabbling family from somewhere in the Far East, they tried to see out the windows.

"Who were they?" Mark asked, almost talking to himself.

"Maybe nothing to do with us. Maybe just a coincidence."

"I don't think so," Allison said. "I think they've got the airport covered."

Kealy felt a flash of anger. They could not have this whole airport covered. She refused to believe it. "It's huge," she said.

They reached the Delta terminal and went to the international ticket counter. There was a wait, though: four people were ahead in line. One of them seemed to take hours. Something major was wrong with his ticket. He spoke no English. "Lagos," he kept saying, "Lagos, Lagos."

"Maybe we ought to break up," Mark said. "How many groups of two teenagers, male and female, and their mother can there be in one place at one time?"

He had a point. To a professional, they'd be easy to spot no matter their appearance.

Finally, the clerk said, "Next, please," and there was nobody there but them.

"I need a flight to London."

"Today?"

"As soon as possible."

The woman glanced at Kealy. "It'll be a full fare ticket."

"Three people. One way. And make it first class, please."

"Very good. We have those availabilities."

She handed the girl her American Express card. As she did, she sensed Allison beside her growing very still.

The clerk worked with the card for a couple of moments, then looked up. "I'm sorry, ma'am, I'm not able to get approval on this card."

Her American Express card had unlimited credit. She could have bought a car on it. "It's perfectly good!"

"Maybe we could try partials. Split it up."

"There isn't any credit limit on that card."

"Mom."

The clerk put the American Express card through the reader again. "I'm trying for fifty dollars, just to see if we can get anything at all." A moment later, she shook her head. "I'm so sorry, but there must be a glitch."

"Mom."

"Allison, *yes?*"

She nodded toward the far end of the lobby. "We have to go, Mom. We have to go right now."

When Kealy saw that the same two men who had been in the British Airways terminal were there, she understood what it meant for your blood to run cold. There could be no question: they were being followed. She thrust her Visa at the clerk. "Try this!"

It didn't take even a minute for it to be declined, and by the time it was the men were hurrying their way. Mark broke into a dead run and so did Allison. Kealy followed.

The wind rushed past her face, making her scalp feel cold as it sluiced through her hair. She didn't look back; she couldn't afford to slow down enough to do it.

As she ran she uttered breathless little cries. She had never been this scared, hadn't known it was possible to feel as if you wanted to run out of your own skin. Allison was fast, but then she would be; she was on the track team.

Now Kealy could hear their footsteps pounding behind her. They got steadily closer, and Kealy glimpsed some kind of cop joining them, a heavyset guy in a uniform with a gun. He yelled something, but she didn't hear because just then the Avis bus started to pull away from the curb.

She caught a glimpse of Mark and Ally out in the middle of traffic, Mark banging on the yellow hood of a cab that just about hit them. Practically with her last breath, she shrieked, "Mark!"

He stopped, they both did. They stood like statues on the far side of the roadway. And then Kealy was there and she saw why they had stopped. They were standing in front of a ten-foot drop. "Oh, God," Kealy said.

Mark grabbed her wrist and then she was being yanked and

the air roared and she hit so hard her teeth went *chomp* and white light flashed in her head. Pain shot up both legs and she pitched forward, her hands slapping the pavement and driving gravel into her palms. Mark and Allison were rolling and so she rolled, too. A bus bore down on them, its grim-faced driver clearly visible behind the huge windshield. He stood on his brakes, at the last closing his eyes. The staggering family felt the wind of the big vehicle's passing, smelled the hot-rubber stench of its screaming tires. But they were not hit; they escaped instead onto the sidewalk and ran into the baggage claim area, all the way to the end.

Kealy was unable to catch her breath. "Kids, kids, I can't go another step."

There was an elevator. They got in. "This isn't going anywhere," Allison said. She hit some kind of a button and it seemed to jerk, then stopped.

"Allison?" Kealy could barely talk. "What are you doing?"

"You push the alarm halfway down, it stops the car without ringing the bell."

"How do you know that?"

"I learned it from Lushawn, and she learned it in the projects. It's useful knowledge."

Kealy could not prevent herself, she sank to the floor. Mark came down with her. "They sabotaged our plastic," she moaned. As she heard the words come from her lips, her insides rocked with queasy terror. "How could anybody sabotage your plastic?"

"Somehow they did it, Mom. The thing is, what's our next move?"

"Look," Mark said, "we can't stay here."

"We can't go out, either," Allison said. "Mark, hold this button down for me."

She braced herself against the wall, inched up. As she fell forward, she pushed against the escape hatch that was cut into the ceiling.

"Okay, it's loose. Give me a leg up, Mom, then I'll reach down and haul you guys up."

It was all Kealy could do to lift her daughter high enough to push the hatch open. Behind them, Mark kept his finger on the button that kept the elevator from moving.

Allison managed to get Kealy up into the dust-caked, greasy hole. She helped Kealy up, then Mark came behind them and replaced the hatch, fitting it carefully down into its opening so that the elevator would look perfectly normal from inside. They were now on top, completely hidden. They could look down into the empty car through the grate that covered the whirring fan.

"How did you ever think of anything so clever?" Kealy asked her daughter.

"Remember Paul Revere's ride?"

"Of course." It was an ancient tradition at Andover. The girls of the Paul Revere dormitory played a prank on the school each year on the anniversary of Paul Revere's ride.

"We got into Mrs. Chase's bedroom this way, climbing up that old dumbwaiter from the basement." That morning, the headmistress had woken up still in bed, but on the lawn. Spectacular, but not as good as the legendary year back in the seventies when the dorm had reassembled a Volkswagen in the library.

"You are a piece of work, Ally," Mark said. "Mom, do you have any idea what a piece of work your daughter is?"

"Apparently not."

The elevator clicked.

In the dim light that shone up from the interior of the cab, she saw the pulleys and cables that controlled the door start working. You put your hand in the wrong place, you lost your fingers.

Another, more decisive click, and a motor began whining louder than the fan that was just beside Kealy's hip. They rose. What if it crushed them against the ceiling? "Careful, kids." Kealy pressed herself down, making herself as flat as she could. She put her hand on Allison's head, drew her down.

It was all greasy and dusty in here and Kealy knew she was getting totally filthy. She detested being dirty. She was a bather.

Then, all of a sudden, there was a voice down there. She strove to listen, couldn't make out any details. She didn't dare move, but she could see that Mark was maneuvering to look down into the car. Peering through the fan, he mouthed a word. Even in the dimness, Kealy could see clearly what it was: "Them."

They started going up again. Kealy breathed a terrified, "Oh, my God," because she was scared they were about to have the life crushed out of them—and then it stopped.

They were all absolutely flat. Kealy had her hands over her head. Ally followed her example. Mark was on his stomach, his hands clasped over the back of his head, as if that might protect it from being crushed.

But the car went no higher. It was like being trapped in some kind of a coffin, or the time she'd had to go into an MRI machine at University Hospital, when she'd had those migraines.

"Damn," a voice said from below. "God damn."

This was followed by more conversation, but it wasn't as loud and the fan again drowned it out.

There was silence. Kealy knew that the men were looking up, she could feel it. But the elevator doors opened and the men left. The doors closed. The car remained where it was.

"Now what?" Allison whispered. "What do we do now? Where do we go?"

It was a hell of a big question. Kealy was still in shock about not having any money, and she did not know how to answer. They were finished with the Davises, they were in jeopardy on the streets, they didn't have enough cash for more than a couple of nights at a fleabag.

The elevator doors slid open. Six or seven people came in, an exhausted couple with a miserable baby, an old man in a walker, a couple of French tourists. The car went up to its second stop, which would be the main concourse of the terminal, then back down again.

After two more loads of passengers had come and gone without their tails reappearing, they struggled back down through the hatch, dusted themselves off as best they could in the car, then reemerged into the terminal.

Walking separately, they went to a bus stop. The three of them put together had only a couple of hundred dollars. They left

Kennedy on the JFK Shuttle, which took them to the Howard Beach stop on the A train. They moved now like hunted creatures, like mice in a field full of snakes, their helpless eyes searching for danger that they all knew they might not have the knowledge to see.

They went down into the subway station, bound for they knew not where.

CHAPTER 21

Lushawn's," Allison said. "We have to go back."

"We can't go there!"

"Mark, she's my *roomie!* Nothing will happen to us. She won't allow it."

"Do you seriously think that some kind of Andover loyalty thing is gonna help us in any way at all? As soon as that man sees us again, he is picking up the nearest phone."

Kealy said, "Then you suggest something, Mark."

They traveled silently, a tattered little family huddled at the far end of a subway car. Kealy closed her eyes, and in her dark reveries an idea came to her. At first, it seemed so ridiculous that she dismissed it. But then—well, it was one hell of a good way to get money, maybe the only way. And lots of it—money enough to take them to the ends of the earth.

Forty-five minutes later they came up a few blocks from the Davises' house. Kealy had a way, she thought, to convince even Ollie to help them. They mounted the long, dark stairs, past the smells of cooking food, the blare of televisions, and the yowling of kids. Allison tapped on the door. A moment later, Lushawn drew it opened. Her eyes registered surprise, then she and Ally flew into each other's arms.

After a moment, Allison withdrew from her friend's embrace. Carefully and clearly, she explained why they had come back.

"Where's your uncle?" Mark asked Lushawn.

"Out. He's looking for straight work for once. But Mom's sleeping, so we have to be quiet."

"What did he do that wasn't straight?"

"He was a burglar," she said matter-of-factly. "But he's just come back from four years in prison. That's why he's so scared of anything that might involve the police. If he gets caught for anything at all, he becomes a three-time loser. In New York, that's a mandatory life sentence."

The three of them crashed together on the couch. So Ollie's reluctance was somewhat explained. But there was also the matter of the reward. Kealy knew he had been tempted.

Mark began compulsively making runs on the TV with the mute button on.

"What'll happen when he finds us here?" Allison asked.

"All hell is gonna break loose the second he comes through that door," Lushawn answered.

Kealy went into the kitchen, took down a glass, and drew some water. As she put the glass to her lips, she saw that it had a film on it. There was no dishwasher, so the sanitation was not very good. She poured out the water and hand washed the glass herself, wiping it with a paper towel. All sorts of germs could be transmitted by a dirty glass.

God, she was tired. She took a deep breath. She was about to put herself in harm's way, to suggest something so outlandish that her kids were going to consider it mad. But it was also the only thing that had any chance at all of saving them.

Her throat just exactly as dry as it had been before, she returned to the living room. She sat in the brown easy chair that Ollie had inhabited. "Kids, pay attention. Mark, turn that thing off. I have a plan."

"Okay," Allison said. "We could use a plan."

"Now, I want you to listen to it all before you start yelling."

"Uh-oh."

"Marko, you *listen.* I'm going to go into our office and get into our safe. I have bearer bonds in there. They can be cashed at any bank. We've got two hundred and six dollars between us and a price on our heads, and there is two hundred thousand dollars in that safe. At least. Jimmy kept a lot of those bonds. You can transport large sums of cash with them, and cash is involved in a business like his."

After a fair silence, Mark asked, "How?"

Allison closed her eyes, opened them. Her expression made Kealy angry, because it said that she thought that she was dealing with somebody very stupid. "I mean, like they're going to just let you waltz in and open Daddy's safe."

"What else do we have? Sitting in the apartment of an ex-con who's going to go for the reward the instant he sees us?"

"What building is it?" Roselle asked. She had appeared from the bedroom.

"Oh, we woke you up," Kealy said. "I'm so sorry."

"You and me both. So where is this office of yours? What building?"

"The Smolen Building. Fifth between Forty-sixth and—"

"I know the building. That place is hell to dust. They got all that carving in there. And the brass—whew, what a job that one is." She stopped to fire up a cigarette.

Everybody was looking at her. "What're you driving at?" Kealy asked.

"You got a smart idea, Kealy. It'll work."

Allison scoffed. "Don't tell her that!"

"Well, it better, 'cause it sounds to me like if it don't, you-all have to give yourselves up and hope the cops aren't your problem." She regarded Kealy out of slanted eyes. "I've got your ticket to get in there easy." She disappeared into her bedroom for a moment, returned with an olive drab coverall uniform on a hangar. "You go in with the cleaning team. After we alter this thing to fit you, that is."

"Will they allow it?"

"They're not gonna notice. You go in as a special order. Shampoo the rugs. Nobody knows special orders, they come from central. I mean, they might know one just by chance, if they've seen him before. But usually they don't. It's, like, part-timers and stuff. They come on all the time."

"I can't shampoo rugs. I've no idea how."

"We'll get a shampooer from that A&P on Ninth Avenue and Fifty-fifth Street. A lot of special orders rent 'em there. It's a piecework business. You spend thirty bucks on the equipment, five bucks on the liquids, you got your fares, you're gonna make a hundred bucks on the job. It's good work, you get enough calls."

"Will you be there?"

"Me? Nah. I'm in the GM Building. Halls, top ten floors." She flexed an arm. "I got that heavin' a Hoover for fifteen years of my life. I look like Mike Tyson in drag, right?" She burst out laughing, a sound like a rattling old lawnmower.

"Mother," Allison said, "you are not going to do this."

Mark added, "Not alone."

"You kids are in disguise, and people can see through disguises. Nobody cares about an old woman."

"This plan is crazy, anyway. It's broad daylight, and—"

"We aren't day workers. She'll go in at ten tonight."

"You don't know what invisible is until you've been female on the streets of New York in a hideous scarf and no makeup. I am not going to be noticed, believe me."

"She's right," Roselle said. "Women like us just plain aren't seen. And with one of these uniforms on, boy, you gonna have to be careful people don't walk right through you. We're the 'not theres.'"

Allison shook her head. Mark came and laid an arm around his mother's shoulder. "We can't lose you, Mom. We need you."

She turned away from him. She had to do this. There was a slim chance that it might work, which was better than what they had now, which was no chance at all. "Let's get that uniform altered, Roselle. This is going to work, you'll see," she said. She wished that she believed it.

CHAPTER 22

Kealy slipped uneasily into the secret world of night workers. They were never seen by the day world, but it revealed itself to them. They were the ones who threw away the empty bottles of celebration and the shredded reports of disaster. But she wasn't thinking about any of those things as she rolled the appallingly ungainly rug shampooer along the sidewalk. The huge machine must weigh a hundred pounds or more.

She looked up the sheer face of the Smolen Building. Now, how was this going to work—carpet shampooers and revolving doors did not seem to mix.

"Hey! Hey, you!" It was the night porter, Ed Damson. He came striding up, his uniform buttons flashing. Ed was the sweetest man, though, as gentle as a kitten. Observant, too, and he would be her first danger.

"Get the fuck off this entrance, you dumb Polack! Speeka da English? Move it!"

She was so amazed that her mouth dropped open.

"Hey, you another one a them damn retards they send over here? I tole 'em, no more fuckin' retards!"

She drew the heavy oblong machine away from the doors. She affected the accent he seemed to expect. "Where I go?"

"You know damn well, you old—ah, shit, come *on!*" He grabbed the front of the machine and went scurrying down the sidewalk to a black door that she'd never even seen. He unlocked it, pulled it open. "You got a dollar for me? You got a tip? Whaddaya think, I'm free of charge?"

He was damned serious. He was actually demanding money from what obviously must seem to him to be a poor old immigrant woman. He was a swine, in other words. She gave him a dollar from the big green patent-leather purse Roselle had loaned her, noticing just at the last minute that a carpet cleaner couldn't very well traipse around with an alligator bag from Gucci over her shoulder.

Pocketing the money, Ed disappeared without a word, strutting back to his luxurious lobby and the imposing desk behind which he played kitty-cat to his betters and viper to the likes of her. She would forevermore know the secret of Ed, that the faultless gentleman was really scum.

Inside was a corridor lined with bins of trash. It reeked of stale cigarette ash and old cold coffee. The debris of the day. She wondered if any of the bins contained relevant papers. And then she wondered if she was going to live through this night.

She was heading toward the scuffed doors of the service elevators, her machine rumbling on the concrete floor, when a voice yelled out, "Excuse me!"

She almost leaped out of her baggy uniform, which Roselle had altered as much as possible. "Yes!"

It was the assistant superintendent, Winslow Mosely. Winslow had been here forever. He was always very professional and very polite. She wondered what he would be like now. She dreaded to find out. "Got your order?" he barked.

Wordlessly, she held out the pink carbon copy that Roselle had given her from her own sheet of work orders. He examined it, glanced up at her. "Okay, Rose," he said, "they've been working nights at Ryerson & Osborne, so you be aware of that." He looked right in her face, and she was again amazed. He did not see her at all. "Go on, now, hon. Have a good night." He smiled at her just as he had at Mrs. Ryerson, with exactly the same kindness. "Lemme help you get this monster in the elevator." He heaved it into the filthy freight lift. "That's too heavy for a lady," he said. The doors closed on the back of a good, hardworking man. She had never thought how revealing all this would be.

As she ascended, she worried. It was one thing to deceive people who rarely saw her, another entirely to get past office staff. And what if Sim was there? Then what?

The service lift opened onto a foyer just behind the kitchen where Monica Moore came in to make lunch on partners' day every Friday, when Sim and Jimmy and the juniors ate together and pretended to do something other than gossip. Compared to men—especially professional men—women's reputation for gossip was most undeserved.

It was quiet in here, very quiet. She glanced at her watch—actually, Lushawn's Fossil. Her own Cartier was in the Gucci purse at the apartment. Roselle had an eye for detail, most assuredly. By noticing just those two things, she might have saved Kealy's life.

Dear God, she prayed, *I want this to be over. I want to live.* She also wanted to pee. She was so nervous, it was just impossible not to need to. But where should she go? Certainly not to Jimmy's suite. They'd throw her out on the street if they found her using his or Sim's private facilities.

She made her way through the kitchen, paused before the door that led into the employee dining room and rest area. She'd decorated this space herself, with comfortable oak furnishings, delft blue walls, and a blue-gray carpet. On the walls were Hiroshige prints, four of the "Views of Mt. Fujiyama." They were reproductions, of course, but they were very good ones. She went into the ladies' room—which had quite an unpleasant stench. She knew at once what it was, too: somebody had vomited in here, and not very long ago.

Finishing her business as quickly as she could, she got out of the fear-stinking place and returned to her machine. Her plan was to haul it into the hall that ended at Jimmy's and Sim's side-by-side suites. There she would leave it while she went into Jimmy's office and got the combination from its hiding place taped to the inside of a desk drawer.

"Shit! We've got a shampoo order here! You sure you're in the right place?" The other woman stood with her arms folded, blocking any movement beyond the central lobby.

"Yes, yes."

"Damn that Bernie, I'd like to give that bald-headed moron a good smack!" She turned toward the sound of a wailing vacuum cleaner. "Lose the vac, Lisa, we got a shampoo job coming in." She waited. Then she turned around, cupped her hands around her mouth. *"Turn it off!"* The vacuum in the hall faded to silence. "I said, we got a shampoo job in here tonight. Go down to forty-one."

Lisa appeared, hauling an ancient industrial vacuum cleaner. "Alright already," she said. "I'm goin'." She glared at Kealy. "They oughtta tell us."

Now Kealy would have to actually run the shampooer. The instructions on the detergent bottle said nothing about making the machine go, and its instruction card was worn away.

Then she heard a voice, and it wasn't any cleaning person. That was Christa Lawrence—and that low drone that had replied, it might be Sim. Oh, God, if he was here—she put it out of her mind. Stick to the job, keep your head down. After all, Henny had walked right past her at the funeral and not seen a thing.

She poured liquid into the machine's bin—but was it the right one? And what about water? It would need water, surely.

At least she knew the office. She could go to the pantry and get the bucket and fill it. She was on her way when she realized that she *couldn't* go to the pantry, because this dumb old Polack didn't know where it was. She stopped, and when she did, heard a snatch of conversation: "don't have . . ." Christa's voice. A silence and then the male voice again. She listened. Was it familiar? It sounded too low, thank God, to be Sim. But he had spoken only briefly, and now there was silence.

It was broken by a very distinct human sound: laughter. Laughter, low and intimate. Then Christa's voice again, "Shit no!" Then a door slammed.

"I need a fill," she muttered to the supervisor.

"Come on, I'm goin' to the pantry."

As she hurried after the supervisor, she heard muffled rage, the voices speeding, rising and falling, Christa and two men.

She got the bucket back to the machine and filled the reservoir.

"Jesus, are you strung out or just straight over from the home country? That's the waste bin. You turn that thing on, you're gonna burn it up. Go empty it, put the water in *here!*" She pointed to a much smaller, less obvious opening.

With the machine working right, Kealy began shampooing. She was moving up the hall when the supervisor stopped her again. "Have you come out of a grass hut or something? You start in the offices." She threw opened Jimmy's door. "In here, then the one next to it, then work back along the carpet to the next set of doors. I'm gonna dock you one dollar for every footprint I find in the cleaned carpet. Is that understood?"

"Yes, ma'am."

This was gold she'd just been given. She went into Jimmy's office suite, entering a place almost as familiar to her as her home.

With its deeply stained paneling and leather furnishings, the sitting room glowed with invitation. Kealy had chosen every picture, every piece of furniture, even the stain on the walls. Now it all looked oddly pretentious. The Kealy who had done this was no more, gone with the powder that used to cover her blemishes.

She pushed the outer door closed and turned on the machine, expecting that she would leave it running while she went into the office itself and got at the safe. The sooner she was finished, the better. She'd exit fast.

But the door opened again almost immediately, and she was appalled to see Christa. They were both startled. They stood face-to-face and simply stared. She saw something flash in Christa's eyes, something complicated. But was it recognition? The girl said, "Oh."

Kealy dared not utter a word. No matter how much of an accent she might affect, she had only to think of her catastrophic experience with Cornell Drama to know that it would be foolish to try to act her way through this.

She plunged at the machine, began fussing with the cord, unwrapping it, looking for a wall socket, anything to keep Christa's eyes away from her face. She hated plugs—they scared her when they sparked—but she thrust the tines in. Immediately and unexpectedly, the machine roared to life. Brushes whirling, it raced off toward the bookcases. She dashed after it, grabbed the handle, tilted the brushes up, regained control of the mad thing.

Christa watched all of this. Kealy could feel her doing it. A glance revealed curiosity in the eyes, and something that might be suspicion. Then she turned and went into Jimmy's inner office. She closed the door behind her.

Whether she had been recognized or not, Kealy couldn't tell. She ran the machine slowly, concentrating on the part of the Aubusson nearest the row of windows that overlooked Forty-seventh Street.

Should Christa be in Jimmy's office? Weren't there probate rules to be followed regarding his records and possessions? Well, never mind, only two people knew where the combination to the safe was, and the other one was dead.

Conceivably, Christa might need to read client files that were kept in here, maybe on an emergency basis if somebody was about to get served or go to jail. But hadn't the files been stolen?

At least she didn't appear to have recognized her. Christa had never seen Kealy except in full dress, so it was perfectly probable. She kept telling herself that, kept watching the closed door, kept running the furious machine as best she could.

She ran it and ran it, but still the door did not open. This was something she hadn't counted on at all. She'd been here for fully twenty minutes when the outer door burst open. "Whassa matter," the supervisor said, "you sleepin' in here?"

"No ma'am! I clin!" She nodded toward the closed door. "I go in?"

"Somebody's working, you come back. Now get off your ass. This job doesn't complete, you don't get called back, Sister."

"No, no! Complit!" She turned off the machine, dragged it over into Sim's office. This time, she'd start in the inner sanctum.

This was exhausting work. No wonder Roselle had the arms of a fighter. As she cleaned the carpet, she looked around the office. Sim's own safe was gone, which brought up a possibility too terrifying to contemplate.

She hauled the machine into his outer office. Now the damned thing was out of water. Hadn't the woman said that it would explode or something if she ran it this way? Whatever, it was shrieking so she turned it off.

She went back into Jimmy's suite. The office door was still closed. Why the hell was Christa working in the middle of the night, anyway? And who else was in here with her?

This was turning out to be another horrible mistake. She just wasn't up to all this cloak-and-dagger. She got out of Sim's office. But she did not abandon her plan, would not. Keep your head down, you're just a dumb nobody from nowhere.

Filling the bucket, dragging it back, she looked again toward Jimmy's inner office. The door was still closed. Dare she knock, dare she ask, "Me clin?" in her newly acquired accent?

The hell with it, she'd been in here nearly an hour. She had to get on with this or it was going to go sour. Bound to.

She tapped on the door. No response. She tapped again. Still nothing. Thank you God. She pushed the door open—and found herself looking straight at Simon Osborne. What was he doing at Jimmy's desk? Almost, she cried out his name—almost. He raised his eyes, a question in his face, on it the slight smile of a polite man dealing with an unwelcome intrusion.

Immediately, she looked down, backed deferentially away like an embarrassed old-world immigrant might. She wanted to just yell out, "Sim, it's me. Sim, you can't go to the cops, listen to me. I'm not crazy. We need to talk." But instead she muttered, "Clin?"

"Don't mind me, I'll just be behind the desk."

Miserably, she dragged her monster into the room.

"Oh, dear," Sim said. "Did we ask for this to be done?"

"Yessir." She sounded ridiculous. Surely he could hear that she was changing her voice.

He got up, came toward her. It was over. "I'll stay out of your way for fifteen minutes, dear."

No it's not! God, he's buying it. Okay, be dour, laconic. Do *not* look at him. "Is goot."

As he withdrew from the room, she turned on the machine. He'd left the door wide open but she did not dare close it. Now it was time to go for the safe, right now.

She let go of the machine, which immediately went out of

control again, flopping like a maddened shark on the deck of a fishing boat. She leaped to pull the plug.

It stopped, crashing to the floor, fluids bubbling out. She was actually dizzy; her blood pressure must be going through the roof. That would be great, to have a heart attack now. She righted the monster, then went to the desk.

"What the *fuck* is this!"

"Sorry! Sorry! I clin!"

The supervisor strode over. "Gimme your order."

Kealy dug the work order out of her pocket, thrust it into her hand. The woman opened it, read. "Okay, you're docked five bucks. Clean it up."

Kealy knelt down, pretending to examine the pool of rug cleaner and water.

"No, no! Run the machine through it! Disperse it. Jesus, are you some kinda moron? Here." She grabbed the machine. "Plug it in."

Kealy did it.

The supervisor moved the cleaner expertly back and forth, raising a froth on the carpet. "It'll come out a little cleaner is all. Just the damn time, hon. I gotta hit you for the time."

When the woman left, Kealy closed the door behind her. The hell with it, and the hell with this accursed machine. Controlling it as best she could, she slid open the right top drawer of the desk, felt the upper surface where the pouch containing the combination was kept. The instructions were coded, but Kealy knew the code because she and Jimmy had devised it together. "If anything ever happens to me, the first thing you do is get these bonds. They'll tide you over through probate or anything else."

She could crack the code on a yellow pad in a few minutes. Or she could have if the combination had been there, but it wasn't.

Increasingly frantic, she searched the rest of the desk. Nothing. Maybe he'd moved it—but no, that was not his style, he was too careful. If he'd done that, she would have been told. He would have made certain that she changed the coded information about its location on her emergency page.

The safe, set into the wall beneath the window behind his desk, was closed and locked.

Okay, supposedly your memory for the distant past improves as you get older. They had used a line of poetry, that she recalled clearly. And you did a back count from each consonant . . . but what poem and which line?

"'Anthem for Doomed Youth,'" she blurted, her voice drowned by the whining machine:

What candles may be held to speed them all?
Not in the hands of boys, but in their eyes
Shall shine the holy glimmers of good-byes.

She'd said, "It's so sad." He had smiled gently and not replied. At the time, she'd not seen it as an epitaph.

It took another five minutes to reconstruct the combination. Now she had to run and check. Silence was obviously a major risk, but she switched off the machine.

The outer office was empty. Somewhere down the hall she heard the supervisor's voice, high and angry, as she punished somebody else. She returned to the safe, turned the knob two, three, four times, dropped the handle to the first click, then fed in the rest of the complex combination. Along the way, one tumbler after another ticked satisfyingly over. Good, better, best: the handle went all the way down and the door came open and thank you, God, thank you for this one gift, at last, at long last.

The safe was empty.

CHAPTER 23

They'd been in here taking her money, Christa and Sim, they must have. Well, to hell with them, she'd get it back, she had to get it back from them right now before they left. She lurched toward the door, her vision obscured by tears, rage clawing her throat. Swinging it open into the silent, soft elegance of the outer office, she hesitated. She stared into the empty room. She was like a trapped animal, that was how it felt, like she was a lady bear driven to the back of a cave who knew she had to fight her way out right here and now or die right here and now. The first thing to do was to start the machine again so that she would not get kicked out of here. Above all things, she needed time.

She dragged the machine out of Jimmy's office and into Sim's. He was there in the inner office; she could see him at his desk. He had piles of papers. He was working at his computer terminal.

They were damn well cleaning this place out, he and Christa, that's what they were doing. She rolled the machine into his sanctum. "I clin," she said.

He started. "Shit!" Then he smiled, and she saw in his eyes his own tiredness and his fear. But she was not willing to reveal herself to him. She was afraid of him now because she did not see the logic of this, not if he was straight. Because Jimmy's bonds were lying on his desk in plain view. She would recognize them anywhere, three on the AXO Corporation and three on the General Services Group, two hundred thousand dollars' worth of bearer bonds.

Could she grab them and run? Yes, maybe so, maybe she could do that right here and now, maybe she *should* do it, just grab them right this second and get the hell out of here. She moved toward the desk, head down, dragging the machine, getting closer and closer to them. "I clin," she repeated, moving as if to lean down, as if perhaps to unwrap the machine's power cord.

She was close to the bonds now, she could see by the way they were folded, and by the numerals she herself had written on their faces that they were definitely hers. She had jotted their checking account number on them the day she and Jimmy put them in the safe.

She was so mad at Sim that it was all she could do not to lift the machine over his head and bring it down with all her force and crush him like an insect. But he wasn't an insect; he might not even be at fault. What if he sensed a threat to security here and he was trying to protect them for her sake?

There could be all kinds of reasons, that was the truth. But still, she had to get those bonds. She needed just a couple of minutes in here, then she would grab them and simply leave. That was the thing, keep it simple, always keep it simple. No problem, just leave, you poor jerk. Just leave.

She fired up the machine and came roaring around the desk, thrusting it at his feet, willing him to go, get out, get out, leave her alone with the damn bonds. But he raised his feet, on his face a pained smile. "I clin," she said, "I clin!"

Suddenly he burst up to his full height, his chair shooting back against the far wall. On his face was a skeletal grin, a horrible, murderous expression that she had never seen before. The Sim she knew was mild and inoffensive. The Sim she knew was not given to violence. But this man—this man was about to kick her senseless or something. "I sorry," she said. "Sorry!" She backed away from him.

"Just hurry the fuck up," he snarled. "And then get the fuck outta here!" He went around the desk, and—yes, oh, yes—he headed for the door. He went out.

Okay, there they were and here she was. Grab them, do it now, there's no time. But he was standing there in the doorway. He was watching her. She wheeled the machine around, moving toward the back of the office, struggling to do the work evenly, to look professional, not to get thrown out.

God damn it, go get a glass of water, anything, do it, get out of here! But he just stood, staring. Now she was getting scared, now she was beginning to worry that he was realizing who she was, maybe something in the way she moved, something in her eyes, even her damn smell—maybe some deep part of him was recognizing her right now.

She had the feeling—the definite, terrible feeling—that he was indeed part of the problem, that Mike's brief words of warning had been meant to include him right along with Henny. She moved around the desk, thrusting the machine, making it rumble and howl, pushing it toward the front of the office, trying to block his view of the desk so that she could somehow—somehow—

He came in, he slipped around her, and she saw him retreating with the bonds in his hand. With a quick motion, he tucked them into the top pocket of his suit jacket. Jimmy had said, "The great advantage of bearer bonds is their portability. They're like compressed cash." And so it was: Sim now had her hundereds of thousands of dollars invisibly hidden on his person.

A flush of white hot fury overcame her. She had to get them. She had to hit him and get them, kill him, she didn't care. But she had to have them, she *had to have them!*

"Get the fuck outta here!"

The supervisor stood where Sim had been, the damned bitch in her frayed green uniform with her fat face and her empty shark's eyes.

Kealy kept right on cleaning. "I sorry!"

"No! No more!" The supervisor took the machine from her. "You're in the wrong fucking building, you stupid moron. You belong in the goddamn GM Building." She turned to Sim. "There's been a screwup. I'll have her outta here in a second."

Kealy saw that she had lost. She backed away. "I sorry! I sorry!"

"You sure as hell are." Again she addressed Sim. "I'm so sorry, sir, so sorry that you were disturbed."

Then Christa came in. "Did you open Mr. Ryerson's safe?" she asked Sim.

"No."

"Then I think we have a problem."

Kealy went down the hall, almost running. She must have left the damn safe open, stupid idiot that she was! She hammered the freight lift button.

"Hey," from behind her. "You gotta take this thing!"

Then Christa: "We need to talk to that woman."

The lift opened. Kealy got in. Once in the basement, she dashed out the way she'd come. She burst out into the street and ran.

Could the carpet machine be traced? Roselle's credit card had been used for the deposit. There weren't all that many places around here that rented them. So it was just a question of time before they were led straight to the Davises. Kealy thought: *I've killed us all.*

Fleets of late-night cabs prowled Fifth Avenue. She rushed out into the street and grabbed one. The driver glanced back at her. She wanted to tell him to take her all the way back to the Davises', but she forced herself not to do that. The risk and the expense were both too great. "Sixty-eighth and Lex," she said.

In that cab, riding up those empty, late-night avenues, she knew what it was to be absolutely alone and absolutely desperate. She turned around and watched the lights of the cars behind her, but could tell absolutely nothing about them.

The cleaning staff was lined up before Henny, as bedraggled and terrified a gaggle of humanity as he'd seen in some time. They were all involved in illegal shit, of course. The thing they didn't understand was, he didn't care. But they would never believe that and he would have to fight them for every scrap of information he extracted. They were tired, they wanted to go home. Their day ended at four and it was pushing five, gray light beginning to outline the windows. He'd kept them waiting on purpose, because he knew they'd be less trouble that way. He grinned at them. "Anyone speak English?"

No answer. They all spoke it, of course.

"No problem," he said, staying cheerful. "I'll take you down to the precinct. They have interpreters there." He looked into a pair of eyes. "For the prisoners."

"I speak."

"Oh, must not've heard me the first time. I know, I mumble."

Osborne had called in a theft report: James Ryerson's safe had been opened and cleaned out. The bust had supposedly been accomplished by an elderly Polack carpet cleaner, as if some old bag could crack a five-star safe like that.

Problem was, the elderly Polack carpet cleaner had something wrong with her records. In fact, her work order was fake. But they had her damn rug shampooer, so they were going to find the old bag. Probably a wild goose chase, some kind of illegal labor scam.

"So who was the rug lady?"

The man—short, his mustache suggesting Greece or the Balkans—gave him a look so completely blank that Henny almost believed it. But he did not, because the man was lying with his eyes, just as the others were with their silence. What he was lying about with his eyes, of course, had nothing to do with the Ryerson safe. It had to do with his green card, or lack thereof, or the reefer in his pocket, or the illegal retsina factory in his apartment.

"Look, folks, you want to go home, I want to go home. I want a nice drink, put my feet up. So let's get this done. You gotta know. Somebody in here has to know who she was."

"Sir, I'm the supervisor."

"Okay, supervisor. What we got?"

"Like I told you, she was from the main office—"

"No, I beg to differ. There was nobody sent out to this building or the GM Building or anywhere, not to shampoo rugs, not tonight. The work order is bogus." Inside, he had that familiar sinking feeling that detectives learn is part of the job. You work half blind, you're always getting surprised, and the surprises are usually negative ones.

The supervisor played dumb. "She wasn't from the office?"

Either an elderly woman had come in here posing as an add-on to the crew and cleaned out Jim Ryerson's safe, or she was some dumb old bag who'd gone to the wrong building, and the cleaning outfit's records were so screwed up they didn't even know it.

But she had not busted the Ryerson safe, no matter who she was. Because who ever heard of an old lady buster who could sweet the lock on a Bechmann pete? The best rippers in the trade had to burn Bechmanns down. So this genius would be known. She would be famous.

White lady, about five-six, salt-and-pepper blond hair pulled back in a bun. Green eyes, Sim said. Kealy had green eyes, but she was not an elderly woman, and there was no possible way that she could have come in here without being noticed, not even in disguise.

Could she?

Henny realized that he was standing there staring at the help, who were staring back, their mouths hanging open. "All right," he said with a briskness he did not feel, "any other descriptions?"

"She wasn't one I'd seen before," the supervisor said, "and she did a lousy job."

"Lousy," he said, "I'm sure. She talk? Have an accent?"

"She didn't talk much."

"You people wear gloves when you work?"

"Gloves? No gloves."

"We need everybody's fingerprints," he said. There was a nervous stirring. They sure as hell spoke English now. "If you give us any trouble, you get sent back to Albania at your own expense. Please line up for the officer over there." He indicated a cop with print kits, who began setting up a work station in the receptionist's area. "Thanks for your help."

He went back into Ryerson's office, where he found Christa Lawrence and Simon Osborne. "Hey," he said, throwing himself down into one of the leather wing chairs that stood before the fireplace. "I like this room. This is where the rich bad guys got told they were probably gonna do time. I can smell the fear."

"Actually, most of them got told they were going to walk."

"Be that as it may, I just don't understand who'd come in

here now, not after the place already got worked over." He gave them one of his best smiles. "As you explained."

"I think I'm getting drunk," Sim said. He rattled the ice in the glass he held. "I've been drinking this stuff ever since we found the safe open."

"You both saw her?"

"We saw the rug lady," Christa said. "Just another cleaning person. Looked kind of Polish."

"Short," Sim announced, as if this somehow settled something.

"Polish women are short, I guess," Henny said. "This one been around before? Either of you recognize her?"

"I can't tell you that," Sim replied. "I must confess that I'm virtually never here at night. But we've been struggling to get our case files back in order, what with the thefts. That's the only reason we're here."

"So what was in the safe? Got an inventory?"

This was where the smart guys playing insurance games always showed their hands. The smart guys always had a perfect inventory, often even a videotape of contents.

"It was his personal safe. If he had an inventory—well, it could have gone out with the files." He paused. "Actually, his safe could have attracted unwanted attention of this kind. Jimmy was a big believer in bearer bonds. He often had a lot of them in there."

"Why would that be?"

"A bearer bond worth a million dollars can be slipped into a suit pocket, turned into cash anywhere in the world. It's untraceable."

"Who issues them, Colombian drug lords?"

"Corporations who want fast cash. They're the kind of things you find as initial deposits in numbered accounts in Panama. Crook stuff."

That crap again, trying to imply that Ryerson was some kind of criminal. The man was no criminal, and the fact that Osborne had lied about that had already made Henny damned suspicious of him. He wished that he could just accuse Osborne of cleaning out the safe, but it wouldn't scare a defense lawyer because he'd know it wouldn't stick. Osborne would be out in two hours, and Henny would be up for a possible reprimand, abuse of authority.

"I have additional evidence regarding Jimmy and Sal Bonacori. I have—"

Henny held his hand up. He did not want to hear it. He was sick of Osborne's crap. "I'll send somebody over tomorrow to take a statement."

"Oh. I assumed it would be urgent. Given that this Polish woman must be connected with all this in some way."

He would have let him go on, but it was really late, and he'd suffered enough bullshit for one day. "We're gonna need prints from both of you guys," he said. "There's a rig set up in the foyer."

"My prints must be all over that safe." Sim's voice had gone high.

"I'm sure they are, Mr. Osborne. I'm sure they are."

CHAPTER 24

Finally the subway arrived at the Church Avenue station in Flatbush, and a very weary, very dirty Kealy Ryerson got off. She moved like a ghost along the silent platform, a shadow under the hard yellow lights. Two people came off the train with her, old men with lunch pails, speaking together in the soft, mysterious accents of the black South. As they continued on their way down the stairs to the street, she hung back watching. Until she had seen them going off down the avenue, she stayed put.

Never could she remember being this tired. Her life these past few days had been like a forced march into the depths of hell and it wasn't stopping, it was getting worse.

She was starting to focus more on her physical needs—which, of course, simply made her all the more vulnerable. She was hungry and thirsty. Coffee and hot food came to mind. Moving down the street, she saw a McDonald's blazing with light. Inside, there was another kind of life—she could see kids in the light, boys and girls huddled over the tables, giggling at each other in the timeless way of teenagers. Their happiness radiated through her like heat through a frozen soul, drawing her toward the fatal lights.

She went in, and as she did a sort of rustle passed through the crowd. Every person in the store was aware of the fact that a white woman had just entered. It was nearly four in the morning deep in a black neighborhood, and no white people appeared around here, not even ragged old women.

"Coffee," she said. "A Big Mac."

The girl in the red-and-white uniform gave her the food and she went with it to one of the tables. One of the kids, she saw, was the Davis boy, Jo-Jo.

Her heart stopped; her world swayed and shuddered. But he kept his presence of mind and did not say anything. His eyes tore at her, though. His eyes would not leave her alone. *Stop looking at me,* she wanted to say. *Ignore me, child. Don't give me away.*

As she bit into her hamburger she realized that not only was she the only white person in the place, she was maybe the only one in the neighborhood. She finally understood that she'd been a fool to come in here, a damn fool. But she was so hungry, she was so tired. She gobbled her hamburger, choked down her coffee. Then she stood up and struggled out.

"She lost," a voice said. "She get off at the wrong stop."

She left to a ripple of laughter, a little mean, a little dangerous perhaps. Had anybody connected her to the reward? She could not tell, but as she left she could feel them watching her, all of them, even the ones behind the counter.

Moving as quickly as she could, she went down the street and around the corner. Dawn was rising in the east, spreading clear golden light along the black cityscape. She slipped into the Davises' building and went up the stairs.

"Oh, Mommy, Mommy," Allison shrilled, leaping into her arms.

"The bad news is—"

"There isn't any bad news! You're back!"

"Ally, let her talk," Mark said. He'd come from the kitchen. He had coffee for her, hot and about half milk, just the way she liked it. "Tell us, Mom," he said as he gave it to her.

She took it to the couch, sank down. She leaned her head far back, closed her eyes. "The safe was empty."

Allison reacted with a sort of weeping sigh, a sound like the breathy scream of a shot deer.

Kealy continued, "Sim took it all. He took our money."

"But, Mommy, we had a combination and everything!"

For the first time, she realized that Ollie was there. He was standing over her, looming really, his complicated face solemn. "You didn't get the money?"

She shook her head.

Allison seemed confused. "Is Sim—not our friend? That's definite?" The kids had called him Uncle Sim. He had been a part of their lives forever.

"He could have taken the money to protect it for us."

Ollie laughed a little, dropping into his chair. "I wouldn't bet on that hand, Fifth Avenue. It looks like your options is all used up."

"Ollie, I have to ask you if you know of any other place we could go, just to buy a little more time? Is there anybody who would take us in?"

"Why don't you go with you own friends? Maybe I'm dumb, but I still don't get that."

She wished that Roselle was back from work. She didn't know how to handle Ollie. She didn't know what had transpired while she was gone and she wasn't sure she should ask. But she had the feeling that she was facing some kind of an ultimatum here.

"You afraid that anybody who helps you, they gonna get hurt for their trouble. Am I right?"

"That's part of it."

"Sure it is. So you out here slummin', where it don't matter who get hurt."

Lushawn marched in from the bedroom. "Ollie," she said, "no!" Her eyes were red with sleeplessness.

"She is, she—"

"I said *no!* These people are here because they need help. End of story. Okay, Uncle Ollie?"

They had been through a trial in the past few hours, she could see that. Her kids were haggard and very frightened.

"She a racist and she don't even know it! Jus' like your friends." He gestured toward her two wonderful children, and she decided that she really did not like this man.

Still, she tried to be conciliatory. "If I am, it's innocent."

"It's never innocent."

"I'm out here with my kids because we need help and this is the only place we could find that was safe."

He regarded Kealy with the sinister care of a hunter evaluating a deer. "You gotta get your money. That's what you gotta do."

"It's in Sim's safe by now."

"Your kids say it's a lotta money."

"We offered him a hundred thousand dollars not to turn us in," Mark said, his voice toneless. "We thought you'd have the bonds."

"A hundred thou—"

"Lady, five grand is waitin' for the man that picks up that phone. I ain't never seen five grand, but I ain't never seen a hundred even more."

Lushawn went to the table where the phone stood, an old red Princess. "Ollie, if you do this to them—"

"Girl, you don't have any right to keep on like this. They tell me she's bringin' the money, but she doesn't have it. Now look, that money could put your brother through school."

Kealy had never felt more defeated. But still, she wanted to help her kids so badly that she actually considered at that moment trying to kill him. "Mr. Davis, we're in need. If you turn us in, we're going to die just like my husband did."

"The cops—"

"Are a big part of the problem! I don't know what's happened. I just don't know. But it's carnage." She gestured toward Lushawn. "How would you feel?"

"Lady, your buddy took your money. Now you ain't got no money. No self-respecting businessman's gonna just sit here and give you charity."

"If Sim has the money, maybe we can get it from him, Mother."

"How can we possibly manage that?"

"You got into our safe."

"Yeah," Ollie said, "you did. How about his safe? Could you manage that?"

"I haven't got the combination."

"Well, now. Looks like you need a little professional assistance. For a hundred gees, I might crack that safe for you."

She was so surprised that she uttered a laugh, a harsh sound.

Ollie gave her a long look. "You've got how much money, now?"

"You'd have your hundred thousand, no problem."

Lushawn said, "Uncle Ollie, don't even think about it."

"Hush now, girl. I've got a business proposition going here."

"Ollie!"

"You want your friends to stay alive, girl? They have no other choice." He crossed his legs, folded his arms. "Lady, if I'm gonna risk jail by busting a pete for you, then I'll need more than a hundred thousand. I'll need a whole lot of whatever money's there. Like, half."

"You're on."

"So how much is it?"

"You'll get a hundred thousand dollars in bearer bonds."

Ollie's smile was a slow thing, building in his deeply sad face until it was as if sunshine had broken out from behind deep, deep clouds. "Hell, Kealy, you've got a lot of guts." Drawing his lounge chair straight, he leaned toward her. He folded his big hands around his knees. "This is going to be a legal caper, isn't it? Legal all the way?"

"The property in the safe is mine."

"If it isn't there?"

"I owe Sim a few dollars for the damage, if there is any. He's not going to press any charges against anybody."

"Well, hell, I'll go for a big dollar that's legal. I'm going in with you!" He stopped. His smile faded. He glared at his niece. "Lushawn, you don't let Roselle know one damn thing about it, because she'll raise holy hell, she hears I'm busting a pete." He gave Kealy a sidelong glance. "Lemme tell you, that gal can raise hell higher than heaven, guaran-damn-teed."

He seemed to reach out to her with his eyes, and she couldn't be sure if it was lust for money making him look like that or something more humane. "You gonna have a stroke, white lady? 'Cause you turnin' red as a radish."

"I'm fine. Just excited."

"What I also have to ask is, get Jo-Jo into that school of Lushawn's. It's been tearing my heart right out of my chest, seeing him missing out when he's just as smart."

"My brother doesn't test well," Lushawn explained.

"I gotta tell you, it's just awful having one of 'em up there getting a real chance, while he has to stay back here in hell with me and Sister, and he's dying in his soul, that boy." His sad, sad eyes met hers. "That's my blues, Kealy. That's my blues."

"I'll do everything I can for him."

"You can talk to Andover? You can convince them?"

"If they can be convinced, then I'm in a good position to do it."

"And you knock off the chip you got on your shoulder?"

"I haven't got one!"

"You look in your heart, Fifth Avenue, you're gonna find out you're scared of me. I live my life with white people crossing the street to get away from me. But I haven't got any hurt in my heart for anybody. Black skin hides a man's truth from white eyes, is what my dad told me."

"Ollie—"

"Kealy, I've been mean. I admit that. And it felt good, I admit that, too. But you've been mean, too, looking at me like I'm some kind of killer. You look at me and you think, that ape is dangerous."

"I don't think of you as an animal, Ollie." But she could not say that she didn't fear him. She couldn't deceive those eyes of his.

"Tell you what, Kealy. You and me, we lift the lid and drop all this stuff of ours in the trash. Because we're both good people. Let's try to say hello." The smile came again, complex, small, just at the edge of angry. "Hello."

"Hello, Ollie." They shook hands with the solemn precision of generals on a spent and bloody field.

Allison, who had been watching all this from her friend's side, asked a simple question: "Mommy, what if we don't?"

"What?"

"Find the money. What if we don't?"

Ollie said, "Tomorrow's Saturday. He's going to be able to cash the bonds on Saturday?"

"I don't believe so," Kealy responded.

"So they'll be in that safe."

Allison persisted. "If they aren't?"

"We'll think about that later."

"This sounds totally impossible," Mark said. "We have to plan expertly."

"I am an expert. It isn't any big deal to get in an office on Saturday. Believe me, I have plenty of experience with that."

Kealy did not know how to tell him that Sim's safe was in his apartment. Best just to spit it out. "Ollie, the safe isn't at the office. He's removed it."

"Where to?"

"It's in his apartment."

"Aw, *shit!*"

Before another word could be said, Jo-Jo burst in and slammed the door. The hollow of his eyes spoke of trouble when it touches the young, how amazed they always are. "You got to get out," he said, and there was no doubt that he meant the Ryersons. "Do it."

Almost as a reflex, Kealy started to bargain. "Well, we—"

"*Do it!*"

ootsteps pounding up the stairs blocked the way in that direction. "Fire escape," Mark said, moving quickly to the window. Roselle had locked the safety grate after the last time he'd gone down this way, and it was still locked. "Key," he said. His calm was almost preternatural.

"It's in Mom's room! I'll—" But Lushawn didn't have time even for that, not with the banging that started on the door.

Still very calm, Mark ushered Kealy and Allison into Roselle and Ollie's bedroom and shut the door. Then he sat down on the bed and buried his face in his hands.

An instant later, excited voices rose as the door burst open. "They in here, they in this building, man," a young male who sounded about Jo-Jo's age cried. "Willy Forest done follow that lady here, the Delwood twins, too. Hey, you-all, it's five grand!"

From the Davises, there was total silence.

"What's the matter . . . you-all?" said another young voice, dropping at the end toward suspicion.

Lushawn spoke, her tone sharp. "Bobby Harper, you wake up our mother and somebody's gonna get his hide tanned."

Another young male said, "Your momma isn't home from work till six."

Now it was Ollie's turn. "And what you doing out at all hours, you boys? You don't have any business coming in here at five A.M. This is a stroke-of-midnight house, I seem to recall."

Jo-Jo: "The subway got stuck, Ollie! I swear!"

The one called Bobby Harper: "We've been in it for hours, Mr. Davis. Really and truly! Some jumper did a salami dive onto the A train express track."

"What're you gonna do when your mother smells your breath, Mr. Hot Shot Bobby Harper? And what about you other boys? You full of crack, or just a lot of sloe gin like this genius?"

"Mr. Davis, we've been at McDonald's. We saw one of them come in and sit there eatin' a Big Mac, just like that. You gotta listen! These're the white people got the reward on 'em! Gotta be! Otherwise, what's some old white bag doing coming in this building? They're in here somewhere, gotta be! So what we need to do is hunt them down, and we end up with so much money we'll be swimming in it."

The one who sounded suspicious said, "You aren't in here, are you, lady? You wouldn't give white people a place to stay, would you Ollie?"

"He hates the white man," Jo-Jo said proudly.

Kealy heard the squeak of a floorboard, then saw the handle of the door move a bit. One of the boys was standing right outside, his fist around that knob. "Then why do I smell white people in here?"

"You're gonna get our mom mad," Jo-Jo wailed, "you go fooling around in there. I'm in enough trouble already."

"I won't let her hurt you, little boy."

Now there was a much louder voice. "Okay, that's enough," Ollie said. Then came the sharp sound of a hand hitting skin, perhaps the side of a head. "There's more where that came from, boy. You want it? You want some more?"

"Nossir! But I got to think, the reason you're running so fast in place is that they're in that bedroom right there."

"Get out." Ollie's voice wasn't even a little bit playful, not anymore.

"Uh-oh," Allison whispered. She knew a seriously mad adult when she heard one.

But this kid was not to be put off. "Just let me peek in, then. I'll be real quiet, she isn't even gonna know."

"Jesus Christ," Mark murmured. His eyes were darting from place to place in the tight little room.

There came a hissing sound, another hand moving along the wood of the door. He was about to turn the handle and burst in.

"Don't you do that, you stay outta there," Lushawn said.

"You've got the white people in there. Everybody knows you

do. Everybody on this end of Flatbush Avenue saw you parading around with them."

These kids were not going to back down, not even to Ollie at his most fearsome, because they smelled money, and they knew damn well that it was right here in this room, three valuable rats cowering in the corner of the box, waiting for the snake to begin his evening slide.

Mark spoke with his breath. "Mom, get in Roselle's bed. Get the covers over your head." He pushed Allison into the badly overstuffed closet, then slid under Ollie's bed. Kealy did as she'd been told, at the last minute pulling Roselle's robe off the back of the door and throwing it on. She slipped under the covers, drew them up, then arranged the robe around her waist to create a more padded appearance. As best she could, she drew the covers up over her blond hair. Hopefully, the darkness would do the rest.

She hadn't even finished before a voice said quite clearly, "Shit!" The door was open. The aggressive, suspicious kid was in the room.

"Damn you, Taylor," Jo-Jo whined, "she's stirring and we don't want that! Now come on out, fool. Come *on!*"

"That a white lady under that cover? I smell white, I smell it real strong."

Lushawn: "*Get*, you dumb monkey. That's my momma, and she doesn't smell like a white lady! Now get."

There was a loud thud, a gasp, then: "That hurt!"

"Damn right it did, now *get out!*"

"You gave me a bloody nose!"

Wham, the bedroom door slammed. The yelling boy was silenced. Hurried whispers followed. Kealy couldn't catch much of it, but it was apparent that the possibility of actually waking up Roselle was a lot more serious to Jo-Jo's friends even than a broken nose.

There was more thunder on the stairs, the sound diminishing quickly. Kealy found herself holding her breath.

"It's okay, folks," Lushawn said, opening the door. "They're gone for now."

Mark and Allison came out immediately, but it was all Kealy could do to rise from the bed. Even this spectacularly frightening situation had not leached any more adrenaline out of her spent body than necessary to get her through the immediate moment of tension. "I've got to sleep," she said. It was all she could manage. She was utterly and completely drained.

She managed to get to Lushawn's well-used bed. The next thing she knew, Ollie was there standing over her. He laid his big hand on her forehead. "You got a bit of fever there, lady. You're just so damn bushed, I guess."

"Ollie, are you going to do it?"

"Hell, Kealy, *we're* gonna do it. I need a whole team, if I'm gonna get this thing put down in somebody's damn apartment."

"I won't let you get arrested, Ollie."

"For that much money, free and clear and no heat on it, I'll take a few chances."

"I'm sorry if I offended you."

"You're just naturally scared of a big black somebitch like me. You've been taught from a baby that black is bad. I'm not offended by what you can't help. But beating into a fancy Fifth Avenue apartment with a damn doorman and all does offend me, though. It sure does." He chuckled. "Hell, Kealy, we've got something in common, you and me. You've got about the shittiest luck I've ever seen, except for my own. So I figure why not try to pull a job together? You won't get your money and I'll end up back in the conservatory. But what the hell, you'll find out black isn't bad, and I'll learn whitebread thinking."

"I think this is the worst, most hopeless situation possible for me, Ollie. I don't see how it could be any worse."

"Oh, lady, you are so wrong. There's always somethin' worse. Always."

CHAPTER 26

Mark looked down the gray street enclosed by the high, hostile walls of another age. He followed along behind lumbering Ollie, very unsure of everything, most especially that it was "walking easy," as Ollie had put it, to steal a van.

Since Mark was here because Ollie himself didn't want to take the risk of doing the actual stealing, he was assuming that the reassurances were just sales talk. "You'll just get a warning an' sent home to momma," he had explained. "Me, I go back in for life, boy."

Mark had wanted to ask Jo-Jo to do it or at least to come with him, but the alternative hadn't been offered and he had not dared to bring it up. He didn't care to get into some fearsome argument about race with this fairly crazy man.

"Okay, boy, go on in there. Get a real beat up one, like I said. They don't rent the shitty ones unless they got a lotta demand, so they aren't gonna see this baby's gone till inventory, whenever that is. Likely we've got it longer than we need it."

Mark pointed at a sign concerning dogs. "Now what?"

"There aren't any *dogs*. It cost money to rent dogs."

"You could get a mutt from the pound."

"No mutt's gonna hurt you. It takes a trained animal to do that."

"A big mutt's gonna do fine against me, Ollie. Do I look like somebody who can defend myself?"

That made Ollie stare off toward the vans for some little time. Mark was hoping that he was reconsidering their need for a vehicle, but he only said, "Hit it with the bolt cutter."

"Ripping a box" or "busting a pete," as Ollie variously referred to the act of cracking a safe, took elaborate and bulky equipment, it seemed. This equipment had to be transported in something, and "'No cabbie's gonna be hauling a black man around after midnight with an acetylene torch in his hip pocket.'"

So Mark found himself confronting a towering chain-link fence topped by razor wire, wondering by what astonishing leg-erdemain any of this would work, beginning with this climb. If he did get across, then there was the question of whether or not he would be able to follow Ollie's complicated and offhand hotwiring instructions. After that, there was the matter of the chain that held the driveway gate closed, a chain that could not be reached from the outside and had to be cut from the inside.

"This is impossible."

"This the easiest boost in Brooklyn."

"Tell me again about that razor wire—that piece-of-cake ra-zor wire up there."

Ollie spread his hand, then made a slow fist. "You keep com-pression on it, so the palm of the glove doesn't slide against the blades. Only thing's gonna happen, you're gonna get a little puncture here and there."

Mark found his own blood detestable, frightening, because of the dangerous mystery that held it prisoner. He raised his eyes up what seemed like a fifty-foot climb. How could he ever do this? He didn't have the muscles, let alone the courage and the hard street intelligence that would be needed if things went wrong. He pulled on the heavy gloves that Ollie had given him. "Wish me luck."

When Ollie made no reply, Mark turned to him—and discov-ered that he was halfway down the block, on his way back to the miserable diner where the others were waiting.

He found himself alone in the yellow dark of an abandoned part of the city, a place where surely only a madman would set up a truck rental station. And yet, maybe it was more active than it seemed, perhaps more than Ollie supposed. After all, there were warehouses not far away, and beyond the warehouses the busy glow of LaGuardia Airport. The place had afternoon hours on Sunday, too, so maybe the loss would be noticed tomorrow in-stead of Monday. Of course it would: he had to cut the huge chain with the bolt cutters he'd been given and allegedly taught how to use. But that was at least as dubious as his ability to hotwire the van.

He put his hands on the fence and began to struggle upward. He'd not passed ten links before he realized that this was going to be far, far worse than it had seemed. He started to think that he might die here. And even if he didn't, a cut would bring infection, and infection was so dangerous for him.

It was curious, but just behind the horror of it he found something appealing about the idea of being cut open, even more so about dying. He felt stupid and angry at himself because he'd gotten sick, and on one level he welcomed his own destruction.

So he climbed the shuddering, complaining links, climbed and climbed until his hands were sending red-hot pulses up to his shoulders and his toes felt like they were being torn off every time he thrust a shoe into a link and pushed.

The top of the fence was so high that when he reached the razor wire coils, he actually had a view of the tops of distant Manhattan towers: the Chrysler Building, the Empire State. New York forever.

There was a breeze coming up from the south, and off that way he could see to the far darkness of the Atlantic. The sky was beaded with convoys of planes, their lights blinking peacefully. The nearby Grand Central Parkway roared, gorged with rushing traffic. To the west, Manhattan was a huge beacon shining into the empty night.

If he could see, he could also be seen and that was not good. In fact, he must be visible for miles. He clutched the top of the fence. He was barely able to hold on, making the same little hurt sounds that had called help to his side when he was three. "Dad," he whispered.

Ollie had dismissed the razor wire like it was nothing, but up close it was a terrible obstacle. Each blade was fully two inches long, and the reason why it was called razor wire could not have been more obvious.

He was going to get cut to pieces here. It was a clumsy, messy thing to climb over the top of a fence. Until you could get a hold again on the other side, you simply fell, didn't you?

He clasped a length of the wire, lifted it. Fiery agony made him yell, made him jerk his hand back. He swung out, clinging with two fingers of the other one. For a moment, he hung there. Immediately, his bent fingers began to slip from the links he was trying to clutch.

He was going to fall right here and right now. He'd topple forward, land on his face. From this height, he would die.

Like all young men at the moment of their dying, he was filled with disbelief. In seconds, he would be no more, *he*, Mark James Ryerson.

His free hand came up, windmilled once, twice, then slammed backward against the fence—and he found that he could lace his fingers through it and reach around, and catch—just—and he could get a grip once more.

So once again he challenged the wire. This time he examined the way that it was hooked to the fence and pulled the smaller wire cutter he'd been given from his hip pocket. He snapped two of the connecting loops, then went between them as cleanly as a steer plunging through a slaughterhouse chute.

The climb down took only moments. When he reached the ground, he rocked back and forth like a sailor on land after a storm. He took off the gloves. He was cut, all right. That had happened, that had to be accepted. He took the big roll of bandage he had brought and was carefully winding it around and around his palm when a tawny and monstrous dog burst out from behind the service shack and leaped at him.

He went over backward, a white streamer of bandage sailing out into the night behind him. Frantically, he clutched the animal's dewlaps forcing its jaws away from his throat. He managed to slide out from under the animal. Warding it off as best he could with one hand, he hauled the bolt cutter out of his belt and slammed it down on the animal's broad skull. The crack made the dog wallow and growl, then bare its teeth and leap at him again. He swung the thing with all his might, and this time the blow came down between the eyes. The dog fell with the finality of a pile of wet rags.

Mark stood over it. He was gasping so hard that he feared he would lose consciousness and be blacked out at its feet when it woke up. He staggered to a nearby row of vans, all of them white, all of them, it seemed to him, equally dilapidated. He was beyond worrying about this one or that one, and simply chose the nearest. Inside, it stank of rotted meat, so horribly that for a moment he thought he was going to black out.

Then the dog's face smashed against the driver's side window and he hammered down the locks and scooted under the dashboard just as Ollie had told him.

The wiring forest was barely visible in the murky darkness. They'd forgotten that he'd need a flashlight. Outside, the dog roared, its claws clattering against the door, its tremendous bark, he suspected, carrying all the way to the 186th Precinct a mile away. He felt along the wires, trying to find the ones he needed, the ones attached to the starter key. Reaching around, he thought to locate the switch on the dash—and found his hand closing on a keyring.

Scrambling up off the floor, he yanked it from the socket, sat staring at it. Joy. Amazement. They were so sure that this place was impenetrable that they left the keys in these things.

When he inserted the key and turned it, he was rewarded by a clattering start. The dog seemed to know that this signaled its impending defeat and redoubled its efforts to get in. Mark guided the van toward the gate. He couldn't get out and cut the chain, not if he wanted to stay alive. So there was nothing for it but to press the pedal to the metal and pray.

Off they went, plunging van and roaring dog together across the slovenly lot. The gate shot at him, he threw his arms up, was hurled forward by the impact—and the whole fence went sagging down amid the wild clanging of alarm bells. He hadn't thought about an alarm. But why should he? Ollie hadn't said there would be one.

The thing was, there was nothing between the van and the street: the gate was under him now. He pressed the gas pedal and went out onto the ragged pavement. As a plane thundered by overhead, he sped off. The outraged dog dropped slowly but inexorably to the rear.

He'd never driven one of these things before and at first had some trouble controlling it and also coping with the tangled mass of blood and bandages on his hand. But he managed, he managed it all. Finally, he even managed to find the little diner where they waited, his sister and his mother. He looked at it, at the strange combination of warmth and—somehow—danger that flowed from its moist row of windows. Beyond them, he could see the shadow of a waitress moving back and forth, and the diners huddled in their booths.

He had thought that he would die for those he loved at the hands of Sal Bonacori. But that had been a fantasy, just a confused fantasy. This moment, though, was different. He felt nothing now but peace. He had the van. They would use it to take the equipment to Sim's. They would get in, they would attack the safe. But if Sim caught them—Uncle Sim—and Uncle Sim was dangerous to them, then things would go very wrong.

What would he do then? How would he act? As much as ever, he wanted his mother and his sister to live and be free of this. But he could no longer tell himself that he didn't care about his own life. He did care; he'd found that out in Sal Bonacori's basement. Sick or well, he wanted to taste all of life that he could. So very badly and with all the hunger of his young soul, he wanted to live.

CHAPTER 27

The van was filthy and it rattled and Kealy could feel cold street air coming up through the holes in the floor. She sat in the hard passenger's seat, huddled in her latest uniform, which was that of a nurse. Mark drove, and she was miserable about it because this was a stolen vehicle. If he was caught, he'd get a record. Not yet twenty, and a record.

Ollie and Lushawn and Allison and a quietly furious Roselle sat in the empty cavern behind them, propped against the hard walls of the interior. This had been one of the very worst days yet, involved with gathering equipment and enduring Ollie's paranoia about his parole officer, plus worrying about further attention from bounty hunting neighborhood people.

Somehow, they had reached this point: while Lushawn and Jo-Jo had bought or borrowed the various esoteric tools that Ollie insisted that he needed, she had spent the desolate afternoon hours listening to Roselle rage about the danger to Ollie if anything went wrong, and privately wracking her brains about how to get the whole impossible entourage into Sim's very secure apartment building.

They had evolved a decent enough plan. The only major unknown was whether or not the Osbornes had an alarm system in the apartment. Kealy had never noticed one, but that meant little.

She and Mark and Allison would go in. The only Davis who would commit this crime with them was, unfortunately, Ollie, because he had to do the safe. The others would remain innocently engaged in guard and spotting duties outside. Jo-Jo was already there, walking the neighborhood, using his practiced eye to spot any undercover activity. At exactly one A.M., he would call them on one of the three cell phones that Roselle had very unwillingly bought today on her overtaxed Visa card. Jo-Jo would give them a signal: He would either whine that he was tired and wanted to be picked up, or say that he was ready to paint the town. "Tired" was the word they wanted to hear. It would mean the opposite of what it said, that all was well and they could come ahead.

"Let's run through it," Ollie said as they crossed the Manhattan Bridge, at this late hour empty of incoming traffic. "Lushawn?"

"I sit on one of the benches on the park side of Fifth facing the building, so I can see Rick Berger at his desk. If he goes into the elevator, I phone Allison. If he makes a call to the outside, then I wait to hear from Momma."

"Ally?"

"I'm in the hall. If I get a call from Ollie, I watch the elevator. If it passes the fifth floor, I phone my mom and she tells you guys he's moving. You close down until we know where he is again and we're sure it's safe."

"Roselle?"

"I wait at the corner of Seventy-seventh. If I see anything from the precinct heading toward the building, I call Lushawn."

Mark said, "I apprentice the rip. That means that I give you what you ask me for, Ollie, control the pressure on the acetylene tank, watch your back, and keep everything as quiet as possible."

"The good part about cutting with a torch is it is the quietest way there is to peel steel. But that torch is gonna pop when we light it, and it's gonna hiss when it runs. You gotta keep the mixture real clean and the flame real tight. That's gonna work for us two ways, 'cause the best flame is the quietest."

"We went over that," Mark said, his voice brusque.

"You never operated a torch before, boy. You don't know what you're doing. So we're gonna go over it again and again."

His tone—soft, strong—communicated competence. In this, Kealy knew that Ollie had found his measure. He was expert at the crimes he loved. "It just feels so good, pulling that door off and getting at all the goodies in there," he had explained. "You get to peeling peters, it's a real addiction." He'd talked about the wonder of finding jewels, stocks and bonds, or—best of all—cold cash.

"Kealy?"

"I guard the Osborne's bedroom at the end of the hall. If I see any sign that they're stirring, I tap twice on the study door."

"How we do a bail, if it comes to that?"

Mark said, "You and I abandon our tools. We leave by going up to the roof, then down the outside fire escape on the back. I go to the corner of Seventy-fifth and Madison, you go to Seventy-sixth. We wait for the van."

"I go down the inside stairs with Mommy and out the service entrance. I wait on Seventy-seventh and Madison, Mommy on Seventy-seventh and Fifth."

"Mother and I take the subway home," Lushawn said. "Jo-Jo picks you-all up in the van."

"And he and I get let off at Grand Central. And that's the end of the Davis & Ryerson Pete Busting Company."

Which is exactly where Kealy thought they'd be within the hour—if they weren't caught first, that is. She and the kids would be going as far as they could in a stolen van that sounded like it had died and gone to jalopy heaven long ago. Nothing had been said about Ollie turning them in if they didn't get the money, and she certainly didn't intend to bring the matter up. "Let's continue," she said, "we haven't finished the run-through."

"What haven't we finished?" Ollie asked dubiously.

"What happens if we find what we're looking for!"

"Oh, yeah, if we hit the big seven-eleven. Okay, in *that* case, Mark taps twice on the study door. You come in, you take everything that's yours out of the safe and we roll the job up the same way, except I got my bearer bonds in my pocket instead of the thirty-eight dollars that's there now."

"In addition to," Mark said.

Not for the first time this evening, Kealy looked long at her son. There was a new, yet more disturbing expression on his face now: the vapid smile, almost, of a Buddha in ecstasy. She reached over and touched his injured hand, which he proceeded to yank away. What did he imagine, that he'd give her his AIDS? It had broken her heart that he'd chosen to tell only his father. But that was the way their life had been: the children were not as close to their mother as they were to their dad. Jimmy had been one of those encompassing people whose charisma used up so much space in his kids' lives that there wasn't as much room as there should be for another parent. Her inborn reserve only made this worse. It must be very hard for him to keep his secret from her now, but it must seem even more important to him to do so, because he wouldn't want her to feel a new anguish just after her husband's death.

Who did he think paid the medical bills that came pouring in? Who managed his care? Within the hour of Jimmy's telling her, she had been researching. She'd found the best AIDS doctors in the world. She'd learned everything there was to know about the disease and its treatment.

Jimmy hadn't wanted to face his son—neither his illness nor the sexual orientation that it implied. But she had sent him to Ithaca to give their son support, having first carefully briefed him and made sure that he would treat Marko with the compassion and love he deserved.

She feared for her boy's welfare, suffered for his unwillingness to share his agony with her. Didn't he understand that a mother's love is without conditions?

The cut worried her. In recent weeks, his immune system had declined somewhat. Even a minor infection could be fatal.

At once, a fierce and familiar thought intruded: *this* young man is going to be one of the cures; *this* young man is going to live. And back there in the dark, his sister with her blond hair as soft as sea foam, with her eyes of Venus and her moist, unabashed smile: she, also, will live and grow and thrive.

She barely heard Roselle talking to Jo-Jo, was barely aware that she said, "We're moving."

"Be sure that phone is on vibrate, Sister. Don't any of you have ringing phones."

"I don't know how to work these damn things. I hate 'em."

"Just get it right, Sister, that's what I'm telling you!"

"All right, you don't have to yell."

They went up FDR Drive to the Sixty-eighth Street exit. Kealy thought, *We're actually doing this impossible, dangerous thing, and it really is our last hope.*

She was so absorbed in these thoughts that she was shocked at how quickly they were passing 2122 Fifth with its cavernous maw of an entrance. It was her job to look over the situation, and she peered uneasily out the window. She thought that she might miss practically anything.

The familiar concrete cherubs still pranced up the heavy door frame, and—most importantly—sullen Rick sat behind the glass door at his big mahogany desk. His feet were up, the screen of his little TV glowing against his sound-asleep face.

"He's on his station," she said. "Sleeping."

They reached the corner of Seventy-sixth and Fifth. Mark began the turn.

Asleep or not, Rick was a danger that had to be dealt with. If there was an alarm on the service entrance on the Seventy-sixth Street side of the building, he would have to be distracted long enough for them to figure out how to get past it and into the freight elevator. Even if they made it to the elevator, her job still wasn't over. Then she had to keep him talking until the faint but telltale sound of its motor stopped.

"Ready, Mom?" Mark squeezed her hand.

"Ready, son."

"Love you, Mommy." Allison kissed her mother's cheek.

"Love you guys."

They went up Madison and turned onto Seventy-seventh. This was the drop run, and she prepared to get out of the vehicle.

This was where the nurse's uniform came in. She would enter by the front, masquerading as an RN sent to render aid to Menton Jones, an elderly socialite whom she had known since he'd chaperoned at the DAR tea dances of her childhood. Mr. Jones was a binge drinker, and nurses were routinely called when he was on a bender.

At the corner, Mark stopped. Nobody spoke except Kealy, who whispered in a voice only she could hear, "God, go with my kids."

Appearing out of nowhere, Jo-Jo took Mark's place behind the wheel as Kealy stepped onto the sidewalk. Mark slid into the passenger seat.

She got out into the cool, gusty night and started walking toward the building. The van pulled past her, quickly disappearing around the corner where it would let off the rest of the inside team with all their equipment.

She had to time herself carefully so that she would be in the lobby distracting Rick at the right moment. She looked at her watch. Ollie claimed that the lock would pick in two minutes.

Right now, the main risk was that a passing police patrol would spot the group with the big acetylene and oxygen tanks. If that happened, they'd be arrested for certain. It was a huge danger: Ollie would go back in for possession of burglar tools.

Again, she glanced at her watch. A minute and a half. Picking the lock would not break it. Once they were in the freight elevator, there would be no evidence of their entrance, not even if the alarm was going off. As long as the elevator was returned before Rick got down there, he wouldn't find anything amiss. He'd assume that the system had falsed. At least, that was their hope.

She arrived at the door, rang the buzzer. He stirred, but only a little. Maybe they should have just left him alone. Maybe she should do that now, just abandon this part of the plan and go in with the others. "It's like what you learn in Rangers," Ollie had said, "keep executing, no matter what hell breaks loose. Keep executing until you complete your task." When Roselle had explained that he'd been decorated in Vietnam, he'd growled so dangerously that she'd shut right up.

So Kealy kept executing, which meant hitting the buzzer again. Rick's eyes were open, but staring straight into the small TV. She tapped on the glass, plastering a nervous smile on her face.

He leaped up so fast that his chair went sailing back toward the elevator bank. Kealy could see by the lights that the three passenger cars were in the lobby, the freight car in the basement. One of the passenger cars was open.

"Yeah," Rick said, opening the door. "What?"

"We got a call for Menton."

"Oh, brother. Him." He opened the door wider. "Be my guest, but please listen to me, don't let him come down here in his pajamas, okay? He does that—have you been here before?"

"Yeah."

" 'Cause I seen you. It's been what—a while?"

She broadened her smile. "I told 'em last time was it for me. But I need the money."

"Yeah, I bet it's golden time, isn't it?"

"Triple gold with an afterhours bonus. Just if I can keep my butt away from the raunchy old creep." She saw the freight elevator begin to move. "When's the last call on him?"

"Oh, Jeez—three, four months. He's been better since his wife croaked, actually."

"She used to lock him in that back bedroom and call us." They were passing three. "How's it work now?"

He shrugged. "Beats me. He musta called you himself."

"Well, that's a good sign. That means he's not totally gone. You know, this type of alky almost always drinks himself to death. Too bad he won't do AA."

He'd lost interest. But the elevator hadn't come down yet, so she had to keep executing. She looked over his shoulder. "Oh, what's that?"

"A movie. Some shit."

"*The Roman Spring of Mrs. Stone!* Oh, I love that! I'm gonna put on the TV as soon as I get up there. Vivien Leigh and Lotte Lenya."

"Did a good job on me, it was puttin' me to sleep. I went to dinner, got a big veal chop. Heavy food means heavy sleep." He burped, then casually turned toward the back of the lobby.

Of course—he was getting his damn chair! He'd see that elevator moving for sure, he had to. Her mind froze—and then she acted, did the only thing she could think to do, she kicked her legs out from under herself and crashed heavily to the floor.

"Jesus, lady!"

"It's the goddamn shoe," she said, picking herself up. She'd hit hard, and her left thigh was singing. He helped her to her feet. "Please forgive me," she said.

"You sure you're okay?"

"I need a new heel is all."

"Well, yeah, these floors are slick. You don't wanta . . . you're sober, now, aren't you?"

"People who work with alkys tend to be real dry. We have a horror of it."

The freight elevator finally reached the basement. Without another word, she walked straight into one of the passenger lifts. "Go up to seventeen," he called behind her. "I'll let you in."

That she did not need. "I've got the service's key."

He didn't react, but as the doors closed she silently cursed herself for forgetting something so basic. Did Menton's nursing service actually have a key to his apartment? God only knew. But Rick didn't appear suspicious. Unless he was calling the police right now.

And then she realized that she'd made yet another terrible mistake. The elevator was on its way to the twenty-first floor, not the seventeenth where Menton lived. Without thinking, she'd pushed Sim's button. The way it had been planned, she was to walk up from seventeen.

It was too late to do anything about it now. Their safety, their future—in the end even their lives—depended at this moment entirely on *The Roman Spring of Mrs. Stone*.

CHAPTER 28

All Kealy could think to do was send the car back down to seventeen and hope that Rick would assume she'd pushed the wrong button. It wasn't an awful bet: who'd suspect a dowdy old nurse who knew all of Menton's details of being anything other than what she seemed?

When the elevator opened, Allison came straight into her arms. "I have to just *stand here?*" She gestured at the ornate hallway.

"We need you here, honey."

Behind them, Ollie was working on the Osbornes' lock.

"With no place to hide?"

As she tried to comfort her poor kid, Kealy saw that there was yet another flaw in their plan. What if Rick decided to come up in the freight elevator for some reason? Allison wouldn't see it coming, not if she was watching for the front car.

"Wait a minute." Disentangling herself from her daughter, she went to the brown steel door that led to the service foyer, drew it open. "You wait here with your back against this door. You can watch all the elevators from here."

"What about the apartments? What if somebody comes out?"

"Allison, there are only two apartments to worry about, and the Steens—you know old Margie and Walt—they've been drunk for fifty years. They don't come out at night."

"But what if Sim comes out?"

"We'll see him inside first."

"Not if he goes through the kitchen, you won't."

Allison wasn't thinking straight. "He's in the master bedroom asleep, so he has to come down the hall past me if he's going to get into the kitchen." She gave her another hug.

"I'm scared of him, Mommy."

"We have to keep an open mind. He might not be planning to cash those bonds."

"Then why are we here?"

"To get our property."

"I think this is real dangerous, more than the airport, more than the office, more even than Sal's."

The family had to do this. They could not abandon their only chance. "You stay here and do your part. We'll be back."

Allison grabbed her hands as if with a vise. "If you don't come back, if it goes all horrible—"

There was a faint crunching sound from where Ollie was working. "We're ready," Mark said softly.

"Now, listen up. I'm gonna push this door open. When I do, if we hear anything sounds like an alarm, we do the bail." He looked from face to face. "We stay calm, but we move fast."

Hissing against the carpet, the door went back.

Allison had scrunched her eyes closed. Kealy found that she was holding her breath.

Ollie disappeared into the dark apartment, was gone what seemed like a long time. Was it too long? What if he was captured, they hadn't thought of that. "Christ," she whispered.

Then he reappeared. "Move it in," he said, "we got a clean entry." Sim relied on the building's security—and with reason. But he hadn't counted on an intruder with Kealy's intimate knowledge of how things worked around here.

It was hard to leave scared little Allison, but she had to do it.

She entered the familiar Osborne front hall with its beige striped wallpaper and that appalling Spanish loveseat that Lanette so adored. Original or not, it might as well be a bad fake. It was a baroque monstrosity fit only for the love of beasts. Lanette, for all her charm, was that most foolhardy of creatures, a self-decorator. Of course, Kealy had decorated Jimmy's office, but she had taste.

To the right were the dining room and kitchen. Straight ahead was a forty-foot living room overlooking the park. To the left was a hallway that led, in this case, first to the study, then to the library and a corner sitting room. The hall then made a turn, and the door of the master bedroom suite was set into the facing

corner. Beyond it were two more doors leading into a guest bedroom and what Lanette called her sewing room, although she did
not sew. They played cards in the sewing room so that Bitsy could
smoke without infuriating Sim, who detested a habit he been compelled to abandon by his doctor. They smoked and drank and
laughed their heads off in there, as a matter of fact. Thousands
could change hands in those bridge games, and there could be
catfights. Outright hair pulling, if Julia was no-bid by Lanette or
something.

She snapped herself back to reality. Because there was a problem. The door to the master bedroom was closed, which meant that
she couldn't actually watch them. If they woke up, she would have
no warning until they appeared.

She wondered if Ollie had meant that she was to open it.
Should she? It struck her as being terribly dangerous. But *should*
she?

Roselle had totally refused to allow them to go armed. "Nobody's got a permit, nobody's gonna carry. It's bad enough these
fool men keep bringing pieces into this house." She had glared at
Jo-Jo and Ollie. "You say you're worried about the paroles coming after you, Brother. But you let a damn kid have a gun."

From the way Ollie had reacted, Kealy had concluded that
there were reasons a gun was needed in the house that he wasn't
telling anybody. She didn't ask, either. Better to be curious than to
know, she thought. But she surely wished they had a gun, now.

There came from behind the closed door of the study a loud
scraping sound, followed by a rumble that changed quickly to a
hiss as if of steam pipes. The so-called silent way of cutting into a
safe made a hell of a lot of noise, especially in the quiet of the
night. They had hollow doors, also, another ghastly feature of
the Osborne establishment. Kealy would never have allowed hollow doors.

She went to the study. They had to do something about that
noise; it was way too loud. Should she enter? If she tapped,
they'd think it was an alert and shut the thing down. Then the
whole popping, rumbling, hissing sequence would have to be

repeated. In one quick movement, she slipped into the room.

The light of the torch was incredible, like a flashbulb that didn't burn out. And the noise was incredible, too—it was actually shaking the room.

She went closer to them. Mark, crouching over the tanks, did not hear her. Ollie, behind his welder's mask and intent on a white-hot spot on the door of the safe, was totally concentrated on his work. If she so much as put a hand on one of their backs, there was liable to be a slip. She hovered behind the little tableau, two shadowy figures hunched over a particle of the sun. Finally, she returned to the hall.

She went to the front door, opened it, and looked out. Allison waved, tried to smile. Then she heard another sound, one that sent a wave of terror right through her. *Keep your cool, girl,* she told herself as she retreated to the apartment.

The thing was, she could not be sure where the toilet had flushed, here or at the Steens. She'd been in exactly the wrong spot to determine that. Should she go back and listen at the bedroom door, or ask Allison if she'd heard it?

No matter what happened, she decided that she couldn't take her eyes off that bedroom door. If he came out, she was going to have to—what? They'd all just pile out and hope for the best.

Unless, of course, she departed from the plan. But she was not going to depart from the plan. She was not going to pick up the grotesque faux jade Buddha that had been such an object of mirth when it had appeared on Lanette's hall table last year. She was not going to do that, and she was not going to take the Buddha with her down the hall, and—

She heard music. *Music!* Had they lost their minds, they were playing Puccini on Sim's stereo!

Her small hairs tickled as if they had been brushed by a stranger's hand. Ollie and Mark weren't playing the music. It was coming from the bedroom.

Without another thought, she got a dining chair and the Buddha—which turned out not to be jade at all, but some sort of glazed pottery affair, lighter than it looked.

She stationed herself on the chair with the statuette high over her head. Sim must be using music to cover the annoying hiss, not realizing how unusual it actually was. He must have gone into the bathroom to try to see if it involved the plumbing.

She was supposed to alert them, tap twice on that door. A problem like this was supposed to mean that everything got called off. But now, in the moment, she experienced her depth of commitment to the plan. It was *not* going to be called off. They were getting in that darned safe. She hoped to God that she wouldn't hurt Sim seriously, that was all, especially if he wasn't guilty of anything. She'd never knocked anybody out before, and she had no idea how hard she should hit him. She certainly didn't want to injure him permanently or, God forbid, kill him. If she killed him, she thought she would die herself.

The door opened and Sim stepped into the hallway. He was much more stooped than he appeared during the day, his hair a white corona.

As she brought down the Buddha, he detected the movement and lunged away. In that moment their eyes met, and she almost screamed, the hate that she saw there was so intense.

He was surprised, he was confused, he probably wasn't even sure who he was seeing. But he was not innocent. That face was twisted with the hatred of a guilty man.

This time when she swung the Buddha, it struck the right side of his head with the dull sound of a melon hitting a kitchen floor.

She hadn't realized that he would collapse this completely or make such a resounding thud when he hit the floor.

She went down to him. There wasn't any blood, but his face was bright red.

Lanette, dear God, she must have been waked up by this.

Kealy raced into the bedroom. Lanette was snoring softly. She was unable to avoid noticing that without her slides and inserts, Lanette had practically no natural hair at all. Kealy turned off the radio. Then she went back to Sim. He was out, his lips slack, his eyes closed. He was breathing rather roughly, she thought. Was that a good sign or a bad one?

Heat came roaring into her cheeks. Was Sim really the enemy, this man who had been her husband's most trusted friend for all these years?

The hissing of the torch filled the silence. How long had they been in there, anyway? Ollie had estimated thirty minutes, based on the fact that the safe was a Bechmann identical to Jimmy's. "Good steel," he'd said. "Good mechanism." He'd paused for effect. "Half an hour."

She went to the living room to get enough outside light to read her watch.

They had been in there just seven minutes. A whole age, an eon, had passed in that short time. She hurried back to Sim. His breathing sounded awful. Was this a death rattle?

A dreadful symphony of hissing acetylene and hoarse, slow breathing filled the air. Ten minutes passed, then fifteen. You didn't stay knocked out forever. Boxers got up in minutes. But surely boxers and sixty-year-old lawyers weren't the same. She waited, pacing.

Sim said, "Oh," in a loud, clear tone. She backed toward the living room, hoping that she would be invisible in the dark. But then Sim began to snore. He'd slid from unconsciousness into sleep.

It took three full rings for her to realize that her phone was vibrating. She lunged into the deep side pocket of the uniform and pulled it out. "Kealy," she whispered.

It was Lushawn. "Momma says there's a car from the precinct coming my way."

Kealy dared barely whisper in reply, given that Sim was only sleeping and either he or Lanette could wake up at any moment. "You see it?"

"Not yet. Yeah. Now I do. Look, I'm gonna leave the line open. If they take me in, you'll hear."

Lushawn was the only human being the cops were likely to see at this hour, and she was black. Roselle could watch from the shadows of a doorway, but Lushawn, if she was to keep an eye on Rick, had no such option. Until the moment she heard the clank of the phone, still open, being put down, and then the voice of the police officer who was coming over to Lushawn, Kealy had not considered this problem. None of them had.

Helpless, Kealy listened.

Cop: "You live around here?"

Lushawn: "Nossir, I don't, sir."

Cop: "You got a place to go?"

"Ah'm hidin' from mah ole man," Lushawn's voice said, her accent ridiculously broad.

"Well, you better hide from him somewhere else, not around here."

"Yessir." It was almost *yowsah*. Kealy wanted to warn her not to lay it on too thick. A moment later, she said in her usual voice, "I'm walking north on the park side of Fifth. They're going the other way. I can't stop, but Rick's not asleep, he's been watching that damn TV show ever since you went in." She hung up, and Kealy thrust her own phone back in her pocket.

God's very curse on *The Roman Spring of Mrs. Stone*.

CHAPTER 29

J esus Christ, Mother," Mark whispered. She almost jumped halfway down the hall. As quiet as it was, she was so concentrated on watching Sim that she hadn't even heard Mark come out.

"You were supposed to signal me, remember? Tap on the door?"

Ollie appeared, saw Sim. "What the shit?"

"I hit him."

"You're a bigger fool than I thought." Ollie went to him, leaned over, and came up with something that Kealy had not seen in Sim's hand: a dark blue pistol, small and streamlined and ugly. "We better get rid of this, in case he comes to."

"Take it," Mark said.

"Not in my van, no way! Leave it here."

"Okay, so let's have a look in the safe."

"It's *opened?*"

" 'Course it's opened, Mother. We did a good rip, real sweet."

"Full of all kinds of shit," Ollie said happily. "Only that guy's head's gonna be hurting enough to wake him up real soon. He's gonna raise a lot of hell, you know it."

The study was dark and reeked of chemical smoke. Ollie gave her his flashlight, and she shone it into the packed interior of the safe. Immediately, she saw something familiar, a distinctive manila portfolio. She took it out, fumbled it opened. "My bonds," she said. "My damn bearer bonds!" She actually hugged them to her.

Anything else here that was theirs? Nothing apparent—but no, look, a folded mass of computer paper, stuffed in behind the bonds. She drew it out, started to unfold it.

"Sim," a female voice called in the distance.

"Lanette," Kealy whispered.

It seemed only an instant later that the four of them were

racing down the interior fire escape, trying their best to maintain what silence they could.

They reached the street without incident. Sim was about to discover the robbery and this neighborhood was going to fill with cops, and they knew they had to hurry. But instead of splitting up like they were supposed to, deep instinct kept them together. Nobody had really expected this to work as well as it had, and the flush of success made them less cautious.

Even Ollie relaxed his vigilance a little once he could no longer be connected with the safe. When they reached Roselle, he clapped his big hands down on both of her shoulders. "We're rich, Sister, just as legal as it gets."

Jo-Jo let out a yell that briefly filled the wee hours' silence. They got in the van. The police would trace the safecracking equipment left in Sim's study. Kealy decided not to even ask Ollie why he wasn't worried about it.

At her instructions, Jo-Jo drove up to Eighty-sixth Street, then turned and went slowly down Fifth until he found a very annoyed Lushawn hanging back in the shadowy portico of the Metropolitan Museum.

"We got the money," Jo-Jo said as she came into the van, scrambling around her mother and into the bay.

Almost casually, Kealy had given Ollie the bonds that were so very important to the Davis family. She was getting more interested in these other papers.

"Folks," she said. "There's something very weird here, and I need ideas." There came silence. "Why would Simon Osborne think that the master list of space holders in the ministorage warehouse we own be important?" She held it up. "This wasn't even in our safe. But it ended up in his."

Number 455 was a big old property on the Brooklyn waterfront near the Bush Terminal. Jimmy had bought it at a tax auction in 1986 for sixty thousand dollars. He had divided the fourteen-story structure into three hundred small storage units and they had been making a profit on it ever since.

"He's got something in there," Ollie said. "Something he's nervous about."

She looked, shining the flashlight along the list of names. "Osborne, Simon, C-1121 A-B. It's one of the doubles on the eleventh floor."

"Is this the only copy of that record?"

"Well, there'd be one on the computer at the office, I'm sure."

"He can erase that. So maybe he's got something in there he doesn't want to see involved in probate. Maybe he trying to make that warehouse just disappear for a little while."

"Nobody's going into his storage area because Jimmy died. That's not how probate works."

"He's in it, Kealy. He's your man."

"I don't know what to think. But we have to look in this space, for certain."

Jo-Jo tooted the horn. "I know a club where we can celebrate! And I'm gonna get me a GTO, man!"

Roselle said, "You're gonna get an education first, a Jeep-O second, if at all."

"GTO, Momma. G-T-O! There's no car called a Jeep-O."

"Well, you aren't getting a fancy car, no way. You take me home now, boy. I've got a chance to get to bed early for once, and after this mess, I need it." It was three A.M., hours before she usually turned in.

"Come on, Sister, think! That guy back there's gonna be fighting mad and tiger-dangerous soon's he sees his safe's been cracked." He regarded Kealy. "I got to explain you something you might not be getting. You want to find out what he has in your warehouse, you've got to go in there, and the time you've got to do that is right now."

"It's the middle of the night."

"He know his safe's open, and he know what's gone. You don't move fast, he gonna get to that warehouse before you do. He's getting his act together right now, you can be sure of it."

"Kids?"

"We do it," Mark said.

"I agree, Mommy."

"You know how to open the place up? 'Cause I could pick you in."

Roselle exploded. "Ollie, *no!* We're finished with this!"

"Hush up, now, Sister! What kinda locks?"

"It's got an electronic locking system. I have the codes on my emergency page." She took her phone directory out of her purse and began flipping the pages, looking for the emergency section at the back. "We shouldn't have a problem."

"But then you've gotta open this guy's space. What kinda lock does he have?"

Roselle said, "I'm telling you, you're not breaking any more locks tonight!"

"I just want to give 'em a few pointers."

"They're padlocked. All the units."

"You got master keys?"

"No."

"Well, I could—"

"Ollie, I told you no!"

"How're they gonna get in there without me? How're they gonna do that? What's the address, Fifth Avenue?"

"It's on the Bush Terminal dock."

"See, Roselle? We can't just leave these folks out there. That's the far side of the damn moon."

Roselle turned to Kealy. "If this guy's on his way there, it's just plain crazy to do what you're doing. I don't want my brother in there, he'll get killed, I just know it!"

"We can go alone."

"You can get killed alone, too," Roselle said. "You have your money now. My advice is to run."

"We should've taken his pistol from him," Mark said.

Kealy was going deeper into shock about Sim. If it had just been the bonds, she might have believed that he was simply being greedy. But this list, this was damned strange. She could not think of a single reason for him to hide a list that was legitimate.

"Kealy?"

"Yes, Ollie?"

"This is what we're gonna do. We're gonna leave you off. Then we're gonna take a long trip around the block. We'll be back in ten minutes to get you outta there."

"What if it takes more time?"

"If things look quiet, we'll do it again. Two times, that's it."

"You're not worried about spending all this time in a stolen van?"

"Yeah, I'm worried."

After that, Ollie was silent for some time. They went down the long, empty avenues of Manhattan, moving toward the Brooklyn Bridge. "Jo-Jo, you go over to the BQE. Take the Sunset Park exit," he finally said.

"Why do you know where Bush Terminal is, Ollie?" Allison asked.

"I've been over that way a few times."

Of course he had. The district was a tomb at night, a tomb that was probably full of safes to crack and locks to pick.

"You've been so wonderful to us, all of you," Kealy said.

"You're a brave woman, Kealy Ryerson," Roselle said. "You're good people."

Ollie looked hard at Kealy. There were no words between them, not across that gulf. But his face was no longer sculpted by anger. He reached back, offering his hand. She took it. "Do me a favor, Fifth Avenue. Try not to get yourself killed."

"I've been trying not to for days!"

His hand went tight, then slipped away.

Lushawn and Allison sat arm in arm, their heads touching, their long legs stretched out before them.

Mark said, "I want the bolt cutter."

"And could we borrow some cash? If we don't connect up again—"

"Mommy, we're *going* to connect up!"

"In the unlikely event that we don't, we'll need cash."

Roselle burst out laughing. "How much do you want? Because we don't have a whole lot—not of cash."

They found another sixty dollars in their pockets and gave thirty to Kealy.

"I want to tell you, you've been heroes," she said. "You saved our lives."

"Everybody saved everybody's lives," Ollie said, patting the pocket where he had his portion of the bonds. "That the fact."

"Kealy, if this is it, when will we hear from you?"

"Sometime, Roselle."

"You mean never, don't you, Mrs. Ryerson? Because I don't see why you can stop running."

"If we find an answer, we might be fine, Lushawn."

"Might be," Mark said.

Allison and Lushawn drew close together. They were two kittens cuddling in the corner of a box, their young eyes opened wide by the hard world.

CHAPTER 30

I
t was a bleak, bleak place, a long row of dark, hulking warehouses without a single light showing. Many of them were
empty, and some were abandoned. Four fifty-five looked different from the ones around it, much cleaner and better cared for.
The sign, METRO STORAGE, was even lit.

"Remember," Ollie said, "ten minutes, then ten more."

"Take my kids with you."

"Mommy, no way!"

"I'm sorry, Mom, but that—"

"Take them!"

Even before the van was stopped, Mark had jumped out.

Allison said, "There's no way, Mommy." She crawled to the
back of the van, also jumped to the street.

Kealy could not help but feel pride. But she knew how stupid
they were being. She got out of the van. "This is a life-or-death
thing," she said. "You're too young to take the chance."

The van sped off, and at once the silence became very deep.

"Don't just stand there, Mother. Sim could be on his way."

She went to the door panel. What if they couldn't get in? Actually, maybe it would be better. They'd wait for the Davises to come
back and it would all be over. But where would they sleep, under a
damn bridge or something? She decided not to think about it.
What mattered right now was putting 4-9-4-6-6-1 into the keypad.

There was a soft whining noise, then the door clicked.

The small office on the first floor contained the electronic control panel that opened and closed the fire doors, a metal desk with
a coffeemaker and a phone on it—not much. The warehouse supervisor was a retired bus driver, as Kealy recalled. She did not
remember his name.

"Everything's turned off," Allison said, moving toward a
light switch.

"Leave it that way," Kealy said. She wondered if the fire doors were opened or closed. She had not the faintest idea how to use the control panel.

Mark called from across the wide hallway. "I've got the elevator working."

It wasn't automatic, but he managed to run it fairly well. Still, it took three tries before they were close enough to the eleventh floor to get the door to slide open, and then they had a three-foot drop.

"Give me that," Allison said, taking the tiller from him. She proved to be coordinated enough to get the thing to a more reasonable position.

They looked out into the long corridor, which was lined with dark green metal doors on both sides. Except for the code lights— single bulbs at the end of each corridor and lit EXIT signs—the warehouse was dark. It was possible to see ahead, but not all the way to the end.

They ventured out, Mark at the lead. It wasn't hard to find Sim's space.

"Okay," Allison said, "do the deed."

He attacked the hasp of Sim's padlock with the bolt cutter, giving it the kind of twist that Ollie had explained would sink it into the hard metal. "Shit!" The bolt cutter went clanging down the dimly lit corridor. He picked it up, returned to the lock.

"Jesus," Allison said, and Kealy saw that her son's bandaged hand was soaking with blood. Instinctively, she reached out to him.

"Don't touch it!"

"You need it re-dressed." She tried again.

He jumped back. "No!"

The time for this was ended. She said, "I know."

He stood as still as a surprised rabbit.

"I'm your mother, Marko. Of course I know!"

"Know what, Mommy?"

"Your brother's HIV positive."

Surprise made his breath hiss. "Mother—"

"HIV *positive?* Jesus, Mark—you're—you . . ." Allison's voice trailed off.

Mark's head dropped, his shoulders began shaking. His dark sobs filled the silent space. "How long have you known?"

"Your father hung up the phone and told me. I did all the research. I got you your doctor. Oh, honey, I love you so!" She tried to embrace him. He drew back.

"From the beginning, then?"

"Of course. And of course I still love you, and of course I'm going to dress that hand. Now come here!" This time, he moved toward her. "A cut is mother's business."

She brought out all she had, which was a purse pack of Kleenex. She and Allison unwrapped the bandages while Mark wept silently. She could imagine his distress and thought it best to ignore it. So he would learn a little something about mother love.

The wound was quite clean, and she was able to staunch the bleeding fairly effectively.

He said, "You have no way to wash, remember that."

"Mark, I want you to understand something. If I get it on me, I'll survive. I have no open wounds. And to tell you the truth, if I could heal you by drinking it, I would drink it."

"Oh, God, Mom!"

The next attempt to hug him succeeded. "We'll fight it together," she said. This had not been the time or the place, but it had to come eventually.

"We all will," Allison said. "What's your count?"

"Low. A little bump recently. I need to get my meds."

"His count is very hopeful. And we're going to begin a new regimen next month. He's going to survive to a cure, Allison. Momma says."

In the darkest part of this terrible night, the three of them held each other. Then, without speaking, or needing to, they began to work as one: Kealy and Allison took the bolt cutter. They attacked the lock with it once more. Each of them held one of its arms, each of them pushed with all the strength she possessed. Mark added what effort he could.

The arms of the cutter bowed, the hasp resisted, the moment began to wear itself out. "It's not—" Allison said.

They stopped. They rearranged themselves to see if they could gain greater pressure by each pushing with both hands.

This time, the hasp finally lost the battle it had been designed to win, giving way with a brisk snap. The lock body clattered to the floor.

Smoothly, quickly, Mark reached down with his good hand and grasped the handle on the bottom of the rolling door. "Here we go," he said, and lifted it on screaming bearings.

Allison gasped, put her hands to her cheeks. Mark laughed, a bitter, angry bark. Kealy thought that she wouldn't cry out, but she did, she screamed out her rage and bitter disappointment.

They all recognized Granny Osborne's fabulous collection of Mission furniture that Lanette had so detested.

"We've found the furniture his wife thinks she made him sell."

"There's something else," Mark said, "or that sheet wouldn't have been in his safe."

"What're these doing here?" Allison asked. She had picked up a small cardboard box. "One, two . . ." She looked up at her mother. "Eleven keys."

"Sim doesn't own but this one space."

"Let's see here," Kealy said. She took a couple of them in her hand. "All GPMs. Like this lock. This is a GPM."

"It's been six minutes," Allison said.

"These are keys to other spaces."

Kealy went to the one next door. It had a Schlage lock. The one beyond that was a GPM, though. She tried a key, then another, then a third. The third key went in, but it wouldn't turn.

"So we each take four keys and go space to space, try every GPM lock that we find."

"Mom, that isn't brilliant."

She put her arm around Mark's shoulder. She had never felt so close to her kids, to him. A wall had fallen tonight. "Why not, honey?"

"We have to try all twelve keys on every lock. That's the only way."

"Plus there is no way I'm going to be alone in here," Allison interjected. "I'm going with somebody."

"So we do it together."

They each took four keys, found GPM locks on nearby carrels and tried them. Then they rotated keys, then went to the next three GPM locks they could find.

Initially, it had been tomb-silent in the warehouse, but there were occasional deep clangs now. God only knew what they were, probably something to do with the heat, which was kept at a low, clammy temperature—it felt like about fifty.

"Nine minutes, folks! They'll be making the first pass."

Kealy made a decision. "We keep going. This is too important."

"But—"

She and Kealy exchanged another handful of keys.

"I need some," Mark called. He was far down toward the end of the hall. Allison went and exchanged with him.

When she came back, the two of them started on new locks. "You didn't know about him, Allison? He didn't tell you, either?"

"Nope."

"Are you surprised?"

"Yep."

"Don't think less of him. He adores you, you know. He's always talking about you, asking about you."

"Mommy, I would never! I mean, *never!* I love my brother totally. I'll love him forever. In a way, the fact that he's gay and coping with AIDS makes me love him more—cherish him more."

Mark came trotting up. "I thought I had one. No cigar, though."

On Kealy's eleventh lock, one of the keys not only slid in, it turned. "Oh, Jesus," she said, "Jesus, *I* have one."

They gathered close. Triumph singing in her blood, Kealy took the lock off the door.

Boxes. Boxes all the way to the ceiling, two dozen or more of them. Each one had a stamped serial number on it and a printed count. All the counts were the same, 105. A hundred and five of whatever was inside.

She tried to pull at one of them, but the fronts were flush and the carrel was packed. Mark tried, same result. So she tore at them with a key, digging in one of the boxes until she had a mouse hole. She put her fingers in.

"Careful, Mommy!"

"It feels like little cases." She found an edge, pulled on it. "It's plastic cards in cellophane."

She managed to pull on one, and one of the boxes slid out through the hole. The three of them stared down at the cards, then up at one another. Mark laughed nervously. "I guess these are Sal Bonacori's stolen phone cards."

"I guess."

"God damn it," he yelled. He kicked the door of one of the spaces, the clang echoing off down the hall, echoing and coming back.

"Your father would never do this," she said.

Mark's eyes were tearing. "I mean, this is so perfect! The FBI thinks that these things are already sold. The crime's been committed. But Sim just bled a few out into the public to generate the complaints. Then he could come along and sell them later without any risk. The FBI would expect complaints to come in for a couple of years, maybe. They'd never realize that most of the cards were being moved for the first time *after* Bonacori was burned down."

Allison added, "And he was keeping them here in spaces owned by Daddy. That's why he wanted the list—so that he could keep them from getting found in probate."

Mark turned on his mother, his eyes gleaming wet in the faint light. "Did Uncle Sim kill Dad? Do you think?"

"It's possible, Mark."

"If Dad knew about this at all, then it had to be something like that. That's what the lunch with Mr. McGarrigle would have been about. Daddy was turning in a crook—Sim, who has been his partner and friend for most of his life. He tells McGarrigle, then he warns us. Then he's shot."

"And we're in danger because we actually own the cards, only we didn't know it. We've got to be killed, too, all three of us. That way the estate goes to the state. Sim can buy the chattel at auction on the courthouse steps—including these cards. And you know what? Then it becomes legal. No matter where the cards came from, he's a bona fide purchaser. Untouchable."

Kealy opened her cell phone. However the cards had gotten here, Sal Bonacori had the right to know about them immediately. He was headed for the federal pen because of these things. But the cell phone did not work, not in the middle of a huge old masonry building with ten-foot-thick outer walls. They built these warehouses like this in the old days so that any fire would be confined to a single structure.

They went down to the ground-floor office. Kealy called Bonacori on the desk phone.

Three rings, then a voice muffled by sleep: "Yeah?"

"It's Kealy Ryerson. I've found your phone cards."

"Whosit?"

"Kealy Ryerson. I've found your missing phone cards. They are definitely not sold, and you can prove that now."

There was a sound of surprise, then a series of grunts has he struggled harder to wake up.

"Where are you, Kealy Ryerson?"

"In my husband's warehouse."

"Jesus Christ, you're right where the cards are? Right now?"

"Warehouse 455 on the Bush Terminal docks."

"That's ten blocks from here. Ten damn years for ten damn blocks."

"You know how to find it?"

"I grew up on them docks, Sister. You'll see me in a few minutes. You okay in there, you got a piece?"

"No piece. But we're fine, it's very quiet."

"Look, I'll be there in ten minutes. Give me ten." With that, he hung up.

It was time for the Davises to make their second pass.

"They're late," Mark commented, looking out the office window.

Nobody replied.

Soon a sleek black Cadillac pulled up, ghosting along beside the ancient trolley tracks that passed before the long row of warehouses. Kealy watched it come in the moonlight.

"It's Mr. Bonacori," Allison said.

"I think you're right."

They had trouble letting him in, because she had no idea how to deactivate the electronic locking system from the inside. So it took a while, but in the end Mark and Allison figured it out and the locks snapped open.

Even as he was coming in, Kealy knew that something was very wrong. This man was slim in the dark, slim and tall.

"Get back," she said to her kids, stepping in front of them. They stood as still as two young rabbits. She stepped forward, moving slowly toward the man with the gun. "Hello, Sim," she said.

CHAPTER 31

L ooks like Osborne's car," Henny said.

"It is."

"This is fascinating."

"Fascinating indeed, Chief."

As Osborne's car slid up to the warehouse, the van that had been circling the block came closer to where Henny and Detective Malone waited in their dilapidated Chevy. "Pass number three," Malone said.

"Want to toss it?"

"We need to stay with Sim."

"Let him get inside and get cooking. He'll be all the more delighted to see us."

Malone jammed her foot down on the gas and the car sped forward into the path of the van. The van jammed on its brakes, slid to one side, and came rocking to a stop in a cloud of dust.

Henny piled out, shield in one hand and pistol in the other. "Freeze!" he yelled. "Police!"

From inside the van he heard a male voice say, "Aw, *shit!*"

He didn't move, just stayed there with his gun pointed directly at the driver's side window. The silence from within spoke eloquently of what was going on in there. He'd order them all down soon enough. Let 'em cook a little bit. Let 'em wait for it.

He was desperate for a break on the case, because if Kealy didn't come in she wasn't going to last much longer, no matter how much damn-fool luck she had.

He'd put this warehouse under surveillance not on the theory that he would find her here, but because Detective Malone, who had penetrated Ryerson & Osborne some weeks ago, had concluded that it was important based on the fact that Osborne had erased all record of it from the database on Jimmy's computer.

Tonight he was here personally because last night's stakeout had reported activity. The videotape showed two unidentified Caucasian males attempting to enter, but backing off when they could not get past the alarm system.

The people in the van were now talking, frantically whispering to each other. They'd cooked long enough: it was time to pop them out of the oven. "Okay, get ready to exit the vehicle! *Do not* open the passenger's door, *do not* open the driver's door. I want everybody coming out the back where I can see you."

The rear door opened.

"Keep your hands where I can see them. Come on down, please."

The most unlikely assemblage of blacks he had seen in a while came struggling down to the pavement.

"So, who have we here?"

A big, fat black lady stood beside her boyfriend or husband or whatever. With them were two teenagers with their knees literally knocking together and their lips so dry they looked like withered orange peels.

"So, you folks work for Simon Osborne? You here to pick something up for him?" They didn't reply, not unexpectedly. "Driver's license," Henny continued briskly, speaking to the driver. Then he went over and kicked on the the van's brake lights a couple of times. "You got a taillight out, you know that? I can't allow this vehicle on the public streets."

Before the man could reply, Henny almost lost interest in him altogether. Another car had just pulled up to the warehouse, and it was a surprising one.

He was beginning to get excited. He could smell a break in this case, smell it very strong. "Okay, Mr. Davis," he said, handing back the license, "now could you tell me—is this your family?"

"This is my family. My sister and her kids."

"So what is a nice family like you doing in a place like this at a time like this? You work for Osborne?"

The girl said, "Ollie, he's *here!*"

"Who's here?"

"Sim! Sim is here! *Look!*"

"You didn't expect him?"

She shook her head. This girl was more than scared—the way her eyes were flickering back and forth as if she was being surrounded in some way, she must be terrified.

There had been a black girl with the Ryersons at Bonacori's place. Was he looking at her now?

"Chief," Malone said, "Davis—that's the name on the shampooer rental receipt." A woman believed to be Kealy had abandoned a rug shampooer in Ryerson & Osborne. They'd traced the rental to a Roselle Davis.

"Do you know Kealy Ryerson?"

All four of them reacted the same way: their faces closed, their eyes flickered away. Even in the thin light of the streetlight, he could see that they knew her well.

The black man spoke. "We don't know anybody name of Ryerson. So are you gonna keep us here all night or what?"

The girl said, "Uncle, didn't you hear him say—"

"Hush, girl!"

"But they're in—"

"I told you to *hush!*"

"Who's in what?"

She set her jaw. He turned to the boy.

"You play baseball, son?"

"Basketball."

"Yeah, well, in baseball you wait a lot. It's a waiting game. Me, too, I like to wait. Everything comes to him who waits. Ever hear that saying?"

"No."

"You have no right to do this," the girl said. "We're not under suspicion of any crime."

This was a very well-spoken girl, sounding quite different from her old uncle, if that's what he was.

"Well, are we from around these parts, young lady? Or what? May I see some ID?"

She handed him a student card. "We are not criminals," she said.

Now he was certain: Phillips Academy at Andover was where the Ryersons had sent their kids for a hundred years. Allison was an Andover student right now. So this was indeed the black girl who had accompanied them to Sal's place. These Davises were involved with them, all right, probably hiding them right this second. And somehow, Simon Osborne was involved.

"I know that the Ryersons have been staying with you folks," he said as if it was knowledge old and common. "I need to speak with them about some police business." His heart was leaping, he could barely breathe, he was so excited. He put the gun away, tried to smile. "They need to come in."

"We don't know what you're talking about."

"Oh, I think you do. I think you're here on the Ryersons' behalf—and I don't fault you for that. I'm here on their behalf, too."

"You're Henneman. You're the enemy."

"They think that, I know. And I understand why they would. Problem is, I'm the only friend they've got."

"They have us," the girl said.

"Do they? Because I think I see burglar tools back in there." He peered into the van. "Are you really here on their behalf, or is this some kind of robbery you're involved with, assisting Mr. Osborne in some way?"

Things went black. There was no warning, but as he lost consciousness, Henny had the impression that it had been the teenage boy who had hit him. When he heard Malone yelling, he realized that he wasn't going completely out. He staggered, tried to heft his gun.

Then Malone was beside him, bracing her own .38, trying to get off a shot at the departing van.

She didn't.

"We gotta give chase," he said.

She helped him into their car.

"That kid hits hard."

The van was headed off in the general direction of the expressway. Engine screaming, they followed it.

CHAPTER 32

Mark's jaw was blasting with pain, his head still ringing from a blow from the side of Sim's nasty little gun, a blow he had not seen coming. He loaded the gas cans into the building one after the other, moving as quickly as he could, doing just exactly what Sim said and praying to God that Ollie Davis would see what was happening and do something to save them.

Kealy knelt beside her daughter with an arm around her trembling shoulder. Allison's head was thrown back, her mouth filled with the gun that was in Sim's hand. Except for the sloshing of the gas in the cans Mark was bringing in, the only sound was her gulping breath.

Kealy's mind twisted and fought, her thoughts the thoughts of a trapped animal. "Remember when they were babies?"

"No."

"You remember 'Unk'? Remember that? She said 'Unk, Unk.'"

"Kealy, you have to understand my position."

"Sim, that's gonna be a little hard."

He had said that the phone cards he had hidden in Jimmy's unused spaces were worth over ten million dollars. "As valuable as heroin," he said, "and a lot easier to turn." He had also said that there was something else that had to be destroyed.

Allison made a gagging sound.

"Take it out of her mouth!"

"As soon as all the gas is in the building."

Allison tasted the steel and oil in her mouth, tasted it and looked straight into Uncle Sim's eyes, pleading for all she was worth. She stifled nausea; pain stabbed her neck and gripped her tight-stretched jaw. She wanted to save her family, but her mind came up a complete blank. If she did anything at all, Uncle Sim was going to pull that trigger.

A huge wave of nausea made her twist and gag. The barrel of
the gun was crushed against the roof of her mouth so hard that
she could taste blood. Mommy had to do something, Mark had to.
She was losing it, she was starting to go crazy, she was going to
panic and pull away from him and he might shoot her then.

Mark lifted the last of the heavy cans out of the trunk. Ten
five-gallon cans—fifty gallons of gas. The ancient warehouse was
fitted with a sprinkler system, though, but he doubted that it
could contain the fire that would result from these. He took the
can in and laid it next to the others. "That's the last."

"I thank you," Sim said.

Mark wanted to kill Sim even more than he had wanted to kill
Bonacori, but he kept seeing an image of his sister's head blowing
apart, the dark blood, the red maw.

"I'm going to make you happy," Sim said.

When he drew the pistol out of Allison's mouth, Kealy enclosed
the sobbing child in her arms. "Why?" she asked him. "Why are
you doing this?"

"Your husband told McGarrigle everything."

"I don't know what you're talking about."

"You know. Now there's work to do upstairs."

In the elevator, Allison decided that he had done something to
the Davises. He must have intercepted them, that's why they
hadn't come back. He might have killed that whole beautiful family. She tossed her head, throwing the little tears that had formed
in the corners of her eyes aside. She would not cry in front of this
monster.

Kealy tried to find a reason to hope. What would happen
when Sal came? He'd said ten minutes, but it had been longer
than that. So where was he? She'd written off the Davises. Either
they'd made their two passes and gone home, or they'd seen the
car and gotten spooked, or Sim had killed them all.

Sim gave them keys, told them to unload the phone cards
from the spaces they were in.

As Kealy worked, she noticed that there were other boxes behind the phone cards, that in fact the boxes of cards were only

one layer deep. What was in those other boxes? She said nothing, but she intended to find out. This was really about the other boxes, of course. Nobody cared about a bunch of phone cards except the crook they were going to put in jail.

Mark worked as slowly as he dared, trying to prolong this as much as possible.

"As soon as they're in my car, you'll be free to go," Sim said. His voice was almost friendly. Mark did not believe him. The cards couldn't fit in his car. He needed a truck . . . or maybe a van would do. Mark had the horrible thought that Ollie might have led them into a trap.

"We won't be free to go. You're going to kill us just like you killed Dad."

He saw Sim's hand begin to move, then there was a flash, screams from Mom and Ally, and Mark found himself lying on his side, his ear blasting with pain.

"Why do you keep hitting him? Why do you keep hitting my brother?"

"Because he can," Mark said dully, getting up from the floor.

They worked briskly now, loading the heavy boxes into the elevator with the help of a dolly. Mark tried to find an opening, but Sim was a careful man.

When we're loading the car, we just to have scatter, Allison thought. *We have to run and just try to dodge the bullets.*

As they rode down in the elevator, she could smell the sweat, could still taste the gun in her mouth.

"I sure as hell never thought it was you," Sim said. He smiled an awful smile, shook his head. "Where in God's name did you ever learn to crack a safe, Keelster?"

In that moment, hope flared in Kealy's heart, because she knew that he was unaware of the Davises. They were still alive, and maybe they had seen Sim's car pull up and gone for help.

Maybe.

Now the last of the boxes of cards were loaded into the main lobby. All that was left to do was to take them out. And then she thought: he probably had the Davises' van out there somewhere, and she was ever more sad for those poor people she had led into this.

The moment she got the chance, she was going to pounce on Sim. She would die, of course. But her kids were smart and they were quick. They would take the time she gave them and use it well.

As he worked, Mark imagined getting his blood down Sim's throat, or, better yet, crushing his head with one of these heavy boxes. But Sim was no fool, and he stayed well away.

"That's quite a disguise, Kealy," he said.

"It's not a disguise."

"You're a clever woman, I have to give you that. Impressively brave. Your husband was right to think the world of you."

"I thought the world of him."

"He was an idiot, though—it took him a long time to figure things out."

"No, Sim. He was honest. That sounds ridiculous to scum like you, I know."

As she spoke, Mother was walking toward him. Mark knew why, too. Mother was going to leap at him. Mother was going to get herself killed to give them the seconds they needed to escape.

"I'm not scum," Sim said. "But I'm trapped. Oh, God, Kealy, I'm so terribly trapped."

The gun wavered. Mark stood frozen, watching horrified as a tension spread visibly through his mother's body. Her face was gray and tight, her fists were clenching. Sim realized it, too. Sim raised the gun. "Kealy, don't break my heart."

A man came out of the control room, a short man with gray stubble on his face. "Don't nobody move," he said. He spoke with force and authority, did Sal Bonacori, and Mark knew at once why he was called a boss.

A great gust of breath whooshed out of Kealy's lungs. She had committed herself to death and suddenly everything had changed.

Bonacori's voice was almost mild. "Osborne, gimme my fuckin' phone cards, you vicious piece a shit."

There came a tremendous, deafening, overwhelming sound, a

clap of thunder, the roar of a waterfall, and with it a flash as if of lightning, the kind of flash that left your eyes seeing white.

And the white rose to a great brightness.

Sim had fired directly into one of the gas cans.

CHAPTER 33

The room throbbed, the floor tossing as if in an earthquake. Kealy saw Mark stagger, saw Bonacori frozen, standing there with Mark's bolt cutters in one hand and a gun in the other, saw Allison with great presence of mind move toward the electronic controls that would close the internal fire doors and open the outer door.

But that was no good: another split second brought a wave of intense heat as the cloud of flames that had burst out of the exploding can enveloped the whole end of the room, blocking the door. The other cans could be seen inside the fire, their surfaces blackening.

Bonacori shot and Sim pitched forward like a man made of sticks. He lurched into the fire, actually fell across the line of cans. He leaped back. He was on fire, the whole front of his body.

Bonacori grabbed Kealy, thrust her away from the fire. "Come on," he howled at the kids.

And then Sim screamed, the most horrible, most intense, most fearsome human sound that Kealy had ever heard. Aflame from head to foot, the shoulder where he had been shot spurting blood that spattered and smoked as it came out, he toppled backward into the piles of cans.

Incredibly, Mark had produced a fire extinguisher. He emptied it toward the cans, toward the burning man.

A column of flames burst up, billows of deep orange flame tattered by black tendrils—beautiful, terrible, like the secret interior of an evil soul. With a roar that snatched their cries away with a hurricane's indifferent ease, flames swarmed toward them.

Kealy felt knives of fire tearing into her legs, and she danced, she ran, falling back, screaming to her kids—but only Bonacori came, waving the bolt cutters like some sort of battle flag. He sped off into the building. "Follow me," he yelled. "We gotta get to the roof!"

He was trying to make it to the elevator. She saw its mesh door sliding closed. "Don't do that!"

He stared at her, his face twisted, full of fear, full of . . . something else. Then the elevator rose out of the bay.

The fire was spreading with gluttonous speed, racing up the walls. With a low boom, it grew twice its former size. The flames danced with the wild intensity of escaped prisoners, licking up the walls in their passion to devour.

"Come on," Kealy screamed to Mark and Allison, who were back at the console, working furiously in a sea of fire.

The whole wall before them was a mass of flame, and now a sheet of it boiled up behind the desk. As both of her children reeled back, Kealy threw herself toward them. In a couple of seconds, the inferno would trap them all. "Upstairs," she shouted. "We'll have to jump out a window."

Her left leg was throbbing—burned, struck, she did not know which. She led them to the narrow stairway, heard the elevator grinding its way upward. She knew that Bonacori was in there, and that there would be no help for him.

They went into the stairwell at the far end of the structure. Here there was no fire, but the windows that looked onto the street were barred on the lower four floors. "The fire doors—" She dragged at the iron door, but its chains were controlled by the system and it would not budge. "Nothing works!"

"We couldn't get the system running," Allison said. "The doors are stuck open."

She'd led them into a trap, damn stupid fool that she was— stupid, stupid *fool!* "Come on," she said, "Sal's right, there's no choice but the roof."

As they passed floor two, she looked up toward a sprinkler head. It was spitting a useless froth.

All the while, coming here, she'd felt they'd been alone. She'd actually felt safe. But why? Ollie had told her that Sim would come after his stuff, he'd *told* her, but she just could not believe in Sim as a murderer. How could Sim kill Jimmy's kids when he had dandled them on his knees? How could he possibly kill *her*—they'd been like brother and sister for twenty years.

Sim had thought it was Sal who broke into his safe. Of course. The safe is professionally cracked, the all-important manifest of this warehouse is taken. He comes out here expecting to find Bonacori and his people stealing the damned phone cards back.

But instead—oh, God, he had the heart of a monster. He'd been a monster inside and they had never even dreamed it. Or, perhaps it had been different. Perhaps he'd been sucked into something, somehow.

There came a shriek as wild as wind in fury, then a lower, deeper, roar, profoundly agonized. Allison clapped her hands to her ears and screamed with him, again and again, as Sal Bonacori died in the burning elevator, died amid blasting thuds that were probably from the poor man trying to kick down the door.

"Keep going," Kealy said. "Ignore it, there's nothing we can do."

Around a landing they went, then around another. The air began blowing past them from below. Then it got hot, then began stinking of rubber and wire on fire, of wood and paper and plastic burning. The building was ancient, built before steel girders. Its walls were designed to hold fire in, but only the modern equipment—the fire doors, the sprinklers—would have been able to slow it down. The entire interior would be in full fire in a matter of minutes.

"We're alone," Allison wailed. "Nobody knows we're here!"

Maybe somebody driving along on the BQE would notice the fire and call in an alarm, but New Yorkers couldn't be counted on to perform civic duties as elaborate as that. Probably they'd figure it was somebody else's problem and just drive on. If the Davises came back again—if they could—they'd be certain to raise the alarm. But they had only minutes, so who was going to save her babies?

"Keep going," she snarled when Allison stumbled.

But then it came upon them, the smoke rolling quietly up around them, dropping the already minimal light level to nothing. It cut into the tissues of the throat like the coarsest sandpaper, and it was hot, so hot! Kealy kept thinking, *It hurts to burn, it hurts to burn,* and she wished that she could knock them out before the fire touched them, if it came to that. But she had no weapon, no tool.

On the tenth floor, they came to a halt. The smoke had made it so black now that she couldn't tell whether they were going up or down. Mark and Allison were gasping. Kealy moved in a syrup of detachment, as if this was all happening to some distant version of herself, another Kealy Ryerson in another age of the world. She knew that this response was a danger sign. And then she realized that the smoke was making her dizzy, that she felt detached because she was in the actual process of suffocation. The reason that she felt disconnected was simple: she was dying where she stood.

"Get down," she said, dragging them to the floor. Here the air was clear, here they could hack the foulness out of their lungs. "Cough," she ordered them. "Get rid of it." They hacked black fluid, and both kids cried, their voices breaking with the bitterness of young life in jeopardy.

The smoke that had been collecting along the ceiling suddenly blossomed with deep, red fire. The fire began to crackle, and sparks from burning ceiling materials started drifting down— melted, flaming sparks that had to be beaten out the instant they touched a head, a back.

Then the doors on all the spaces began banging, as if there were people behind them, or all the possessions inside wanted to escape. Allison crawled over to one, started trying to raise it.

And it did rise.

"No, baby," Kealy screamed, going to her, throwing her arms around her. "That won't work, you can't get in!"

"Mommy, it will! It's not on fire in there and it has a steel door!"

Allison peered into the space. It was one they had emptied of phone cards. And she saw those boxes that had been behind the cards. And she thought maybe, somehow, she could, and despite the situation, the desperate urgency, get behind them.

She dug into the boxes, pushing them out behind her. They spilled out at Kealy's feet, and she saw then a deeper, more terrible evil. She saw luridly illustrated boxes with pictures of women being dismembered and titles on them like *Snuffing Sally* and others with children, little girls and boys, engaged in grotesque intimacies.

"My *God*," Mark shouted.

The boxes kept falling, and Allison and Mark saw them in their hundreds: snuff films, kiddie porn, the worst, the most filthy things in the world.

"We can hide in here," Ally screamed. "We can hide!"

As Mark had a few nights before, Kealy slapped her—not hard, for this was not a hitting family. Allison blinked, turned shocked eyes on her mother. "We have to keep doing that," Kealy said. "We have to try for the roof," she added. "Wait for rescue up there."

"It'll burn through," Mark said. "Dad told me all about how they designed these buildings."

"Me, too," Allison said. "Oh, Jesus, we're *burning!*"

"Why did I ever let us come here," Mark burst out. "I knew it was stupid!"

It got real hot real fast. Above them there was a red haze shot through with orange flames. It was like being in a broiler.

They were all crying, none able to reconcile to such a bitter fate, all in terror of the agony that was beginning along their backs and necks.

Kealy tried to cover her babies with her own body. There was no more time to think: this was the end; she had led them finally to their deaths. She lay over them, hugging them, trying not to scream as the heat rose.

Distantly, there was a sound different from the fire, perhaps something exploding in one of the spaces, something that died with a surging hiss. But then it started again, went on longer, became part of the background of roaring and fearsome crackling.

"Mommy!" Allison screamed, *"Mommy!"* She was feeling the heat now, too; she was realizing that she was about to burn. Mark lay quietly. His head was on its side against the floor. Kealy kissed his cheek.

Then Allison was struggling, was trying to leap to her feet. "No! Stay down!" Kealy's voice was so hoarse that she could barely get the words out. There was no stopping Ally. She squirmed and struggled with the undulating energy of a snake. She must not raise her head, not into that broiling air, she would be killed instantly.

Kealy lay fully over her, pressing her head and face into the floor while the poor girl screamed and screamed.

Between her shouts, Mark asked, "Mom, how far is the nearest fire station?" His voice had that preternatural calm of his, but it was shaking, it wasn't going to be long before he joined his sister.

"I don't know," she said miserably. Then, to her panicked daughter: "This is gonna be visible all the way to New Jersey, honey. Firemen will come."

Mark said, "Come *on*," and she realized that he was crawling, pulling himself along on his stomach.

"Ally, we have to go, baby. We can escape, Mark found the way."

She came speeding on her belly, gasping relief. But Kealy had no idea if Mark could get them out, just that he was doing something, and anything was better than staying where they were.

The stairs were full of smoke that sluiced past like a scalding river. "We've got to keep going," he said.

"Too much smoke!"

"We have to!"

There was a crash below them, followed by roaring even deeper, even more powerful. The enormous old structure began to tremble as if it was almost alive, as if it had a soul, and that soul was dying in agony. Then the smoke around them turned white, letting a strange, moon-shadow glow in through the dim stairwell windows.

They went up a full flight before Kealy started to gag. It was an awful sound, she knew it, but she couldn't stop herself. She pitched all the way forward, throwing herself down, seeking for air. Somewhere far away, Allison had begun to scream something, a long, complicated sentence.

Then a hand came around her upper arm and what appeared to be a great bat loomed out of the shadows, striking directly at her face.

She pushed away from it, until suddenly she saw bulging eyes and a sweating face, the lips pulled back, the teeth gritted tight, the black skin shimmering with sweat.

Ollie got his big arms around her and then she was off the floor and flopping over his shoulder.

"Ollie, my kids—"

"You gotta worry about Roselle, she done gonna kill me, I don't get you-all outta here."

She hammered his back. "My *kids!* They're somewhere in here!"

Then she saw a strange being in the shadowy smoke, a creature from a science fiction film. As Ollie heaved her off his shoulder, the creature disappeared. She thought she must be hallucinating.

Ollie coughed, grabbed the mask off what proved to be the face of a woman. He thrust it against Kealy's mouth and nose, and suddenly her lungs were filling with the sweetest, purest air she had ever tasted. It was the deep country on a dew-touched morning; it was the seaside in June.

As she got her air, she saw through the eyeholes of the mask the dim shape of the woman who was giving it to her. No matter the situation, the confusion, her amazement at the rescue, she cried out because of what she saw—or rather, who. It was like being transported to some surrealistic other version of her life. Because this was impossible. This could not be real. And yet it was, in the flesh and blood, indisputably.

Of all the unlikely, impossible people, Christa Lawrence from the office—Sim's executive assistant—was the one who was helping her, was using this bulky rescue equipment with the assurance of a pro.

As quickly as she would have avoided a striking snake, Kealy leaped away from the woman. "She'll kill us," she cried, her voice rasping. The oxygen mask went rattling off into the murk, and once again her lungs filled with smoke.

"Hold her," Christa said, and ironlike arms grabbed her from behind.

She had to make him understand. "Ollie, let me go! She's with Sim, she'll kill us both!"

Christa got the mask and gave it to Ollie, then took a long pull from it herself. "Okay, sweetheart," she said, "you take a deep breath." She was wearing jeans and a heavy sweater; she had on a black knit hat.

When Kealy stood rooted by amazement and disbelief, she came back and took her wrist, drawing her firmly along. Kealy went not five steps before she yanked free. "My kids?"

"Your kids are with Chief Henneman upstairs. They're waiting for the cherry picker."

"Henny?"

"Who else would it be? We've been watching this place for days."

Henny, helping the kids? Christa here, doing this? What in the very name of hell was going on?

"Christa, I need to understand—"

"Come on, Mrs. Ryerson, there's not a moment to spare." She grabbed the mask off Kealy's face, pressed it tightly to her own.

When it was replaced, Kealy sucked greedily.

There came a loud beeping noise from somewhere—the pack on Christa's back. "That's the three-minute warning," she said. "We're low on air and I don't like this smoke, it's getting real hot again."

"So we'd appreciate it if you'd get your tight white ass in gear, otherwise we're gonna leave you to bake!"

Confused though she was, terrified that there were things about this that did not add up, Kealy did the only thing she could. She went with them.

er kids were there, two statues in the stinking haze that was gushing from the door through which she'd just emerged. And there also was a familiar figure. His face was blackened, his beautiful suit was a wreck, his eyebrows were singed off, but she would recognize Henny Henneman anywhere. He stood almost formally between Mark and Allison. The three of them were hand in hand.

A huge machine appeared behind them, drifting in and out of the billows of smoke. In it stood a fireman, who proceeded to cry out: "Over here! I'm over here!"

They turned around and began walking like people might on their way up the stairs of heaven, as carefully as if they were in a formal procession. Beneath her feet, Kealy felt rough, continuous shuddering. Simultaneously there was a huge, cracking noise.

Christa howled, "Move, move, move!"

Kealy told her feet to walk, told her legs to run, but she couldn't move at all. She could not climb the stairs to heaven, not when they led only to Henny and another kind of death.

"I'm sick of carryin' you," Ollie said.

"You don't have to carry me!"

But the roof shuddered again.

"Christ," Christa Lawrence said.

They went to the edge, leaning over to breathe, as the cherry picker came slowly back up, nosing its way through the smoke, speeding away with an agitated whine when billows of flame lunged from the windows that lined the floor below.

Another huge cracking sound came, and Kealy found herself falling in a heap of Ollie's and Christa's arms and legs. Behind them, the roof looked like a collapsing hammock as it sunk down into itself. Red fireballs burst out of the center, moving lazily into the hard night sky.

Then there was a rope, white, snaking down across the three struggling people. Kealy was fighting to grab onto Ollie or get the rope, whichever she could manage.

"C'mon, lady, take it easy," a male voice said. "What's your name, give me your name." Then she realized that she was in the cherry picker. She was being rescued, and she hadn't even realized it. Smoke was incredibly disorienting. You lost touch with up and down, left and right, you were too totally involved in the process of coughing and suffocating. "Your name, lady?"

"Kealy . . ."

"Keep your eyes open, Kealy, take deep breaths." Then, into a radio, "I got all of 'em, all conscious, one needs O_2 pronto."

She understood that she was curled up like a dog in the bottom of the cherry picker's bucket. Three inches from her face, she could see Ollie's gigantic feet. He was wearing scuffed old high-tops, with socks pulled down over the tops. The fireman's feet were stuffed into gleaming rubber boots, and Christa had on white sneakers, one of which was scorched.

They went through a gushing storm of rain that proved to be a hose dousing them for safety's sake each time they passed a blazing window. Then the thing hit something so hard that Kealy saw stars. Its door opened then, and she started trying to get out. But she didn't need to try, people were helping her, and then she was inside another oxygen mask, one that at least left her eyes free. Mark's face came down out of the welter of faces and lights and shouting voices, came down and looked into her eyes. "Mark," she said behind the mask, "run, run . . ."

Allison's voice: "Mommy, we're safe. Henny's here and it's all right."

"It's not all right! It's not, *it is not!*"

Christa appeared again. "I've been on undercover assignment in Simon Osborne's office for three months."

Kealy pulled the oxygen mask off. She was confused, yes, and disoriented. But she was very far from stupid, and she was finally taking in this new piece of information.

"You're a cop?"

"A cop. My name is Malone."

"Working in our office? What are you working on?"

"I need to let Chief Henneman tell you that." She replaced the mask on Kealy's face, did it quite firmly. "But not now. Now is not the time."

Kealy wanted to just close her eyes and let things happen, but she couldn't do that, not even as she realized that she was on a stretcher and the men around her were lifting it, they were carrying it somewhere—and that was not acceptable. Coughing her brains out, coughing and crying at the same time, she tore the mask off and forced herself to her feet. She wobbled around looking for her kids. And she saw them, both of them standing there with Cokes in their hands, the fire behind them like a backdrop painted in shades of Armageddon. The thing was, they were standing with Henny, and she had to be certain that he was not dangerous to them. She ran forward, only vaguely aware that the savage, wildly inappropriate roar that came with her was issuing from her own throat.

Mark was in front of her then, clapping strong hands down on her shoulders. "Mother, these people are our friends! There's been a huge investigation going on all along!" She tried to fight past him, to get to Allison, to place herself between Henny and her children.

Then Henny was there, his face so deep with sorrow and compassion that instead she sank against him, and felt again the Henny of the good times, whose love had once given her life meaning. "I'm sorry," he said. "I'm so sorry."

She wept now, for the gentle past and the hard past, for present terror and, more than anything, because his eyes had told her what words could not: as bad as he had been, as difficult as their memories must forever be, she and her babies were safe with this man.

She let them take her to a rather awful hospital, a sprawling Brooklyn institution, name unknown until somebody said it was called King's County. She let them wheel her through the green-tile halls of King's County with her kids walking alongside her, with Henny behind them and Christa Lawrence who was really Detective Malone behind him.

The entourage clattered into some kind of a holding area, a place full of olive-drab screens and nurses who moved with the swift precision of people who spent their lives with the injured. "Am I dying?"

"Mother, you're fine. It's smoke inhalation is all."

"I'm not burned?"

"We're gonna make you cough, dear," somebody said, and then she was sitting up, and then her face was in yet another mask. Steam came out that smelled of mint and Lysol. "Breathe deep," the voice said.

Over the better part of half an hour, she underwent the treatment, inhaling and coughing up the remains of the fire. Henny sat on the bedside holding her hand, and she allowed that. "You are some kind of a lady," he said. "I had eighty people trying to run you down, did you know that?"

"What about Sal?"

"Who?"

"Sal! Where's Sal!"

"Mom, it's all right. Everything is all right."

She sat up. "Sal?"

"Sal is dead, Mommy," Allison said.

She could think of only one thing: "What about that poor little boy?"

"Oh," Detective Malone said, "that's . . . we have to do that, Chief."

"Let the precinct do it."

"I have to help that baby," Kealy said.

"Mother—"

Then she was lying down again, she couldn't help it. "I don't feel so good." Her head was whirling, her heart rumbling like artillery.

Then she saw Ollie. "The cop you've been running from turns out to be the same cop working the case. He's on your side, fool."

"She didn't know who she was running from, but she probably saved all their lives doing it."

"I did?"

"You might've called me once or twice, given me a small reason to think that you weren't dead at the bottom of the river." He shook his head. "Not knowing made for some hard nights, Kealy."

"Henny, I thought I was running from you."

He glanced up. "Could we have a little space, here? I need just the family for a few minutes."

The Davises stepped away, but not so far that Henny didn't have to speak as if he was in a confessional. "This is a very tight investigation. I've got four people directly involved in it besides myself. I report to the commissioner and the mayor."

"I thought you said eighty people. Eighty people were looking for us."

"On the manhunt, yeah. Not on this investigation. Point people are getting killed on this sucker."

"Point people?"

"Like Sergeant Phillips. We lost him about six weeks ago, an investigator assigned to Matthews, Locke, Trimble & Ford. That's another one of these places."

She knew Matthews, Locke as a competing firm.

"Henny, this is over. Sim is dead. The danger is past."

"Sim is dead, but this is not over. By no means."

The fact that she was just so exhausted was what made her burst into tears.

Ollie came roaring back. "What you doin' to her?" He shoveled her into his arms. "Okay, Fifth Avenue." He glared at Henny. "She's sensitive, man, and she doesn't take being pushed around."

"I know she's sensitive. I was married to her once. I lost her because she's sensitive."

"Well, I'll be damned."

Henny addressed Kealy again, this time more gently. "There's something we have to talk about." He made a head movement, signaling Ollie to leave.

"But we're not in danger? My kids are safe?"

"I want you to meet with Howard Bass in the morning. If you're feeling up to it."

"What does that mean? Because if this is over—"

"There's no further danger from Sim. He's really and truly dead."

She closed her eyes. No further danger. It must feel like this to be told you're in remission, that wonderful flush of sweet relief that washes through you.

"Then I don't want to meet with Howie. I want to turn my back on this whole thing."

"There are loose ends, Kealy."

"A lot of loose ends?"

"You need to hear what Howard has to say."

The commissioner of police had been a friend of Jimmy's. They were both members of the Century Club, among other things.

"What sort of loose ends, Henny? You're not giving me enough information."

Detective Malone spoke. "I've been inside Ryerson & Osborne for three months," she said. "Mr. Ryerson was used by his partner to lure Sal Bonacori to the table. Mr. Ryerson didn't want an organized crime client. But Mr. Osborne convinced him that Sal was innocent, so he took the case."

Henny continued. "When he understood that what was really involved wasn't representing a client, but scamming him in a ten-million-dollar deal that left the poor bastard holding the bag, he went straight to the DA."

"Henny, you have to be certain we're safe. I need you to be absolutely sure."

"My best guess is that you're going to be left alone."

"No revenge?" Mark asked. "We're responsible for the death of one of their main people."

"He was just another cog. And the dark side of corporate America doesn't have emotions like revenge. You were dangerous to them because you controlled that warehouse. Now that it's gone, you'll be left alone. Nobody involved in this takes unnecessary risks, and a revenge killing would be an unnecessary risk. These people are not like the mob. They're better."

"Except there's a huge problem," Mark said. "The fact that we know all this makes us a target all over again."

"Mark, we have that handled. We are going to let Sal Bonacori take the fall for the whole thing. The story will be that he killed your dad. The Mafia's known to hit lawyers it distrusts, so that'll be believed. Then, to cover himself he killed the DA who knew the skinny. He kidnapped you guys and set the fire that killed Osborne—"

Mark sprang to his defense. "But he didn't! He didn't do anything! And it's wrong because what about his poor little boy, to have to live with that."

"Except that your dad didn't so much as cheat on a parking ticket, and Sal's probably got ten murders to his credit, not to mention a lifetime in the rackets. The kid has to live with his father's past. He has to face it."

"I'm going to help him," Kealy said.

Mark flared up at Henny. "If you keep saying in public that my dad was mixed up with Sal Bonacori—"

"Hear me out. The press is gonna get the story that Bonacori did it all to stop his phone cards being turned over to the Feds. He'd stored them in Jimmy's warehouse to hide them where the law wouldn't think to go. Jimmy discovered them and did his civic duty. If an attorney finds evidence of a crime, he's obligated to tell the police."

"What about all that porn? There were snuff films in there, DVDs of children having sex. It was vile."

"And it's better off burned."

"There'll be more."

"Until we crack this thing, yes."

Kealy looked a long time at Henny Henneman. They took her back, Henny's eyes.

"Kealy?"

She didn't know if she wanted to hear that tone from him. "We have plans for you," he continued. "Important plans."

"Look, I've had it with plans." Her body felt like a dead weight. "I've just plain had it."

CHAPTER 35

She woke up as they were bringing in the first fairly decent food she'd seen in days. It looked ghastly, actually—greasy bacon and eggs that looked like hockey pucks—but it was just amazingly delicious. Life returning.

"Ouch," she said when she tried to raise herself up.

"You have second-degree burns on your back, Mrs. Ryerson. They're going to be sensitive."

Sensitive was not the word, but Vicodin and anesthetic-loaded burn packs helped a great deal. By noon, she was ready for discharge, still living in the state of wonder that comes with cheating death.

Ally and Mark, who both looked as fresh as if it had never happened, took her home at noon. Vee was there waiting, and they embraced like the sisters that in truth they had been for years. Vee cried, Kealy cried. She was frightened when she heard noises in the apartment.

"We've got men working in Daddy's study," Ally said.

"It's going to be cleaned up and the closet repainted, Mom. No trace of what was done."

She went into her bedroom suite, followed by Ally and Vee. "I'm fine," she said. "Let me freshen up." After they left, she lay down on the bed and had a good, long cry, hugging Jimmy's pillow to her chest. "I will never leave you," she whispered. She opened a little door in her heart and went in, and there was Jimmy where he would always be, beside her in this bed, reading a brief while she cuddled close, waiting for her time with him. "One day, love, one day . . ."

But not today. She opened her eyes, sat up. There was life to be lived and work to do. She went into her bathroom and had as luxurious a shower as you can have when contending with burns.

She lathered herself with her lovely, soft Floris Serengia shower gel until she was foaming with fragrance.

Afterward, she made herself up, but lightly. Like magic, the old Kealy reappeared, with all the sparkle, all the brightness that she loved. Her hair, however, was hopelessly, fantastically Medusaed. She looked like she was carrying a head full of asps. Well, she had some lovely hats, and she'd wear one this afternoon. Tomorrow, first thing, she was going to spend some time with Rosie Franklin, who had been doing her hair for ten years.

She chose a Dolce & Gabbana suit, black with red stitching. It was designed to display the female body at its best. She hadn't been wearing it lately, due to a certain interruption in the line of the hip. One thing about terror: it causes your weight to plummet.

When she made her entrace into the living room, Marko and Ally and Vee applauded. It was a big joke, she knew, but it felt good. And she felt good, too, this glowing woman she saw in the mirror behind the couch.

Vee fed them a lunch of ham and cheeses, olives and preserved veggies, washed down with a delightfully fizzy *Vinho Verde*.

The new phone in the kitchen rang. "Chief Henneman," Vee said.

Kealy took the call. "Henny, hi."

"Hey, Keelster."

He still called her that after all these years. And she found that she rather liked it.

"Hey."

"Howie can see you at three. You want him to come over there?"

"I can go to his office."

"You're sure?"

Life was pouring back into her like the sunlight that was pouring into the apartment on this crackling October day. Out the kitchen window, ragged white clouds raced across a heartbreakingly blue sky. "I'm absolutely sure."

She left shortly thereafter on a mission that was, if anything, more important to her than the meeting with Howie. Just because she could, she waited on the street for Ned to show up with the car. The wind was lovely, rattling the tails of her coat, making her hold down her hat.

"Hi, Ned," she said as he let her into the car.

"Now what am I gonna do with you? You're the most famous ride in town."

"I am?"

He'd arrayed the papers across the back seat. There were a lot of stories, a whole lot.

"Where to, Mrs. Ryerson?"

"I'm going out to Brooklyn, actually. Sal Bonacori's house."

You didn't need to give Ned directions or tell him addresses. Part of his professional pride was to know all of his clients' locations so that they didn't need to remember things like that. He headed over to the drive.

She sat listening to WQXR and watching the golden, wonderful city pass by outside the windows. She thought of the vast, impoverished world out there. She'd never known before how damn lucky she was to be rich. Never again would she fail to notice the realities all around her. It was all too easy to make reality disappear if you lived in the world of Manhattan wealth.

She had not realized that she was sleeping until she heard Ned say, "We're here, Mrs. Ryerson."

How small it seemed now, squeezed in between two much wider row houses. Its drapes were so firmly drawn and it was so very quiet that he added, "Are you sure this is right, Mrs. Ryerson?"

"Wait here."

The steps to the front door were made steeper by the task at hand. She rang the bell and listened to the echo. Surely they weren't gone.

The door made a loud click, then came open a crack.

"Hi, Paulie."

It shut.

"Paulie, I'm here because I have a message from your dad."

It opened. "My dad is dead." The voice was surprisingly mature, but just as sad as would be expected—maybe sadder.

"I was with him, Paulie. I was there."

He stepped aside, nodded for her to come in. She noticed that he was wearing a blue suit, of all things, with a red necktie that had been so inexpertly knotted it looked as if he'd tried to hang himself.

She knelt to him. "Did your granddad do this?"

"My granddad got so upset he forgot how to talk English. Then he went to bed."

"I'll teach you some proper knots," she said as she redid his tie. "Do you wear this at school?"

They had gone into the living room. "No way," he said, "this is for my dad's funeral."

"When is that going to be?"

He shrugged. "Whenever they say."

"Who is 'they'?"

His bottom lip came out, and all of a sudden he was bawling. She opened her arms and he flew into them, his heft almost knocking her down.

"My daddy got no friends, just dumb wiseguys that're gone to jail and I don't know how to do no funeral, and I got no momma and Granddad . . ." There were long sobs, the weeping of a child who is truly lost. Then he pulled back. He swallowed the tears. He gave her a narrow, ugly look. "So what the hell do you want, lady?"

"I came here to tell you the truth about your daddy, even though there are going to be some bad things said about him."

"We'll waste 'em, they try that shit on us. They're all liars!"

"Your dad was a very brave man. He saved my life and the lives of my kids."

He shook his head. "I'm real glad for you." The face screwed up into tears again. Again he swallowed them. "What in hell am I gonna do, lady?"

"You're going to go on. We all go on. Your daddy and my husband were working together on something very, very dangerous.

They were like secret agents. They both got killed, but they died as heroes."

"Lady, I wasn't exactly born yesterday. My dad was the big boss. That doesn't add up to hero in anybody's book."

Life had aged this boy far beyond twelve years. In that sense, he was like too many children, wiser than he should be. It would be a source of anger later, when he looked back and saw that he'd had his innocence stolen from him.

"Paulie, I also came here to let you know that you have a friend. You can call me, you can count on me." And she thought: *Never again will I turn away from need. Wherever I see it—and I will make myself look for it—I will act.* "I'm going to be here for you."

"Except not now."

"Absolutely now."

His face screwed up again. "Please help me have a funeral for my daddy. I don't have no idea what to do, and my granddad is, like, brain-dead. All he can do is cook."

This child's agony had been waiting here behind these closed shades for her, and she took it now into her heart. "I'll take care of everything. I'll make it just like your dad wanted, to honor him."

"Will we have a white hearse?"

"Certainly not."

"The boss gets a white hearse, lady."

"Your father is to be buried with honor. That requires a black hearse."

"The boss gets a white hearse!"

She had to go, she knew that, but she also didn't know what to do with him. She couldn't leave him alone here with his ga-ga grandfather. So what was the alternative—call family services? Then what would happen? The grandfather would be found incompetent. Paulie would go into foster care. Her sense of this proud, tough, half-criminalized child was that he would not make it in care.

"Come with me," she said. "We'll leave your granddad a note, let him know where you are."

"We're gonna have the funeral now?"

"Not now. But I'll bet you'd like to have a dessert at Sant Ambroeus with me. Ever been there?"

"Nope."

"It has fantastic sweets. Gelati and cannoli, all kinds of fabulous stuff."

"Espresso?"

"You drink coffee?"

"I'm an Italian. I smoke cigars, too."

"Not on my watch, young man."

"My dad has real cigars from Cuba, boxes and boxes of 'em down in the basement. Men come and get them all the time. He was teaching me how to cut 'em and smoke 'em, and to take off the band like a gentleman. Wiseguys leave the band on because they don't know any better. But the boss knows."

Could she cope with Paulie Bonacori? It was going to be interesting.

"Wow, a real limo with a driver," he said as they approached the car. "My dad just had a Mercedes he drove himself. We don't trust no drivers, they might be in on some fuckin' hit." He turned to her. "Did my dad burn to death in an elevator?"

"He was overcome by smoke. It's like going to sleep."

His brown eyes were boy-soft, but they bore a terrible knowing. It was as if the eyes of a suffering man had been embedded in the face of a child. "He didn't go to sleep, lady. He burned."

Hard though it was, she met those eyes of his. "That's the truth," she said, her voice as gentle as she could make it.

He slid as close to the door as he could. "Where is this place?"

"In Manhattan."

"Is it fancy?"

"Very fancy. The suit's perfect for it."

Silence for some time. When they crossed the Brooklyn Bridge he opened the window and hung outside.

"Don't do that."

"My dad lets me."

"Well, not now."

He came back in. "It's a real pretty day," he said. Sal's voice echoed in his son's.

"Yes, it is. Call your granddad on my cell phone, see if he's up."

"He won't be. I made him take a Nembutal."

"You *made* him?"

"Somebody's gotta be responsible for him. He wets his pants, you know, if he ain't helped to the john."

The poor little guy had no idea how alone he really was. She thought, *What if I take Paulie in? What if I put the old man in a nursing home?*

"Jesus Christ, this is One Police Plaza!"

"I've got a meeting here. You can come in and see the commissioner's office."

"Lemme out! Cops!" As he began piling out the door, Ned put on the brakes.

"Come here, you!" She got him by the tail of his jacket, dragged him back. "Park the car, Ned."

Paulie glowered his way up to the top floor, but his eyes became interested when he saw the computers and digital maps in the commissioner's communications suite.

"Well, who's this," Howard Bass said as he popped out of his office. "I didn't know you had one this young, Kealy."

"This is Paul Bonacori," she said.

Very formally, Howard shook the boy's hand. Then he laid one of his long hands on the boy's head.

"Lay off the pompadour," Paulie snarled.

"You call that a pompadour? When I was a kid, we knew from pompadours. Fenders, all that."

Paulie shrugged away from him. "Whatever."

They settled Paulie—to the degree that he could be settled—with the office staff. Their uniforms did not help matters.

"I've got Henneman with me," Howard said. "You're comfortable with that?"

"I don't know. Sort of."

"Well, I guess I can—"

"You need him, I know. It's not a problem."

"You're sure?"

She followed him into the office.

CHAPTER 36

Henny was standing in front of the window in a dark suit. His face was flushed. His shaved eyebrows made him look spectacularly sinister, like an evil clown. " 'Lo, Keelster," he said.

"Hi, Henny."

He smiled, but, she thought, a little too carefully. "You look like a million bucks, Kealy."

"Okay." She addressed herself to Howard. "I'm here as requested."

Howie Bass was as gnarled as Henny was tall, as shabby as he was handsome. He chewed on unlit cigars, among other ghastly habits. He'd once been a marvelous jazz pianist. She could remember some fun, fun parties, back when she and Jimmy were newlyweds and Howie was a legal aid lawyer with a wild nightlife.

"What I don't understand is why you didn't pick up a phone and call me? Even if you distrusted this piece of work. Kealy, we've known each other for years."

"When our funds were frozen, I thought there must be high-level official involvement. It was very scary and it looked like somebody really powerful had to be behind it, like maybe the whole police department."

"Osborne did it," Henny said, "using a bent judge called Garrison Lake."

"I saw any contact with the official world as high risk."

"We're dealing with something that amounts to a fundamental change in the culture of crime. We have a clever and well-educated adversary now. The hard-bitten, honor-bound gangster is becoming extinct. It's the turn of the gentlemen."

"All I cared about was running. Getting the money for that. Plus, I have to admit, when I realized that Sim was stealing my bonds, I got damn mad."

"So you became a burglar," Henny said.

When Howard chuckled, Kealy bristled.

"Sorry," Howard said. "But it's just the damnedest story." He glanced at Henny. "He's a good detective. He figured it out."

"Just in time, too," Henny said. "Keelster."

"So how does it feel to have survived a thing like this, Kealy?"

"Like it isn't over yet, Howard."

"That's perceptive of you," Henny said.

"Nobody's been arrested. So it can't be over. I won't let it be over. Unless Sim was the whole thing. But he wasn't."

"No, he wasn't," Howie said. He was about to continue, but Henny interrupted him.

"You know you're still in danger."

She considered that. "Even with Sim dead?"

"Even with Sim dead."

"And my kids?"

"Not them, not anymore. With the warehouse destroyed, nobody has any reason to need them dead. They're not going to inherit any phone cards or that . . . that damn filth the scum had in there."

"Kealy, we want you to help us."

"I know you do, Howie, and I want to."

"Hold on, hold on. You need to know that there's a way out for you."

Howard chomped the cigar. "Henny?"

"She has a right to know, Howie!"

"Just let me float our proposal, for Chrissakes!"

"No! This woman's life is involved!" Howard turned a dirty pink, and Kealy understood that they'd been fighting about this proposal of his. Henny went right on. "There is a way to get you out of it, to make you safe."

"Which I don't necessarily want, if it means we don't get the rest of these people."

"You listen! It's very simple. We blame everything on Bonacori. He killed Jimmy, he kidnapped you and the kids. That lets the bad boys think they're in the clear. *Not* hitting you then becomes the wise move. If they touch you, they reopen a case that appears to be closed."

"Appears?"

"Of course it's not closed," Howard snapped. "Thing is, Kealy, if we let you walk out of it like that, we're in trouble. But if we do it another way, we might be okay."

Henny looked at her with the eyes of a wet dog. His whole body urged toward her. He looked like he might want to hold her. To restrain, or to love? His signals were as mixed as they were powerful. She did not want to be held by him. And she did not want any more danger in her life. "I've been through enough, Howie."

"Hear me out. We want you to work for us—with us. Go to parties, socialize, listen."

"And report back," Henny added. He shrugged. "It's his idea."

She was being asked to become a spy in her own life. "Why don't you just arrest these people?"

"Evidence is lacking," Howie said. "But they run in the same social circles you do."

"I'm not going to socialize with murderers! Especially not the murderers of my husband."

Howard began to sell, as was his very political nature. "You could get us that evidence, Kealy. You could go places where we can't, right into people's homes, penetrate deeply into their private lives—"

"No! No way! I practically had a heart attack when we were in there cracking that safe. I died a thousand deaths in the warehouse. *Howard, I went through hell!*"

"Nobody but nobody is gonna suspect sweet little Kealy."

"Howard if this is some sort of macabre prank—"

"If we don't nail these people while we still can, this could get too big for us. It could get too big for every police force in the world."

"I'm off your list. I'm not a James Bond."

"No, but you're a good van thief, an excellent safe cracker, a master of disguise. You do have some skills in this area, Kealy."

"You're laughing at me, Howard, just like you used to."

Henny, she was amazed to see, was gazing at her with liquid eyes. Despite her history with him, her natural tenderness made her reach out a tentative hand. He grasped it harder than he should have. He did not let go.

Finally, she had to withdraw it. She regarded Howard. She was about to do something to him that he had always had a great deal of trouble with, which was to tell him "no." He was a man who liked to be in society, to glory in his status as a successful importer and now a high official and confidante of mayors. He hated to be thwarted. In this respect, he was a spoiled little boy.

"I am absolutely not ever going to do any of this. I'll end up right back in the trap I was in. This is final."

Henny bowed his head, closed his eyes. When he looked up, he was fighting a smile of relief.

"If you *don't* do it, is where your danger lies."

"Okay, Howard, try to make me believe that. Since it's a blatant lie, I'm very interested in your reasoning."

Howie's glasses practically fogged up, he was so angry, but his voice remained steady. "Now, that's hasty. Very hasty. Chief Henneman will provide all the security you need."

"There is no security against these people, as you well know. Anyway, I don't have the faintest idea how to be a—whatever you want to call it—a shamus."

"Undercover, is the term."

"You fooled me with that old lady disguise," Henny said. "I mean, I remember those three old bags in that church. That was astonishing work, Keelster."

"Stop calling her that! Can't you see it grates?"

It did grate. She hadn't wanted to tell him.

"Force of habit."

"It wasn't a goddamn disguise," Kealy muttered. How little they understood the reality of life as a woman. "This is the disguise," she said, brushing her cheek with the tips of her fingers. "To disappear, all a woman in my age group has to do is reveal herself as she really is."

"You can act up a storm, make them think you're a complete ditz—all the while, you'll miss nothing."

"I was tossed out of Cornell Drama like a rotten turnip."

"There's a colorful metaphor," Howard commented.

"Look, all I've been doing is what any mother would do, trying to save her kids. I've done that, so my double-oh-seven days are over."

Howard gave her a hollow look. "Kealy, there is going to be a party. You're going to be invited. But it won't be an ordinary party. It'll be something akin to a trial. And you will either be declared innocent, and allowed to live, or you will be found guilty, and die."

"Henny, you told me I could get out of danger!"

"At the party. You play innocent, they're going to leave you alone. We feed that by announcing that the guilty party—Bonacori—is dead. Problem solved."

"For her," Howie said acidly.

"I can't stand this! I can't stand it for another second!"

"Then help us bring it to an end!"

"What trial, Howie? Who's going to put me on trial?"

He leaned back in his chair, in the process almost disappearing below the desk. She noticed that his fingers were gripping its edge as if it was a lifeboat and he was clinging for all he was worth. "At some point, you'll be invited to a party. Quite soon, would be my guess. At that party, you'll be tested. If we've planted the Bonacori story and you act dumb, leaving you be will become the route of least resistance, and they will take it. If we have not, then they'll endeavor to find out if you're working with us in some way. If you are, you'll be hit just like your husband was, at their earliest opportunity."

"I'm scared! Way too scared! And what is this trial? I certainly won't go, I'll stay home."

"Kealy, you have tremendous reserves of courage and intelligence. You can do this." Howie leaned forward. "You can get these people and you can put them in prison for the rest of their lives. Because you are a careful, brave, and effective person who is in a unique position to help us. We need you, your children need you, and the unquiet ghost of your husband needs you."

She had never felt such an awful foreboding as this. This would come to no good. But she could not refuse him, she saw that. She lowered her eyes, and in that gesture they saw that she had assented.

They did not speak. They let her absorb what she had done, let her taste the reality of it in her own way.

"There's another thing," she said at last. "The little boy in the outer office. I want you to bring that boy in and explain to him that you know his dad did not kill my husband. His dad's name is going to be dragged through the gutter, no matter what happens."

The boy came in still spitting with hate to be in this despised cop sanctum, but now also awed by the drama of Howard's big office with its rich paneling and his museum-quality gun collection that was displayed in cases against every spare wall.

Howie explained carefully, but Paulie understood only that some crime his dad hadn't committed was being pinned on him, and he became even more belligerent.

"Your dad was helping us catch crooks. He died a hero."

"Yeah, catch the crooks, I believe that."

Wrong move once again. Paulie was not going to be easy to reach, it seemed.

Henny walked out with them. "Kealy," he said.

She knew that tone of voice and she did not want to become involved with this man again. "Good-bye, Chief," she said.

He did not follow them down the elevator.

In the car, Paulie was withdrawn. "My dad didn't do nothin'. You got a problem with that?"

"No."

He grunted, seemed to sink into himself, absorbing the believability of this answer. "It's bullshit."

"What's bullshit?"

"He did things. It was our business."

"But he saved my life at the cost of his own. Me and my two children."

Paulie was silent until a sob escaped from between tight lips. "I hate you and your two damn kids!"

"Paulie, I promise you this: one day, I will let the world know that your father was a hero. No matter what else he did or didn't do, that fact remains. In the end, that's what defined him."

"You know what a zoo is, lady?"

"Yes, I know what a zoo is."

"I never been to one."

"You want to go to the Bronx Zoo?"

"Not with you, bitch."

She soldiered on with him to Sant Ambroeus. With its long brass dessert bar and elegant, silk-hung dining room, it was as dear and wonderful and familiar as ever. Paulie had lamb chops and a Coke, and after that a double espresso, and the dessert that he ordered was huge.

"You want to go to that zoo, don't you?" Kealy asked afterward.

"Whatever."

"But you'll go? With me?"

"I could give it a try."

CHAPTER 37

There followed the saddest and most beautiful days she had ever known, days filled with memories and desires, spent in the cold autumn sun with a frightened little man who was slowly discovering that if he allowed himself he could recover his boyhood.

The funeral of the has-been don was a pitiful affair, which Kealy endeavored to make impressive with flowers. Even the wreaths could not disguise the lack of mourners, though. The sun had long since set on Sal Bonacori. Still, Paulie solemnly shook hands with each one of them, even the funeral monsters and the scruffy reporters from the *Post* and the *Daily News,* and the bored FBI photographer there to record the presence of any stray mob figures.

Paulie's sensei came, a squat man with eyes like raisins, whom Kealy thought had a rather unhealthy way of gazing at the boy. She resolved to get him a karate teacher with a reputation she could check out.

After the funeral, in the privacy of the guest room where he had taken up residence, he had thrown his arms around her waist and howled out his grief. She held the poor creature tight. Hearing his misery, Mark came in. "We gotta do this together, guy," he said. "All of us grieving kids."

Kealy fell in love with the baby-faced, hostile little tough guy. She found his helplessness impossible to resist. There were numbers of things about him that appealed to her—his stubborn ways, his spunk. In him she saw an echo of his father, as she saw in Mark an echo of Jimmy. And so the two men haunted her in the forms of the boys they had left behind.

Vee brought her young niece Billie to work, too, now that the flat was hopping once again with young people. The Davises appeared and sat stiffly in the living room with coffee cups balanced on their knees.

"Roselle stuffed that vacuum cleaner so far up her boss's ass, he's suckin' the sky," Ollie said when Kealy asked how they were doing. "We're gonna move to Ozone Park. If I get me a little bleach and a toupee, I'm gonna fit right in."

"There are African-Americans in Ozone Park," Jo-Jo said.

Ollie laughed. "Nigger get a little cash, he ain't no nigger no mo'!"

His family glared at him.

In any event, they moved to Greenwich Village and Ollie began to dress himself in Soho boutiques. In appearance and in the way she conducted herself, Roselle remained as she had always been. She hired a maid, though, because she absolutely hated even to dust a table. Kealy began shepherding Jo-Jo's application through the Andover admissions process, hoping for the best.

She also helped them with their money, introducing them to various financial advisers, whom she privately admonished with stern warnings that she would be examining the books herself.

Ollie began to appear at the apartment more often. This, it developed, had to do with Billie, who was twenty-four, shaped like a tennis star, ravishingly pretty and a *habitué* of the night world that Ollie was so eagerly beginning to explore.

The apartment was often so busy that it seemed like it had been in the lost days when Mark and Allison were young, and it was always full of kids.

Vee emptied the cookie jar of cigarettes, but when she filled it with homemade chocolate chip cookies, Paulie announced to her, "These things are pure shit."

In Vee's opinion, Kealy did not correct his language or his manners forcefully enough. "You ever get your tail whipped, kid?" she asked him with deceptive mildness.

"Nobody touches me. 'Specially no nigger."

So Vee gave him a cuff that would have knocked most children his age senseless.

He set up a yell and Kealy, who had been going through her

mail in the study, came out to the kitchen to intervene. "I don't care for that," she told Vee. "No hitting."

"He called me a nigger, Mrs. Ryerson. For God's sake!"

"You know, Paulie, what if we call you a wog?"

"I'm not a fuckin' wog!"

"See how it feels?"

"I'm a greaseball."

Kealy sighed a little and laughed a little. "Okay, greaseball, if you call any of the black people in this household 'nigger,' they have my permission to punish you in whatever way satisfies them. Because that's as mean a thing as you can say to them. It's more insulting than 'greaseball,' because it reminds them of slavery."

Only when she was on her way back to her desk did she realize that the letter she was still holding in her hand was an invitation. It was her first since the funeral, and it was quite an early one, she thought.

Cocktails with Judge Allen and his wife, Mary. To her surprise, the gathering was in her honor. She knew the Allens reasonably well. Morris was a state supreme court judge before whom Jimmy had sometimes practiced. His father and hers had been great friends, both of them yachtsmen, both involved in the Cup. Morris, however, was a poor sailor and an extremely annoying golfer. But he knew poetry, of all things, vast quantities of it, which Jimmy said could sometimes be surprising in the courtroom.

She thought nothing of the invitation—accepted with some pleasure, in fact. Mourning was no longer the stringent affair that it had been in her mother's day, and a cocktail party or a small dinner party were considered perfectly acceptable after the first few weeks.

Over the next days, she forgot the invitation in a flurry of activities. Paulie pined for his father and his grandfather, who was cooking happily away in a nursing home in Ossining. Henny made a date to take the boy to a baseball game. He didn't want to go with a "fuckin' cop" as he put it, but the lure of the Ryersons' box at Yankee Stadium proved impossible to resist. So off they went, two solemn enemies drawn together by their Yankee caps.

When they returned, Paulie announced that "the fuckin' Red Sox are a buncha fags."

One piece of good news was that Mark's disease was again going into remission.

Paulie had formed the habit of coming and sitting on the foot of Kealy's bed late at night. He liked to talk. One night he suddenly said "Mom."

"Do you want to call me that?"

"Fuck no."

"Like now? Do you want to do it now?"

He came up the bed, lay on his back beside her with his hands behind his head. "I hate your guts, you know. You kidnapped me."

"You want to go to family services? You're welcome to anytime."

It was a moment before she realized that his silence concealed tears. "You can cry in front of me," she whispered. "Moms are used to it."

"I wanna go home, Kealy." He said it quite calmly. Then he burst into tears. She held him as best she could. He was big and it was awkward. Slowly, his grief subsided.

"I could be your secret mom," Kealy said. "If that helps."

"Shh! Don't let nobody hear!"

"Nobody will hear, honey. It'll stay just between us. You'll have a secret mom."

He sat up. Then he got off the bed. "Screw that," he said. He stalked out. She heard the door to his room slam.

Deep in the night, she would hear him walking the floors, and once he stole into her room and stood a long time at her bedside. After that, she kept her door locked at night.

"Mrs. Ryerson," Vee said on the morning that she was to attend the Allen party, "Commissioner Bass is on his way up."

At the sound of that name, she stopped what she was doing. "Howie? Here?"

Then the elevator opened and he stepped out, his suit looking as if it had been put through a washer.

"Howard, please come in. This is an unexpected pleasure."

He was all business. "Kealy, let's go in the study, please."

She didn't need to go in any study to be told what he wanted. "You're hear about this crazy trial business, aren't you?"

"Oh, God," Allison said from the living room. Howard's proposal had been discussed with all three kids, and they were all dead against it.

Paulie shot at her from the back of the house, threw his arms around her.

Mark appeared, bleary-eyed, from his room. "What's going on?"

"The trial," Allison said. "The damned Allen cocktail party is the trial!"

"You're sure, Howard?"

He nodded. "How many people know about this? This is very poor security, Kealy."

"The kids have a right to know."

Ollie appeared from the kitchen, where he had been romancing Billie. "Know what? What's goin' on?"

"Ollie—"

Howard interrupted her. "Ollie, it's better that you not know."

"If Kealy's in trouble again—"

"Ollie, he's right. It's better."

He hesitated in the doorway. "Don't you shut me out, you need a helpin' hand. I'm damn good at it, as you well know, Kealy Ryerson."

"If there's anything you can do," Howard said, "I'll certainly make sure you're called upon."

With that, he ushered Kealy into the study. Ollie hung back, but the kids did not. The kids insisted on coming.

"Nobody does nothin' to her," Paulie cried. "Nobody, see! I'll get Sal's guns, I'll blow their fuckin' brains out." He glared at Howie. "My dad's got a fuckin' Uzi."

Howie put a kindly hand on the boy's head.

"You got a thing about the pompadour," he said, backing away.

Henny came up then, very subdued, looking as if he hadn't slept in days. "We need to lay this thing out," he said, glancing at the kids.

"It's family business," Kealy said. They all went into Jimmy's study. Paulie hung back.

"You can come," Kealy said. "I trust you."

"I ain't in your damn family."

The magnificent portrait of Jimmy done in 1981 by the genius Alice Neel hung once again over the mantel. She specialized in naked portraits of the rich and mighty. Jimmy hadn't been comfortable with the image of his own nude body looming over him, but Kealy would never see it removed again, not as long as she drew breath.

She felt that his eyes commanded them all to have courage.

"Okay," Henny said, "here's how it lays out. Allen we've been watching and we feel he's deep in this thing. He probably isn't the big boss, but he could be. In any event, he's close to the top. We're going to have a complex situation at that party, but we're sure you're going to be fine."

"If I'm not fine?"

Henny's eyes flickered. He turned to Howard. Howard cleared his throat. "Now listen to me, I don't want a big eruption in here. I want you all to hear me out, what I'm gonna say. If they feel that you know too much, Kealy, they are going to try to kill you."

"I know it."

"There's a particular approach we want to take," Howie continued. "Be naïve. Come across as a complete idiot, a ditz."

"Oh, I intend to pass the test."

Howard lowered his head like a man facing into a blizzard. "We want you to fail the test, Kealy."

"But if I fail—"

Paulie burst into the room. He'd been at the door, obviously. "They're usin' you as bait," he shouted. "Your mom's gonna get her ass shot off!"

His words fell onto silence. Kealy looked at Mark's stern face, at Allison's pale one.

"How much actual danger will there be?" Mark asked quietly.

"We think it's relatively minor. They dare not do her when she's in the building. The attempt will take place after she's left. We'll have her covered. When we've got that shooter and he's talking, this whole thing is going to fall apart very quickly."

"How will I know?"

"You won't know. Go to the party, do your act, and leave. Just totally normal in every way. At some point, a call will be made. That call will trigger the hit. We will monitor it."

"What if it comes from a digital cell phone? You can't monitor that."

"Son," Howard said, "that's an urban legend spread by police departments to keep crooks off their guard. We will be monitoring every cell phone frequency in use in the United States, in addition to the landlines to that apartment."

Mark said, "Don't do this, Mom."

"Yeah, it's dumb," Paulie said. "A cop thought it up, for sure."

"Paulie, honey, I might have to do it. Think of your dad. Wouldn't your dad have done it?"

"Are you fuckin' *kidding?* 'Course not!"

Well, that was probably true. "The thing is, my husband certainly would have."

"Dad got shot," Allison said.

"We didn't have him under protection."

"You did Mike."

That brought silence. Kealy knew that it was a bigger gamble than Howie wanted her to believe, or, no doubt, that Henny was allowed to tell her.

The people who killed Jimmy, the monsters who had broken her life into little bits, would be the ones she would be destroying. She looked at the kids, meeting one set of those eyes after another. Allison was miserable, Mark scared. Paulie, as usual, was unreadable. "I have to," she told them.

Paulie got up and stalked out. "Cops are damn assholes," he yelled as he disappeared into the back of the house.

"It's okay," Kealy said after him.

"It's not okay." His bedroom door slammed. He was right. It was way not okay. But she was going to do it.

CHAPTER 38

Allison and Mark wanted her to go in armed. Ollie, who had pretty well figured out what was going on, announced that he'd be here having supper with Billie if he was needed. Paulie stayed in his bedroom. When Kealy tried to come in, he told her, "I hate you."

Henny came back later with detailed instructions.

"You have to understand that these people aren't cruel. They're dispassionate. They work by the numbers. You're going to be asked a series of questions. It'll seem casual, off the cuff. But what you need to say is that you know that Sim was part of a larger conspiracy. Say that you've been able to help the cops. That you're trying to find information for them—but then you get coy. You can't talk about it. Be charming, you know how to do that. Puff yourself up a little—be self-important. You're working with the police, it's all very hush-hush. Speak of the commissioner on first-name terms."

"Do *you* want me to do this, Henny?"

"Absolutely not."

"Howard overrode you?"

"The party will seem completely normal. Nobody'll bat an eye. You won't know when the decision is made or when the call takes place. But we will. We will hear that call."

"I just play the dumb ditz that they all think I am anyway. It's another kind of invisibility, and believe me, I'm all too familiar with it." She smiled a little, remembering. "Jimmy and I had a system. When he wanted to know what people at a party thought of him, he'd signal me and I'd go stand near them. The second he walked away, they'd start gossiping about him. As far as they were concerned, the little wife-o just didn't exist."

"Well, tonight you're going to enjoy that kind of invisibility all over again," Henny said, "but this time you're gonna ram it down their throats."

"And that is not going to be unpleasant."

"You're a ditz who, unfortunately, knows too much for her own good and is just too dumb not to go to the cops. She doesn't even begin to understand the danger. She's so naïve, poor thing. They'll put you down like a lame horse."

While she was dressing, Kealy actually felt fairly okay. She was even eager. Wrap it up, put the guilty in jail. But, as the hours swept past, she felt less and less confident.

Sitting here in the back of the car on her way to the party, she thought she might be sick.

Sensing her mood precisely—as he had so often since they'd begun to work together—Henny said, "This is one of those 'don't look down' situations. You gotta just do it."

"Yeah, that's good. Don't look down."

She felt him gazing at her.

"I'll survive," she said. "God willing."

He did not reply, not for a long time. Then he said, "I hope what we're doing is right," in a husky voice that Kealy sensed contained feelings that she had not known he still had. She looked over at his profile. He stared straight ahead.

The car moved swiftly on. To all appearances, it was an ordinary black sedan, the sort of car that commonly ferried the affluent through the streets of New York. If you'd looked in the glove box, you'd even have found that it was registered to a limousine service. But the man in the livery was not Ned. It fact, he was no ordinary driver at all. Like Henny, Captain Greer was a trusted member of Howard's small task force.

"You're precious to a lot of people," Henny murmured.

He meant, "to me." She wondered, *Has he stayed in love with me all this time, or did it come back?* She looked at him again. A sudden, powerful memory of being under him made her blink her eyes from the shock of old passion.

"Don't wait around. If it looks like *anything* is not as we expect, bail out."

"What if I can't bail out?"

He didn't answer and she knew why: there was no answer.

The Allens were uptown on Eighty-eighth and Fifth, so they'd had to go around and up Madison. Traffic was heavy. "Come on," Henny muttered.

"Nothing I can do, Chief."

"I know it!"

Kealy opened her purse and took out a roll of Tums, ate three of them.

Suddenly his hand was on hers. It was clumsy, blatant, just like it had been in the old days. "You're not moving away from New York?"

"No."

In other circumstances, he might have tried to kiss her, and perhaps he did this in his heart. When she removed her hand, she brushed his fingertips in a way that that left a little promise behind. Immediately, though, she thought, *Why did I do that?* Even this slight suggestion of interest from another man made Jimmy come racing back to mind. She had knelt at her husband's grave, knelt among the bobbing flowers on a day of small, blowing rain, and made a promise to his spirit. *I will not fail you,* she had told him, *before God, I will not.*

She leaned her head back and closed her eyes, and let him out of the secret room in her heart. He ghostly took the hand that Henny had pressed. She told him of her doings and wove the cloth of vengeance with him.

She watched as 4800 Fifth came closer. She looked up the cliff of windows.

Henny took a deep breath. "Okay," he said. "Okay."

"I'll be fine."

"You come down, you get in the limo, you are driven home. The only other person you'll see will be Greer. It's when you leave the limo and start for the apartment that the danger will be highest. Remember that there are over a hundred plainclothes in the stakeout positions, and we've got vehicles all along the route. The point is to nail this shooter, not get you shot."

"I couldn't agree more."

He nodded toward a Parks Department van at the corner of Eighty-ninth and Fifth. "That's us. Also that cab over there. Us."

The captain in his chauffeur's livery got out and went around the car. Henny pressed himself against the far door. There must be no chance of his being observed.

He murmured something, and she knew that it was a word of love, although she had only seen his lips move. But how could she ever let him back in her life? She did not know, not right now, but she also knew that a human heart is a garden of many forked paths.

She stood before the building, another familiar entrance, a place she knew well. Ahead of her, she could see Joe Ross and his wife, Pat, going in. She hesitated, unable to bear the thought of riding up with anybody.

When they had disappeared, she proceeded. "Good evening, Walt," she said as she passed the doorman.

"Evenin', Mrs. Ryerson."

He met her eyes and delivered his version of the "it's so sad" smile that she had come to detest.

On the way up, her courage began to melt away. She started to feel that she could not do this after all. For all she knew, they were going to seize her and torture her for information and then kill her without her ever getting the all-important chance to leave.

Her heart stared hammering, but she quelled it with the thought that they would never do anything foolish like that, which would lead the police back to them.

Still, she arrived at the Allens' floor so scared that she had to literally lean against the wall and close her eyes for a few moments before she touched their bell.

"Kealy, I'm so delighted! It's just wonderful to see you getting out a little." Mary opened her arms. "Oh, darling, I'm just so full of feelings, love!"

Kealy smiled and bussed cheeks. She wanted a damn big drink, anything to dampen this sand-packed mouth of hers, anything to quell what she was sure was shaking that could be seen from across the room.

The living room was flooded with people. A gigantic spray of roses stood in an urn on a table in the doorway. It was an odd, overdone way of using flowers, but she loved roses and their scent was a welcome friend.

As she came into the room, everybody stood, women as well as men. They were actually pretending to honor her.

Bitsy came up, Bitsy who was her oldest friend. Surely she and Sam weren't involved. "Stay away from my Sam, you devil," Bits whispered as they traded kisses. "That's the sexiest mourning I've ever seen, my dear."

"That's the tackiest thing you've ever said, my dear," Kealy whispered back.

Sam and Bits were so wealthy that more money would be nothing but an annoyance, so maybe they were just guests, innocent filler.

Julie, Minette, and Claire appeared and disappeared in succession, a whisper of Boucheron, a sigh of Chanel, a flutter of Petite Cherie, this last much too young a scent for any of these women. They had been trusted friends, too. But nobody's status was the same. Nobody was to be trusted now.

And then Morris was standing before her, his eyebrows raised, his hands extended as if in supplication. Fighting herself, she smiled at the man who had probably imprisoned Jimmy in her heart.

She did it well enough, she thought, but she could see from his eyes that he was far from convinced.

"Oh, Morrie," she said, throwing herself into his arms. It felt like holding a wooden Indian.

"Okay, okay," he said as he drew quickly away. Clearly, he hadn't expected her to do that. His tension was reflected in the stiffness of his body and his rush to seperate himself from her. "You lovely woman," he said, "you lovely, brave woman."

"Where's Ames?"

He glanced around, signaled the servant. She asked for Glen-
livet with a splash.

When it came, she sipped the drink gratefully. "My," she
said. Miserably, she thought, *I'm a terrible actress. Terrible!* At
least she wasn't expected to stay long. Honoree or not, it was unattractive for a two-week widow to linger.

She forced herself to go deeper into the living room—and she
was immediately surprised. Not because Michael Dilbert popped
up off the couch and gave her his hand, but because he was so
radically changed. This ebullient man was now a sunken shadow
of his former self. He looked like a drug addict.

He was CEO of SecureLink Technologies, an enormous computer network security company. He'd taken her to a fancy dress
ball when they were ten or eleven. She'd gone as the Fairy Queen;
he'd been a matador. Nowadays, they traveled in what Bitsy called
"parallel crowds." It was a nice way of saying that he wasn't really
there yet. Maybe it was that his money was too new or his jokes
perhaps too old—you never quite knew why somebody like him
didn't manage to arrive socially.

"Kealy," he said, "I want to tell you how proud we all are of
you. I've wondered what to say. I've thought of a lot of things."
He shook his head. "But there are no words." Was he here because he'd been carrying a torch all these years like Henny? Or
were there other reasons? With a company like his, she supposed
that he could potentially steal computer files worth billions.

Then she knew. His too-steady eyes told her. He was part of
it. He was part of Jimmy's murder.

Small talk began quickly, as people sought to cover the awk-
wardness of having a grieving widow as the center of attention.
There was discussion about how pushy George and Lenny Brit-
tain were being about the Robert Lustig installation they wanted
to put on display at the Whitney Museum of American Art.
Everybody knew that they had warehouses full of his sculptures
and were trying to raise his profile.

"Tom Boulton's up for a judgeship," Michael Dilbert said.

He didn't seem to be talking to anybody in particular, but she could tell by the way Morris lowered his eyes, seeming to look into his drink, that the statement was of interest to him.

The she realized that it had been directed to him *through* her. This was part of the test. If she was working with the police, she'd be interested. Her underarms were getting wet. They were soaking. She needed to pee. The scotch was hitting her harder than it should. She glanced from one man to the other, feigning interest.

"Boulton?" Morris said. "He's with—I want to say Conrad, Ray. Isn't he one of old Bill Watkins's protégés? Rising young star about ten years ago?"

"That's your man," Michael said.

She recalled Howard telling her how worried they were about the bench. "We're afraid they'll get their people into more judge-ships, and that's going to sink us." A crooked judge had almost sunk her and the kids. It had been a crooked judge who had closed their accounts.

When Morris spoke again, his eyes were on her even though he was talking to Dilbert. "Tom was always the free spirit."

"Tom? I don't know any Tom," she said.

Dilbert answered Morris as if she hadn't even spoken. "That's his great strength."

Superficially, they were treating her like a decoration. But they were watching her very carefully.

Bob Thomas of Lunden, Thomas, Claypool & Foreman came strolling over. He took a long pull on his drink. "I think he'd be welcome, Morris."

Kealy wondered how many other people in this room knew what this conversation really meant. She was cataloging names, wishing that she could go somewhere and get everything written down in her little notebook. They'd discussed sending her in with a wire, but it was too risky. Bugging the place, equally so. Morris had to think he was completely safe in ordering the hit. At the least sign of police interest, he would slip away down dark strands of his web.

"Who is he?" she asked again, her voice louder. "I'd love to know who we're talking about." She grinned right into Morris's face, making it as fallacious as she could.

Morris continued to speak right through her. "I don't know how I could help a guy like that, Bob."

"I'm helping the police," she said to nobody in particular.

"Oh, that's excellent," Dilbert said. "Very important. But didn't the papers say—"

"The Bonacori thing is just a blind. They're after somebody else."

"Really," Morris said. He was interested now. "Any ideas?"

"Oh, now, Morris, there *are* such things as official secrets. And I happen to have one." She actually managed to smile at that point, and that made her proud.

"Good girl, Kealy," he said affably. "Fine work!"

Despite herself, she felt her cheeks beginning to burn. Thankfully, he turned away to another guest, giving her a welcome chance to move away from him. She went to a side table where some unattractive crudités had been arranged on one of Mary's wonderful Bellini trays, fodder for the dieters and vegetarians among them. She bent over the raw vegetables and thin sauces, trying to catch her breath. That had been sheer hell, and now she was absolutely terrified that they'd all been wrong and Morris would have some goon come out of a damn closet and drag her away.

Struggling against herself, she forced the corners of her mouth to rise, her eyes to crinkle, her lips to spread in the famous Kealy smile. She swiped a bloom of broccoli through curried mayonnaise. Holding it between her fingers, she turned around and faced them all again.

"It's so lovely that you've all come," she said, drawing the room to silence. She wanted to add, "I know who you are, I know that you killed my Jimmy, some or all of you, and I am going to see you burn for it." But she smiled the smile and kept talking. "I really didn't see how I could manage this. Even to see old friends— well, I just can't get away from it. Somebody is not here. Somebody is missing."

Bitsy made a soft sound. Julie fought melting eyeliner.

Morris, less wooden now, came to her and took her hand. "There," he said, "there now. Know at least that you have good friends."

"And a future," Michael Dilbert added. "I know it doesn't seem like it now, but it's true."

"It's true," Morris agreed. And then it came: "Our Kealy is being very brave. She's giving evidence."

The room seemed to rock back and forth. "I'd hardly call it that," she said.

He smiled affably. "Well, I think that our brave little soul is way too modest. You're important to the police. Without you, what would they have?"

She gazed at him with melting, teary eyes. He saw nothing of her hate for him, nothing of the reality behind the invisible woman. "Not much," she said. "Apparently I've got a lot of important evidence swimming around in my innocent little head. At least, they think so."

Joe Ross, who had been silent until now, suddenly said, "Is that why Chief Henneman was in the car with you on the way over?"

She fought for composure, but she was so surprised that she couldn't manage it. She coughed, sputtered. She felt her cheeks go hot.

"She was married to Chief Henneman," Bitsy said quickly.

"He's been a great comfort to me," Kealy managed to whisper.

"You should have brought him up," Norm Halstead said. "We might enjoy meeting the chief of detectives."

"That would hardly be appropriate," Bitsy said. "And this line of conversation isn't appropriate, either. I suggest we try a new subject."

"No new subjects," Kealy said. "I'm afraid the party's over for me." She glanced at Norm Halstead. "I must say that Henny's been a help to me. He has a policeman's wisdom. He helps me through."

"Nor*man*," Bitsy said, "look what you've done. Now she's leaving."

Kealy didn't notice until he was returning that Morris had slipped out of the room. He had passed her death sentence out there on his hall phone, she suspected. If she didn't get out of here right now she was going to faint. Actually faint.

She went to Mary. "It's been lovely, dear," she said.

"Norman, I'm furious with you! She really is leaving! Oh, Kealy, all I can do is apologize!"

"Norman asked a perfectly ordinary question. Perfectly appropriate." She turned her eyes to him. "It's natural for people to reach out to old friends when they're suffering grief. And Henny and I do go back."

"Is he going to pick you up?"

Such an innocent question Morris had asked, innocent and loaded.

"No, no," she said, "I gave him a lift was all."

Morris sipped his drink, gave her one of the blandest smiles she had ever seen.

Amid another flurry of kisses, Kealy left.

CHAPTER 39

Bitsy followed her out into the hallway. "Norman is such an ass."

"I'm not dating Henny," Kealy said. It was actually better that they'd seen him—unless, of course, it scared them off, which had been his fear. "He's trying to date me."

"Oh, dear, that must be awkward."

"I think he wanted to take me to dinner."

"It's far too soon. And you've been there and done that, anyway."

"The man I married was not the same man. Henny's grown a soul."

Bitsy tossed her one of those awful social smiles she was so good at. "Some people just do not have manners," she said. In her heart, Kealy was miserable, because she knew that this little private moment that Bitsy had manufactured might well mean that she and Sam were also part of it. This might be an interrogation.

What was she thinking, of course it was. If Henneman had been with her on police business, they had to know. And if he was going to be around later, they had to call off their hit. "He's gone home," she said. How could she sound so artificial? She thought that she must be the most dreadful actress ever born.

At that moment, another apartment door burst open. Kealy recoiled, started to scream—then a dark swatch of jacket moved quickly past, and a teenage boy roared out and hammered the elevator button. As she recovered herself, she saw that her old friend was watching with a cold eye.

"You're on edge," Bitsy said.

"Yes—yes, oh, God, Bits—"

"I don't know how you've survived, darling."

Her words were kind, but her voice was flint. She'd never heard Bitsy sound like this. Her heart was breaking as they kissed good-bye. She thought that this was probably her last good-bye to her oldest friend in the world.

Henny and Howard were in the mobile command post that had been parked in the lot of the Central Park Precinct, well away from any chance of anybody on Fifth Avenue seeing it. They didn't have any listening devices in the Allen apartment, but they had video and sound in the hallway and the elevator, so they were listening and watching as Kealy and Bitsy had their exchange.

"Thank God she came out," Howard said.

Henny could not reply. He was beyond speaking. He watched as Bitsy expertly questioned her. What had gone wrong in there? Why was his name in use at all?

Paulie had decided it was time to call this whole damn thing off. He was going back home. He'd hire people to take care of him. He had a load of money, Kealy had told him. If she was going to keep doing crazy things like this, then the hell with her. He was not going to any more funerals, they were too damn boring. Tears welled up in his eyes. Furious, he wiped them away.

"Where are you going?" Allison asked as he went toward the door.

"Out."

"That backpack looks loaded."

"It is."

"You going hiking? It's after dark."

"Look, it's none of your business, okay? I'm just going out. End of story."

The elevator came and he got in.

"Good-bye," Ally said as the door closed.

On the way down, he had to keep wiping his damn eyes. Damn that Kealy, what business did some old bag lady have living dangerously? Didn't she care about anybody else? Helping the cops! That *always* got you in trouble, couldn't that moron figure that out? Duh!

On his way out, he passed Timothy's station. They'd gotten to be good friends. Timothy was cool. He was dynamite on a skateboard, and he'd taken Paulie up and showed him some wild-ass Egyptian stuff at the Metropolitan Museum. Too bad he worked here, because this was it for that friendship.

"Hey, guy. Going on a trip?"

"Yeah."

"You okay, buddy?"

He'd seen that he was crying, the jerk. "I'm fine!"

E very sound that the elevator made, every click and shudder, seemed invested with significance. The closer it got to the lobby, the more Kealy allowed herself to hope that maybe the police were right, maybe she was actually going to make it out of the building. But of course they were right. It was all perfectly logical.

Then the elevator stopped, but not in the lobby. It stopped on the fourth floor. The door began to slide open.

I t's off," Morris Allen's voice said from the speaker overhead. "She's not worth it." There was a click, then a dial tone. The tech killed the feed.

"ID'ed," he said. "We got it. Both ends of the call."

The call had gone from the apartment's wire line to a cellular number. A moment later, the location of that cell phone was pinpointed on the glowing map of Manhattan on the screen of one of the open laptops in the van.

"That's him," Henny said. The shooter was in a car directly across from Kealy's building.

"Damn," Howard said. "She passed the test! Not guilty. How the hell do you like that?"

Henny didn't say it, but he felt like he was spinning around like an unwinding spring, he was so relieved. "Too damn bad," he growled. He managed to sound fairly unhappy, despite the burst of joy that had filled his heart. She was a changed woman, and she had just plain captured him. When he'd seen her back to her old beautiful self, he would have gone nuts anyway. But she was so much more than the mean little ditz he'd married. *This* Kealy was not only glamorous, she was courageous, compassionate, and just plain decent. She was the best damn woman he'd ever met, all over again in a new way.

And she wasn't going to get herself killed because her damn heroics had failed, and he was just plain glad.

The shooter had understood the signal. It was double blinded to reduce the danger if there was an interception. "It's off," meant that it was time to kill Kealy Ryerson. He began to affix the silencer to his pistol.

Kealy moved through the lobby as stiffly as a little girl on a stage. Ahead was the limo. Damn Henny for coming with her. He'd almost ruined everything.

As she approached the car, Greer got out, walked around, and opened the door for her. "You have the moves down perfectly," she said. He winked.

Inside, he said, "It's a bust."

"A *bust?* You're kidding!"

"The chief just called me. They've decided you're harmless. They've called off the hit."

Kealy realized immediately that this meant she was safe. But nobody was going to get arrested now. "I think I'm disappointed."

"You're alive, Kealy. Be thankful for that."

Yeah, but that was going to be true anyway. She would have survived, it was all planned. No, she was disappointed as hell. She was furious.

Paulie was sitting on the ground behind the wall that separated Central Park from Fifth. He was thinking about the subway. He was thinking about how dark it was upstairs in his house, and did he know how to get the heat up? He got up to go. Better just get where he was going and then think.

He looked toward their building. He counted floors. There was their apartment, all lit up. "Mom," he said. He didn't try to stop his tears. Nobody could see him here, nobody could hear him. "Mom," he said again, "oh, Mom."

He was going to go down to Fifty-ninth Street and get on that subway, for sure. But maybe not yet. She wasn't going to be at the party long, that was the plan. So he decided that he was going to wait here and watch her get safely home. Then he was outta here. This whole deal was just too screwed up for him. He didn't think about his real mother much. She'd died in childbirth. Dad used to take him to her grave. He had a picture of her in his wallet. He kissed her picture sometimes.

Howard chewed his cigar "Let's pull it all back," he said. "I don't want to take any further chances."

"Are we certain?"

"You heard the bastard, the hit is scrubbed. They live to see another day. Somewhere along the line, we fucked up, that's all. She's such a ditz, maybe they just couldn't believe she was dangerous enough to take the risk."

"She's not a ditz, Howard."

"So maybe she overacted! Damn! We had these people!"

"Some of them." He flipped a switch, spoke into one of the mikes on the steel equipment counter. "Greer, can you hear this?"

"Yessir. She's in the vehicle safe and sound."

"Drop her off and take it back to the Fugazy garage. Do the whole drill. We need to pull out of this thing very, very carefully, because they spot us, they'll be after her at some unknown future time, and that is very damn dangerous."

"You got it."

He said to Howard, "Let's be damn sure about this. The whole stakeout goes away like a ghost."

"If it can."

Kealy should have felt relieved but she did not feel that way at all. "Something's not right," she said.

"Yeah. We had a great shot and it didn't work out."

"I did all the right things."

"You're just not a believable threat, I guess."

Had Bitsy come out on her own, just out of concern for an embarrassed friend? She wanted to believe that, much preferred to. But she did not believe it. "Something's not right," she repeated.

Or maybe it was. Maybe it was very right. If they didn't see her as a threat, not even after the act she'd put on in there, then maybe this was really and truly over for her. But not, of course, for Jimmy.

Vengance is mine, saith the Lord.

She wanted vengance, and she was furious at her failure.

The shooter spotted the limo. He was going to come in close, do it just as she reached the entrance to her building. The day before, he had sneaked into the building and cut the wires of the security camera in the lobby. If the doorman was there and saw it go down, he would get it, too. The key thing was that the limo be pulling away at that time.

He knew those drivers. They were like old horses, ever alert to head for the barn. The limo would go in a flash.

He wasn't worried. It would work fine.

Howard, I have to tell you, I want to leave the protection on just a little longer. I don't want it gone until she's safely inside the building."

"Look," Howard said.

On the screen that covered the Allen hallway, the party was breaking up. People were chattering and laughing as they left, including some of the probable principals.

"Those people aren't in the process of having anybody killed. Not those people."

"Yeah, I guess you're right." Henny got on the horn. "Waste it," he said. "Call it a wrap."

That did it. Operation concluded, no result.

P aulie spotted the limo. He watched it approaching. Three people were on the sidewalk near where she would get out: a guy on blades, a nurse with an old lady in a wheelchair, and an obvious tourist who had just gotten out of a car.

The guy on blades sailed off around the corner. The nurse sped up, rolling the wheelchair off in the opposite direction.

The tourist was eating a Snickers. Paulie wanted one.

H ere we are, Mrs. Ryerson."

"I'm awfully sorry, Captain, but I did try."

"There's always another day. In this line of work you learn that. It ain't over till it's over."

She got out of the car. It was a crisp, pleasant evening. She decided that she would spend the rest of it playing Scrabble with Paulie, trying to do what she could to improve his atrocious vocabulary. That boy could not be sent to Andover, not until he was more academically fit. She was planning to have him interview at Friends and at Ethical Culture. Both schools would nurture and nurse. He was a primitive, poor child, but such a darling. She'd always enjoyed noisy little boys, and he was one very noisy little boy.

T he shooter was eating a candy bar because broad-beamed young men with candy did not look dangerous. He slipped his free hand into his pocket.

Look at her, she was a real stunner. He'd be quick with her. Base of the skull, drops 'em like a sack of shit, hardly bleeds at all.

Paulie saw the hand go in the pocket, saw the black shape that appeared there, it's telltale butt just visible in the guy's fist. That goddamn tourist had a pistol.

He leaped up, grabbing the top of the wall. But it was higher from back there than it had been on the other side, and he would have to chin himself up if he was going to get a leg over.

The tourist was a shooter, and there wasn't a damn cop in sight. There was no stakeout on this place. He'd seen a dozen of them at home, and that was not happening here.

There were only seconds left. He began to struggle, scrambling to reach the top of the wall. "Mom! Mom!"

The limo pulled away, but a bus was coming down Fifth. He did not care to do this in front of a busload of people. He calculated. She was coming across the sidewalk toward him, and the bus was getting closer. No problem. He'd follow her into the lobby, do her there.

Paulie was skinned, he was bleeding, but he was also on top of the wall. A bus roared past, blinding him to a view of the front of the building. When it was gone, he saw Mom heading for the door. Candy Bar was not ten feet behind her. Paulie dropped down onto the sidewalk.

Good evening, Mrs. Ryerson," Timothy said as he swung the door open.

"Good evening, Timothy."

A moment later, somebody was pushing her from behind,

pushing with astonishing force. The thought that flashed through her head was that the police had seen something after all and they were trying to get her under cover. But that was not the right thought.

The shooter showed the doorman the pistol that he had in Kealy Ryerson's back. "Take it easy," he said. He tried to sound affable. It didn't help to sound vicious. Victims were thrown off by a pleasant attitude. Then you did it quick and clean, when they least expected it. That was the way.

Paulie raced straight across Fifth. Cars bore down on him, brakes screamed, horns blared but he didn't care, all he cared about was getting over there, getting to where Mom was being killed.

The shooter felt the almost automatic motions start in his arm, the stiffening of the muscles, the tightening of the finger against the trigger, that in another second would complete the task at hand. He knew that the woman would flop like a great rag halfway across the lobby, that the doorman would cringe away from the scene, then die in terror as a bullet ripped into his face.

He knew it because he'd seen it all before. This was his fifteenth job, and they all went kind of like this. This was part-time work for him. The rest of the time, he ran a marina on the Hudson. Nice marina in Tarrytown.

Paulie lost the backpack and the hunting knife that was in it on his way across the street. But he did not lose his karate.

He burst through the doors. In front of him was the shooter's back. In front of the shooter, Mom. The shooter was holding her with one hand, raising the gun with the other. Timothy was frozen behind the doorman's counter, his jaw open. He was pushing a button again and again, hammering it.

Paulie did a leaping assault on the killer that caused him to fly forward, arms akimbo, gun sailing in one direction, silencer in another. Kealy was thrown against the elevator. She cried out, "Oh!" like somebody who'd been tackled unexpectedly in football. The shooter didn't make a sound.

They hit the floor together, tangling in a mass of arms and legs. Paulie had only one thought: kill. He had only one wish: save Mom. And so he went in with his elbow, connecting with the throat.

The man was strong, though, stronger than he looked. He also had moves, and the next thing Paulie knew, he was on his back and frantically trying to get out from under the raging huge guy. The guy stretched out an arm. Paulie knew that he was reaching for his gun.

That hurt, Jesus, that came out of nowhere. But hey, this was a little kid. The son? Well, it was still together. He'd just do all three of them. The doorman was still frozen, too surprised and scared to move. That wasn't unusual. The shooter knew from experience that a lot of people freeze when they should be running like hell. He got the gun, thrust it into the kid's mouth. Good night, moon.

The lights went out.

Ollie Davis looked down on the inert form of the man who had been about to blow Paulie's face open. "Damn," he said, "muthafucker got a fuckin' *gun*, man!"

Kealy was disoriented. She couldn't quite understand what had just happened. Most of it had been behind her. It had been very fast. "Ollie! Oh, Jesus, where did *you* come from?"

"Outta the elevator. We were going out." Cowering behind him was Billie. She wore a long pink dress that Kealy seemed to remember from Allison's wardrobe. Ollie was marvelous looking in a brand new and very well tailored suit, a huge, rippling man with a face now dark with fury.

He had knocked the gunman senseless with a single blow with his huge closed fist, had brained him. He now picked up the pistol. "He was gonna kill you all with this."

Timothy came to his senses. "Mrs. Ryerson! My God!"

"Call the police, Timothy."

"I've been pressing the silent alarm for hours!"

Sirens were rising outside. Henny and Howard came rushing in, followed by what seemed a whole company of uniformed cops. They quickly made sure that the killer would wake up in hand-cuffs.

A flush of relief went through Kealy as she realized that this was the hit man who was supposed to have been called off. The flush of relief turned to joy as she began to see that this also meant that it was really over, and not only over, but that Jimmy was going to be avenged.

Billie was crying. "It's okay," Ollie said clumsily.

"It is not okay and I'm not going out to any club!"

The shooter groaned as Ollie lifted his head and popped it against the floor with a loud smack.

"Leave him alone, asshole," Henny yelled.

"He ruined my date!"

Kealy thought that there was something odd about what had just happened. The shooter—he'd been in trouble before Ollie appeared on the scene. Surely the jerk hadn't simply tripped. No, there had been a blow delivered, and with great force. "So who hit him from behind?"

A small voice: "You sure are one dumb bitch."

Paulie stood before her, his T-shirt filthy, his cheek and left arm skinned, tears pouring down his face.

"Paulie!"

He flew into her arms. "Mom! I hit him, Mom!"

He was calling her "Mom" right out here in public. That was fine; that was good progress.

"Thank you, son, thank you for saving my life."

He was too heavy for her and in three months he'd be too tall for this, but she lifted him anyway. She would not dream of doing it any other way. For the first and probably only time in his life, Paulie was going to be a child in a mother's arms.

The elevator doors opened and Ally and Mark burst out.

"Hold it," Henny shouted as they came forward. "I want everybody to stay in the apartment until we've made our arrests. It's gonna be a day, maybe two."

Kealy put Paulie down in the elevator—and thankfully. He was a heavy kid, not made for the kind of hugs he needed.

She found herself facing Henny, who was hanging back in the lobby, looking like a lost dog. As the doors closed, he seemed about to say something, and she thought—hoped—she knew what it was. She pressed the DOOR OPEN button. Their eyes met.

His lips parted, but he didn't speak. His eyes were silently pleading. "I—" he said.

The doors tried to close again. Annoyed, not wanting anything to interfere with this moment, she hit the button, bounced them open. She held the button down.

"Mother, we need to get out of this lobby," Allison said.

"Just one second." Either he was going to turn away right now, or he wasn't. He wanted to come up, she could see that, and that there was more to it than just a short visit. He was deciding whether or not to try to enter a new life with her. She knew men well enough to understand that she must not interfere in this. He had to make this decision on his own. She waited, surprising herself with just how much she wanted him to do it.

He glanced over his shoulder. "This is covered," he said. His fear was written on his face: he knew, also, that this was a crucial moment. If she told him no, it wouldn't just mean don't come up, it would mean, "Stay out of my life." He'd been hurt plenty in the past, she was aware of that, and she could see that he really, really didn't want it to happen to him again.

Fear of rejection was freezing him. She knew that "no" would not hurt that much unless he was in love . . . and she found that she wanted him to be in love with her. She searched her heart for some indication of why that would be and found that she was ready to try again with him, on the more solid foundation of adulthood.

"We were kids, then," she said.

He laughed ruefully, nodded.

So she raised an eyebrow, gave him enough of a smile to encourage him a bit more. He just stood there, a big old helpless powerhouse of a man.

"Mo*ther!*"

"Allison, please!" She looked into his eyes, let a sense of welcome flow through her.

He stared back, still frozen.

She tried more encouragement, smiling broadly now, putting welcome into her eyes. "Henny, what do you want?"

His eyes replied, "I want you, my love." His voice said, "Uh, you got any beer up there? But, uh, you know, it's not a big deal. I mean, uh, if you don't."

That was it, at last, his request for admission into her life. It was up to her now.

"Would you like to come up with us?"

"Oh, Kealy, I sure would."

"Well, if you're gonna come, come," Allison said impatiently.

Henny got into the elevator, stood next to Kealy. A moment later, he suddenly grasped her hand. It was about as inept a gesture as there could be. But she did not pull away. He came closer, moving with all the grace of a scared adolescent.

This made her smile, then she suddenly felt his warm breath next to her ear. "Is it too late to start over?" he asked in a husky whisper.

She leaned her head on his shoulder and whispered back, "It's never too late, Henny." Then he kissed her and it was familiar, yet so wonderfully, deliciously new. She realized she wasn't invisible to this guy.

Paulie said, "Yuck!" Mark and Ally were red-faced, staring at the floor.

Kealy pulled away. For a moment, she'd forgotten the kids were in the elevator. "We have Heineken and Bud, I think," she said.

"Great," said Henny.

The elevator stopped. The doors opened onto their apartment. Kealy took Henny's hand, and they all walked inside.